"WYRDRUNE, BEHIND YOU!"

Merlin cried.

"All right, you want to play samurai?" said Wyrdrune. He gestured towards his assailant and the sword in the scabbard on his back unsheathed itself and floated free.

The man's eyes grew wide as the sword came flashing towards him, as if wielded by an invisible attacker. He parried desperately as the blade repeatedly and relentlessly lunged. The flashing sword bit into his upper arm, sliced into his torso, and moved faster and faster, until, with a speed impossible to defend against, it finally delivered the *coup de grace* and drove itself into his chest.

The remaining gunmen took off running. Merlin sent bolts of thaumaturgic energy lancing after them. Each one found its mark and the assassins fell. All save one, who kept on running.

The man grabbed for his sword, but it sprang out of its scabbard. He then reached for the pouch on his belt, but his trousers suddenly fell down around his ankles. Panic-stricken, he struggled out of them and took off.

"A man should not go running about without his trousers," Merlin said. He chuckled and gestured at the discarded pants. The pants got up, as if filled by invisible legs, and gave chase...

* * *

Also by Simon Hawke

THE WIZARD OF RUE MORGUE
THE WIZARD OF SUNSET STRIP
THE WIZARD OF WHITECHAPEL
THE WIZARD OF 4TH STREET

ATTENTION: SCHOOLS AND CORPORATIONS

WARNER books are available at quantity discounts with bulk purchase for educational, business, or sales promotional use For information, please write to: SPECIAL SALES DEPARTMENT, WARNER BOOKS, 666 FIFTH AVENUE, NEW YORK, N.Y. 10103

**ARE THERE WARNER BOOKS
YOU WANT BUT CANNOT FIND IN YOUR LOCAL STORES?**

You can get any WARNER BOOKS title in print. Simply send title and retail price, plus 50¢ per order and 50¢ per copy to cover mailing and handling costs for each book desired. New York State and California residents add applicable sales tax. Enclose check or, money order only, no cash please, to: WARNER BOOKS, P.O BOX 690, NEW YORK, N.Y. 10019

THE SAMURAI WIZARD

SIMON HAWKE

WARNER BOOKS

A Time Warner Company

WARNER BOOKS EDITION

Copyright © 1991 by Simon Hawke
All rights reserved.

Questar® is a registered trademark of Warner Books, Inc.

Cover illustration by Dave Mattingly
Cover design by Don Puckey

Warner Books, Inc.
666 Fifth Avenue
New York, NY 10103

Ⓦ A Time Warner Company

Printed in the United States of America

First Printing: April, 1991

10 9 8 7 6 5 4 3 2 1

For Connie Willis
a good friend and a better writer

PROLOGUE

THE SERPENT TOOK FORM TO THE MUSIC OF THE WIND. THE plaintive, haunting sound of the *shakuhachi* filled Kanno with a deep sense of calm and serenity as he sat cross-legged on the tatami mat, dressed in nothing but a white *fundoshi*, the traditional Japanese loincloth. As he sat, eyes closed, concentrating on the ethereal music of the bamboo flute, he barely heard the tapping of the *Irezumi* master's tools and he experienced the pain without being overwhelmed by it. He allowed the sensations to flow over and through him, as he did the sonorous notes of the *shakuhachi*, and he held himself perfectly still, controlling his feeling of eager anticipation. Today, after nearly a year of visiting the master, the work would at last be completed.

Irezumi was an exacting and demanding art, involving consummate skill and patience. The traditional Japanese tattoos were not executed with the electric needles that were used in the West, but with the difficult, age-old awls and chisels. The *sumi*, brilliantly colored inks made from pressed charcoal, were inserted only after the design had first been drawn in outline, and unlike the more limited, simpler western tattoos, the *Irezumi* designs were far more intricate and complex, often

1

covering the entire back and buttocks, as well as the thighs, shoulders, upper arms, and forearms. It was as much of an art form as was *Ikebana*, the ancient Japanese art of flower arranging, and its mastery was as demanding as that of the tea ceremony.

Takahashi Sakuro, who worked out of his tiny parlor in a small back alley in Shinjuku, was the undisputed master of the form. The design he was executing on Kanno's back, shoulders, arms, and legs was a masterpiece of fine line and shading, perfect down to the finest detail. Over the months, as the wiry little old man had worked diligently on his task while Kanno suffered patiently, the design had slowly taken form in brightly colored ink, agony, and drops of blood. Week by week, the dragon slowly took shape. Kanno could almost feel its power coiling across his back.

He had worked the spell with great care, spending hours at home in the elaborate thaumaturgic ritual after each visit to the master. Soon he would know whether or not his efforts had all been in vain. He dreaded the possibility of failure. It was unthinkable that he should not succeed. In a sense, he had been preparing for this day ever since his early childhood, when he had first embarked upon the thaumaturgic path. The effort and expense his parents had gone to in order to secure a place for him in the proper preschool, followed by the stringent and unceasing competition of Japan's rigorous school system, had only been the first steps taken on that path.

In order to gain admittance to Tokyo University's School of Thaumaturgy, it had been necessary to prepare almost from birth. Admission to the university depended upon first being admitted to the right high school and passing all the exams with only the highest marks. And admission to the high school had been dependent on securing a place in the right preparatory school and so on, all the way back to childhood. And only those university graduates who had achieved the highest honors could seek admission to the postgraduate School of Thaumaturgy, which required surviving *Shiken-jigoku*, the period known as "Exam Hell." Students often quite literally did not survive *Shiken-jigoku*, as the intense pressure and the opprobrium of failure drove many of them to suicide. Those who passed experienced a joy that was transcendent, but short-lived. Life as a warlock demanded a total immersion of the student in the thaumaturgic arts, a complete self-sacrifice that left no time for any sort of social life. Nor was graduation a release from the rigorous obligations of the Way. Even then, successful completion of the courses in the School of Thaumaturgy did not guarantee that one would ever pass beyond the rank of warlock.

Following graduation, those students who had passed the rigorous battery of tests had to embark upon a minimum of three years as a warlock apprentice. Three years was the minimum, but it could last as long as six or eight or even ten. And it was first necessary to find a wizard master who would agree to take them on. The competition for apprentice slots was fierce. Becoming a licensed adept was far more difficult in Japan than in the western nations, where one could simply take the various level examinations at one's own pace. In Japan, nothing was *instanto*, least of all certification as a magic-user. Finding a wizard master and convincing him that you were worthy to be taken on as his apprentice was a difficult task. Without a master's sponsorship, the certification exams could not be taken. And the mandatory years of apprenticeship could easily be wasted if the master felt the student was not worthy to stand for certification. In such a case, it was a foregone conclusion that the apprentice would commit *seppuku*. Being found unworthy after having gone so far was a disgrace impossible to bear, reflecting as it did not only on the apprentice, but on his family, as well. The ritual suicide of *seppuku*, carried out with proper form and dignity, was the only way to save the family from disgrace.

Upon completion of the first levels, a warlock became certified as a lower-grade adept in some specialized branch of the thaumaturgic arts. Depending on performance, one could become licensed, for example, as a transportational adept, of which there were various levels. Some demanded relatively simple spells, such as levitation and impulsion in order to operate a cab or truck or limo, others required the more intense forms of concentration necessary to the task of operating bullet trains. After six years as a lower-grade adept, one could apply to take the more advanced certification levels that would allow the lower-grade adept to advance to the rank of wizard. There were many types of wizardry, involving such occupations as engineer adept, which entailed mastery of the spells that maintained power plants and factory assembly lines, or wizard pilot, which required peak mental and physical conditioning to hold airliners in the sky, or thaumagenetic engineer, an art form demanding years of study to master the spells involved in creating magically hybridized life forms. And, finally, there was corporate sorcerer, the highest pinnacle to which most adepts could aspire.

A very select few could, upon completion of ten years as a sorcerer, qualify for the exams that could allow them to advance to the rank of mage, but so demanding were final levels of certification that only one Japanese had ever succeeded in passing them. The number of mages in the world could be counted on the fingers of one hand. First and foremost among them all had been the legendary Merlin Ambrosius, Father of the Modern Thaumaturgic Age. It had been Merlin who had brought back the forgotten discipline of magic after awakening from his long, enchanted sleep. He had brought the world out of the dark age of the Collapse by founding schools of thaumaturgy, administered by his most gifted pupils, one of whom had been the Arab prince, Sheikh Rashid Al'Hassan, the first of Merlin's students to attain the rank of mage.

Like Ambrosius, Al'Hassan was gone now. He had been seduced by necromancy, a crime punishable throughout the world by death, and it was rumored that he had met his end in mage war between himself and his old master. Others said that he was consumed by his own spells, black magic run amok, and the ruins of his splendid palace, left untouched since he had disappeared, stood as a frightening object lesson to all those who might be tempted by the dark side of the thaumaturgic arts. In any case, no one knew for certain what had happened. Both Al'Hassan and Ambrosius had disappeared, never to be seen again. There had been no sign of Merlin ever since the day his Beacon Hill mansion was totally consumed by flames, yet there were those who continued to believe that Merlin was still alive. Kanno doubted it, himself. He believed that the master and the student had destroyed each other. And that meant the two most powerful mages on the planet were no more.

That left only Zorin, the aloof and implacable Russian, who disdained to use a magename; the venerable Tao Tzu of Tibet, an aged recluse whose magename meant "Son of the Way"; and Kanno's own former sensei, Yohaku, whose true name he had never known and whose magename translated as "white space."

Yohaku had studied in America, under Ambrosius himself, and the master of masters had once remarked upon his pupil's selfless dedication, his total openness and lack of preconceptions in approaching his studies of the art. He had referred to him as a student who came to his teacher as if he were a "blank slate" upon which knowledge could write freely. So deeply affected had the warlock been by that remark that he had translated "blank slate" as "empty space" or, more literally, that space that is purposely left blank or white upon a canvas. That was how Yohaku got his magename. Kanno had lost track of how many times Sensei had told that story.

At first, he had been thrilled and deeply honored that Japan's highest ranking adept had seen fit to accept him as an apprentice. With his standing in his graduating class, there had been many other wizards whom Kanno could have approached and most of his fellow students had thought it was the height of arrogance when he chose to petition the venerable Yohaku, but Kanno had always been ambitious and his pride and the strength of his desire had seen him through the ordeal of sitting on the master's doorstep at his small and modest home in Kyushu.

The mage had known about his presence from the moment he arrived, and yet he had let him sit there, through all hours of the day and night and through the rain that soaked him to the skin. He had kept him waiting for a solid week while Kanno sat there, unmoving, numb in his extremities, without food or sleep, subsisting only on the cups of broth that the master's housekeeper brought out to him three times a day. It had taken all of Kanno's will and concentration to endure the wait of his petition, mumbling spells under his breath to keep himself awake and give him strength, even while those very spells served to sap his energy. But Kanno had endured and at last the housekeeper came out and spoke to him for the first time since he had arrived.

"The master wishes me to ask you," the housekeeper had said, "what makes you think that you are worthy of his tutelage?"

Kanno had a long time to think about how he would reply when the inevitable question came. The question itself was like a koan. It was fraught with pitfalls. If he gave some reason for his worthiness, regardless what that reason was, he would appear too proud and would undoubtedly be dismissed. If he gave a humble answer and said he was not worthy, but hoped to prove his worth, then he had no doubt that he would also be dismissed, as why should the master waste his time with one who thought he was unworthy? So he had given long and careful thought to the answer he would give.

He had said, "It is not for the student to measure his own worth. This humble student can but measure his desire, which is greater than that for life itself."

Whereupon the housekeeper had produced a *tanto* and placed it on the ground before him, the squared point facing him. And, without another word or a backward glance, he turned and went back into the house.

Kanno felt as if his heart had stopped. As he stared with horror at the keen blade of the knife, he realized that the housekeeper would never have taken such an act upon himself. The master had anticipated him. And he had called his bluff. With a sinking feeling, Kanno damned Yohaku for his cleverness. The master did not wish to be bothered with petitions from eager and ambitious warlocks, and so he had settled upon this diabolical manner of discouraging all future applicants.

If Kanno walked away—and there was nothing stopping him—he would be shamed. The stigma of his failure would cling to him like a remora. Though it was twenty-third-century Japan and most modern Japanese had been thoroughly western-ized for generations, there were certain things that never changed. His arrogance in petitioning the mage, his audacity in even *thinking* that his petition might be granted, and his being hoisted on his own petard would become a story told among all students of thaumaturgy for years to come and he would never be able to look any of them in the face. Nor would any other wizard accept him as an apprentice after he had made such a complete fool of himself. His entire education, his whole life, would be wasted. He would shame his family. He really cared very little about that, because of his arrogance and selfishness, but he couldn't face the prospect of seeing the smug expressions on the faces of the other warlocks, hearing their whispered remarks behind his back, or seeing their malicious, knowing grins. Or, worse still, their looks of pity. There was simply no way out.

He gazed at the knife before him, and suddenly everything took on a shocking clarity. The glint of the sun off the razor-sharp steel blade; the faint whisper of the wind; the singing of the birds; his very own heartbeat... Everything became sharp-edged and amplified. His senses had never felt so acute. Death was looking him right in the face and Kanno calmly met its gaze with a profound sense of resignation. He had gambled all and he had lost.

He seemed to be drifting somewhere outside himself as he watched his hand, as if it were somehow not a part of him, reach down toward the knife. He felt his fingers close around the hilt, as if they were doing so of their own accord. He picked up the knife.

The sun had never seemed so bright. The sky had never seemed so blue. He opened up his shirt. He was profoundly sorry that he had to die, but somewhere deep within, in a part of him that he had never known existed, he had accepted it. He held the *tanto* by the hilt with both hands, the blade pointing toward him. He took a deep breath and let it out slowly. Quickly, he thought, do it quickly. Resolve is everything. With all the force that he could muster, he stabbed....

And the blade stopped, of its own accord.

His arms trembled with the shock. It was as if he had encountered some sort of invisible wall, an impenetrable barrier... but no, the blade had pierced his skin, only just barely. He looked down, awestruck, at the tiny trickle of blood welling up out of the small cut where the point of the knife had just barely broken his skin and suddenly realization dawned.

Yohaku.

The master had been testing him. He had never intended for him to die. He had only meant to measure the sincerity of his intent.

And in that moment Kanno had felt weak and dizzy, on the verge of passing out, yet at the same time, he had an almost uncontrollable urge to break out in laughter. He stifled it, because the significance of what had happened suddenly broke upon him like a tsunami. Like a tidal wave, it overwhelmed him, because he realized in that instant that he had prevailed over the master. And that knowledge made him feel giddy with power.

He had fooled Yohaku. The master would believe in his sincerity, in the depth and strength of his honor, in the truth of those ridiculous, melodramatic, empty words that he had spoken, when the *real* truth was not that Kanno's desire to be worthy of the master was greater than his desire to live. Far from it. The truth was that the worth he placed on his own self, the value of his monumental ego, was so great that he would rather die than be humbled in the eyes of others.

Yohaku would now believe that he was humble, worthy, selfless, when in truth Kanno was none of those things, but quite the opposite. And the strength of his own ego had given him the power to deceive the master. Yohaku would never realize it, but in that one incandescent instant when he had magically stopped the blade, Kanno had become the master.

And the choices he had made since then were rendered that much easier for him, because there was no need to question his own decisions, no room left for doubt, no necessity for self-justification. Yohaku was Japan's highest ranking and most venerable adept, one of the greatest living magic-users in the world, and Kanno had outwitted him. In that moment, he felt himself reborn. There were no longer any limits.

He had served Yohaku faithfully for ten long years, hiding his true colors during all that time, exercising the greatest of self-discipline, swallowing his pride, and effacing himself. *Ten years.* The bastard had made him wait ten years before he pronounced him worthy to stand for his first levels and agreed to sponsor him. Kanno had passed with flying colors. Even then, when he could have struck out on his own, he has asked the master if he could remain with him, to study further and refine his knowledge. Yohaku had been proud and pleased with him. The fool. He never suspected Kanno's true intent. Yes, Kanno meant to learn, but not out of selfless dedication and a sincere desire to improve his art, but out of a driving ambition to increase his power.

He had been careful, oh, so very careful. He had successfully resisted the overwhelming temptation to peruse Yohaku's thaumaturgic scrolls when the master wasn't looking. He forced himself not to delve into the master's secrets. At least, he had resisted until he was absolutely certain that Yohaku trusted him completely and would never even entertain the faintest glimmer of suspicion concerning his pupil's duplicity. Kanno had waited until he was absolutely certain of the spells the master used to unlock the invisible, thaumaturgic seals on his ancient scrolls and leather-bound tomes. And even after he had learned all those spells by heart, backward and forward, he still resisted the temptation until he was sure, beyond any shadow of a doubt, that there were no other warding spells that might entrap him or alert Yohaku to what he had done. For years, Kanno bided his time patiently. And then, when he felt totally secure in his duplicity, he broke the sacred bond between master and apprentice, a bond that he truly felt did not apply to him, for after all, had he not proved *himself* to be the master?

Twenty years to the day after he first approached Yohaku, the master agreed that he was ready to advance to the rank of wizard. And once again, Kanno achieved the highest scores in the exams. It was at that point that, with a great display of false regret, he parted from the master, expressing his desire to dedicate himself to the lifelong mastery of the art of thaumagenetic engineering. And once again, Yohaku had been pleased, for while there were a great many other branches of the path that Kanno could have chosen, paths that led to a potential for far greater profit than what Kanno had selected, none were regarded as being more spiritual, more demanding, more harmonious and aesthetic as the art of bringing into being new forms of life imbued with magic. Yohaku was proud that his pupil had not chosen the path to wealth and power, but the spiritual way of the true artist. And yet again, he was deceived.

Power was the be-all and end-all of Kanno's whole existence. And once again, displaying the ruthlessly methodical patience he had schooled himself in over the years, Kanno waited, biding his time, opening a small "magenics" shop in the Shinjuku district, with two young apprentices of his own. He started unpretentiously, by producing fairly common magenes such as snats, a magical hybrid of a snail and a house cat, which resulted in a purring, affectionate little life form with no legs that was capable of clinging to walls and ceilings much like a snail in an aquarium, and paragriffins, a hybrid of a parakeet and the mythical griffin, a sort of enchanted avian cyborg with metallic-scaled wings that was capable of speech.

Only as common as those popular and well-established magenes were, Kanno's creations were truly works of art that stood head and shoulders above all the others. His snats were derived not from ordinary house cats, but from miniature ocelot, panther, and Siberian tiger hybrids that he himself perfected. And his paragriffins were likewise based not on ordinary parakeets, but on bonsai raptors and frigate birds, with variegated, iridescent scales of titanium, silver, and gold, with jeweled eyes and immaculately cut talons of emerald and amethyst. And every one of them was engineered as painstakingly as a haiku was composed. Kanno's reputation as a thaumagenetic artist grew by leaps and bounds. Yohaku positively beamed with pride in his former pupil.

After he was elevated to the rank of sorcerer, Kanno respectfully declined numerous and highly lucrative offers of employment from several large conglomerates, humbly and politely stating his opinion that true art could not be corporatized and produced on an assembly line. After he took such a stance, the offers soon stopped coming, at least from Japanese concerns, because no one wanted to offend a master, but very soon thereafter, possession of a Kanno magene became the ultimate of status symbols. Kanno pretended discomfort at having to continually raise his prices, but apologetically gave the reason that only by doing so could he limit the demand and continue to insure the highest standards of thaumagenetic craftsmanship.

And, not long after that, the backlog of orders was so great, despite the lofty prices, that Kanno closed his shop to orders from the public—though he left it open as a gallery where those who could not afford his magenes could at least come in to view them—and started working only on select commissions.

In the meantime, after his shop closed for the day and his apprentices had left, Kanno worked diligently, late into the night, pursuing his true calling—the art of necromancy.

Beneath his shop, in a long abandoned and forgotten excavation, was a small underground mall that dated back to the days just prior to the Collapse. The site on which his shop now stood had once been an entrance to an underground arcade of exclusive boutiques, galleries, coffee shops, and hostess bars. After careful research through old city records that no one ever bothered to examine anymore, he chose the site for his shop precisely for that reason. Years ago, the subterranean mall had been completely sealed off, buried and forgotten beneath new construction, but using his magical skills, Kanno had broken through to it. The magically warded and camouflaged entrance was now located in the basement of his shop and not even his apprentices, who passed by it several times a day, suspected its existence. Each night, after he locked the doors of his shop, Kanno descended into his secret necromantic enclave, to practice the black arts.

Necromancy, Kanno felt, was the pinnacle of the sorcerer's art. Dangerous, demanding, forbidden, and intoxicating. It demanded the ultimate in skill and concentration on the part of the necromancer, whose own life hung in the balance with each and every spell attempted. But, unlike the white magic of the thaumaturge, black magic was exponential in its rewards. White magic could never increase the power of the sorcerer the way that necromancy could. It was both intensely fulfilling and intensely addictive.

Necromancy—literally, the sorcery of death—had a price, just as thaumaturgy did. Magic had its own immutable laws of metaphysics. Matter and energy could not simply be created out of nothing. The energy, the fuel, had to come from somewhere. To the white magician or the thaumaturge, the energy came most frequently from his or her own life force. On occasion, and only under the strictest licensing and observation of the codes administered by local Bureaus of Thaumaturgy and overseen by the International Thaumaturgical Commission, a thaumaturge could draw upon the life force of carefully screened volunteers, but only in the same way as blood could be taken from a donor—a little at a time and under carefully controlled conditions, allowing for natural replenishment. But in most cases, white sorcerers and wizards drew on their own life force, which placed strict limitations on their powers. The more demanding a spell, the greater the drain on a magician's life force, for which reason magic-users such as pilot adepts needed to be in peak physical condition and could only put in limited amounts of flying time, interspersed with periods of recuperation. But necromancy did not have the drawbacks of such limitations.

The necromancer could and often did draw on his own life force, but rather than take the time necessary to recuperate, he could replenish it immediately. With the life force of another. Or if the spell was more demanding—and necromantic spells usually were—the sorcerer could draw directly on the life force of another, consuming it entirely. The more demanding and ambitious the spell, the more energy in the form of life force was required and the necromancer could, by casting certain spells, increase the strength of his own life force. In effect, he would consume the souls of his sacrificial victims until his power was magnified many times. And that was both the intoxication and the addiction of necromancy. Once "fixed" with the appetite for souls, the necromancer became hooked for life. He killed to increase his power. The more his power increased, the more ambitious—and more dangerous—were the spells he could attempt. And the more ambitious his spells, the more power they consumed. And the more power they consumed, the more he had to kill.

Ambrosius had called it the "dark circle," a circle from which, he had claimed, there was no escape. But Kanno did not believe that. It was a lie, he thought, fostered by Ambrosius and perpetuated by his disciples, by the B.O.T. and I.T.C., meant to control adepts and keep them from gaining too much power so that they could be controlled by the thaumaturgic hierarchy. Forced to function within the limits of the bureaucracy, governed by codes Ambrosius had laid down. Ambrosius himself, Kanno was certain, had been a necromancer. How else could he have attained such power? What about those stories, which could neither be substantiated nor refuted, of how the legendary archmage had brought the world back from the Collapse?

He awoke from his enchanted slumber of two thousand years to find the world plunged into anarchy and darkness. No more fossil fuels. An environment that was poisoned beyond measure. The machines had all stopped. Governments and economies were in a state of collapse. Riots. Lawlessness. Starvation and disease. Two thousand years had passed since Merlin fell victim to the enchantment of Morgan Le Fay and mankind had learned nothing. And so Ambrosius had stormed throughout the world like the Four Horsemen of the Apocalypse rolled into one, selecting men he could control—as he had once selected Arthur, though he had learned from his mistakes and he carefully avoided all clay-footed idealists—and reuniting governments, propping up their collapsed economies, supporting the technology of the pre-Collapse days with the reborn magic of the Second Thaumaturgic Age. And anyone who tried to stop him ... simply disappeared.

Yet Kanno knew what had become of them. What happened to *their* life energies, eh, Ambrosius? What kept *you* going all those years, living so far beyond any normal human lifespan? What gave *you* such power?

Necromancy. It was the obvious answer, of course. It was the one truth that no one ever dared to speak out loud. It was like pointing out the emperor's new clothes. Oh, warlocks whispered it among themselves, but even then, they chose to cloak it in mystical, sentimental hero-worship. Merlin had done only what he had to do, what his fate had demanded of him. He had shouldered the heavy burden of his sins to save mankind, as if he were some sort of Christ figure. And during his lifetime, he had indeed been treated as if he were the Second Coming.

It was not for nothing, Kanno thought, that Ambrosius had instituted the proscriptions against necromancy. The reasons were twofold. First, it fit in with society's long-standing proscriptions against the taking of human life, and in following that old, humanistic tradition, Merlin had reinforced his status as a benevolent lawgiver. And second, it insured that once the knowledge he had spread was assimilated by the society of the Second Thaumaturgic Age, no adept would ever attain the level of his power. Ambrosius was no fool.

But Ambrosius was gone now. Zorin hardly ever left his country. Tao Tzu was a recluse. And Yohaku . . . well, Kanno had already proven himself the master of the aptly named "empty space."

He suddenly became aware that the tapping had stopped. He had lulled himself with the music of the *shakuhachi*, retreating deep within himself, lost in his musings, and he hadn't even felt the pain. Takahashi had finished. Slowly, the old man had risen to his feet and he was now standing behind Kanno, casting a critical eye over his work. He grunted once in satisfaction.

"It is done," he said.

Kanno tensed with anticipation. He took a deep breath and got up, walking over to the three mirrored panels set up opposite where he was sitting. He stood before the mirrors, naked except for the *fundoshi*, slim and muscular, his long black hair worn in the style of a sorcerer, cascading to his shoulders. He gazed at the tattoo with awe.

It was, indeed, a masterpiece. The dragon coiled across his back, its varicolored, reptilian wings spreading out across his shoulders, the paneled decorations and thaumaturgic characters surrounding it, spelling out the complicated incantation in Japanese, covering his upper arms and sides. Its serpent tail stretched across his buttocks and coiled round and round his left leg, more characters, highlighted by multicolored paneling, hummingbirds and flowers, descended down his right leg. The scales of the dragon seemed iridescent, almost metallic, highlighted in delicate shades of gold and green and silver. Its head was huge and fearsome, its jaws open, teeth gleaming. Roiling flames spouted from its gullet. It was terrible and beautiful. It almost seemed alive.

"You are indeed the master of your art, Takahashi-san,"

Kanno said with admiration. "I have never seen such exquisite workmanship."

The old man flushed with pleasure and bowed. "Coming from a master such as yourself, Kanno-san, that is truly a great compliment. I have labored long and hard to render a design that would be worthy of your stature. I thank you for your patience. It is the crowning achievement of my entire career. I do not think that I will ever be able to duplicate such an achievement."

Kanno turned around and smiled. "Then it is only fitting that your crowning moment be your last," he said.

He stretched out his arm, hand open, palm out, fingers extended. And suddenly he clutched his hand into a fist and squeezed.

Takahashi screamed and clutched at his chest. He gasped for air, sank down to his knees on the tatami mat, then pitched forward onto his face, dead.

Crude, thought Kanno, an execution of technique lacking in style, but nevertheless effective. When the body was discovered, it would appear as though the old man had died of a stroke. At his age, no one would have any reason to suspect otherwise. And Kanno had made certain that there would be no record of his visits here. No one would know and his secret would be safe. Now, all that remained was the completion of the spell over which he had labored so long and hard. He dressed quickly. He was anxious to get back to his sanctuary and begin the final preparations.

Soon, the dragon's coils would writhe.

CHAPTER
One

Kanno stood over the altar in his hidden sanctuary below street level, naked, the knife in his right hand dripping blood onto the floor. The altar over which he stood had once been a fountain in the center of the underground mall, a circular pool inlaid with tile, with a short wall around it on which patrons of the mall could sit and with a work of unimaginative abstract sculpture done in bronze placed on a stone pedestal in the center. The pipes had run up through the sculpture, so that the water could cascade down over its plane surfaces. All around the fountain were the small shops that once held boutiques and bars and coffeehouses, but that had long been standing empty, shrouded in dust and shadow and infested with large rats. It was like a miniature, underground ghost town, surreal in itself, but rendered even more surreal by the sight of Kanno standing nude over the pedestal where the sculptured fountain had once stood.

He had removed the fountain, blasted it right off its pedestal, and now the slab on which it had once stood was stained rust red with the dried blood of his victims. A corpse lay upon it now, the nude body of a young woman that had, moments

17

earlier, been alive and vibrant with terror. Her screams had echoed through the darkened mall, which was illuminated only by the burning braziers placed around it at various points. But her frenzied screams had been to no avail. No one could hear them up above. The tiled floor of the pool, once filled with water, was now painted with the sign of the pentagram, the Seal of Solomon, with the altar standing at its center.

Kanno's eyes were glazed as he stood over the body of his victim, spattered with her blood. He felt numb with disappointment. All those months of preparation. . . . What could have gone wrong? There was no written record he could check, no scroll or ancient book in which he could look up the spell and see if had missed something somehow, because the spell had been completely of his own devising. Yet he had drawn upon ancient and authenticated sources, assembled the spell painstakingly and carefully, empowered it with the life energy of his victims. . . . It *should* have worked!

The thought of starting over filled him with anger and frustration, but if there was one thing Kanno had learned over the years, it was patience. To the patient man comes everything. Somewhere, somehow, he had made an error. He would go over it once more and start from the beginning. He would not accept this failure. He would go back to the Ginza, where the young people prowled at night—the young ones always had the most vibrant life force—and he would start anew. He sighed with resignation and turned away from the altar. . .

. . . and she was standing there, just beyond the circle, outside the pentagram. Standing there and watching him.

For a moment he simply froze. It was unthinkable that anyone could have known about his sanctuary, much less penetrated through to it. The only entrance was carefully, magically concealed and warded with his strongest spells. Only a sorcerer—or *sorceress*—much more powerful than he could have defeated them. And that simply couldn't be. He stared at her with shock and disbelief.

She was not Japanese. She was tall and slender, with long, flaming red hair and skin that was a shade of copper-gold unlike anything that he had ever seen. Her eyes were a bright, metallic green, like glowing emeralds, and she was dressed in a long black robe that came down to the floor. Her beauty was staggering. Kanno felt incredible force emanating from her. A power that was almost palpable. He was astonished by the strength of it. He felt suddenly very vulnerable in her presence, and it wasn't just his nakedness.

"Who are you?" he asked nervously. "How did you get in here?"

"My name is Leila," she said. "And you called for me."

"I *called* for you?" He frowned. Something had gone wrong with his spell. Had he inadvertently summoned up a fellow adept somehow? Or was she *more* than an adept? He began to feel excited. Had he summoned up a demonic entity? If so, then he had not failed at all. He had merely succeeded at something other than what he had set out to do. Something that could prove very useful, indeed. "You came in answer to my summons?" he asked.

She smiled faintly. "No one *summons* me, Kanno. You presume a great deal, and falsely. It was your necromancy that called out to me. I felt the trace emanations of your spells."

He stiffened. "You are with the I.T.C.?"

She chuckled. "What I represent is something far more powerful than the pathetic amateurs of your Thaumaturgical Commission. You think yourself a mage and you dabble in things you can't even begin to understand. You are stumbling blindly on the Way. I can show you the true path."

"*You*?" said Kanno. "What do you know of necromancy?"

"Fool. I *am* necromancy."

Her green eyes suddenly flared with hellish fire.

"You have studied the grimoire and the history of the black arts," she said, "yet you have not heard of the Dark Ones?"

Kanno quickly made a warding gesture, defending himself from whatever spell she was about to cast, but her power had not been aimed at him. Just as suddenly as it appeared, the unholy glow faded from her eyes and Kanno heard a faint rustle of movement behind him. He spun around . . . and saw the corpse of his sacrificial victim rising from the slab.

He sucked in his breath sharply and his eyes grew wide with shock. It was merely a trick of manipulation, he told himself at first; she was merely moving the body like a puppeteer. But then he saw that the corpse of the young woman breathed and her eyes, which seconds earlier had been filmed with the mask of death, now gleamed with life as they gazed at him. He saw the unacceptable reality before him as she climbed down off the pedestal and he knew it was not possible, and yet, she lived. *She had no heart*. He himself had torn it from her chest, yet he could see that something pulsed within the gory cavity where her heart had been, something vague and indefinable, something seen and yet not seen, like the misty tendrils of an early morning mist. Something dark and terrible.

"It cannot *be*!" he said as the resurrected woman, naked and blood-spattered like a piece of butchered meat, approached him slowly. "No one has the power to reanimate the dead! *No one!*"

"No *human* has the power," Leila said from behind him. "But there is nothing an Immortal cannot do."

The reanimated corpse came up to Kanno and placed her hands upon his shoulders, then brought her bloody lips to his. He cried out with revulsion and shoved her away.

"Your thirst for power has set you on the Path of Darkness," Leila said, her throaty voice echoing throughout the shadowy and long-deserted mall. "And I am that to which your path has led. I can grant you power beyond your wildest dreams. I can fulfill your heart's desire. In return, all I require is your unquestioning obedience. Serve me, Kanno, and I can give you *anything*. Observe."

She stretched her hand out toward him and a beam of pure thaumaturgic force leapt from her fingers, striking him and bathing him in an incandescent aura. It burned like a cold fire. For an instant of searing agony, it felt as if his skin were being flayed away, and he sank, screaming, to his knees.

It lasted but an instant, and then the aura dissipated. The pain went with it. Kanno kneeled, doubled over on the floor, gasping for breath. *Then he felt something start to writhe beneath his skin*.

His flesh literally crawled. And then the pain struck. Pain so intense that he couldn't even scream. It felt as if he were being torn to pieces. His left leg felt as if it were being squeezed inside a giant steel vise. The coils tightened. His leg shot out as if of its own accord, out of control, and he was flung onto his back as it whipsawed back and forth, lashing like a tail. He couldn't breathe. He bucked and thrashed like a trout thrown up on a riverbank, flipping over onto his stomach. His back arched like a cat's. His skin bulged outward, rippling as the iridescent coils writhed beneath it. And then he found his voice and screamed as the flesh and muscle on his back started seeping blood and tearing with a sound like ripping cloth. And his hoarse scream mingled with another, louder sound that drowned it out as the dragon raised its head up from his back and roared.

"Hunnnnh!" Billy Slade gasped and sat bolt upright in bed, sweat beaded on his forehead. He was breathing heavily. For a moment he felt disoriented, and then he recognized the familiar surroundings of his own bedroom and exhaled heavily, running his hands along the short hair on the sides of his head and through the thick, luxuriant crest that rose up in the middle, combed back like a horse's mane and descending in a long ponytail down to the middle of his back. "Gor' blimey, what a bloody awful dream," he mumbled in a thick cockney accent.

His hand started to reach for the cigarettes on his nightstand, then hovered uncertainly over the pack and instead picked up the pipe and tobacco pouch that lay next to it. Without thinking, he started to fill the pipe, then suddenly realized what he was doing and grimaced.

"Oh, no, you don't!" he said, and flung the pipe and pouch away from him.

The deeply curved, Algerian briar pipe sailed across the room, as did the pouch, spilling tobacco, then both stopped abruptly, frozen in midair. They started floating back toward him. He batted them away and reached for the cigarettes.

"Forget it," he said, pulling a cigarette from the pack. "I need a *fag*, not that bloody peat moss!"

"A fag," he echoed himself, speaking suddenly with a voice that was not his own, but deeper and more cultured, with an accent that was not cockney, but a curious blend of Welsh and Celtic. It sounded strange and incongruous, coming from a teenage boy. "The word is *cigarette*, you bog trotter. It's bad enough you have to smoke those abominable things, must you continually pervert the English language? Besides, you're in America now and here, that unfortunate expression has a considerably different connotation.''

"Bugger off," said Billy with a frown. "Go back t'sleep."

"I *can't* sleep, not while you're awake."

"I 'ad a bleedin' nightmare, right?"

"I know, you young idiot, I had it with you."

"Right, then. So what do you want from me?"

"Lower your voice, for one thing. There's no need to wake the others.''

"Lemme alone!"

He got out of bed. He was wearing nothing but a pair of jockey shorts. His build was slight and wiry. His facial features were delicate, foxlike, and androgynous. To offset this elfin cuteness, he had cultivated a slightly drooping lip, a challenging, aggressive sneer that had become habitual. His ethnic background was impossible to pinpoint and he himself did not know what it was. His skin was the shade of coffee with a lot of cream in it and his eyes looked somewhat Asian and exotic. He might have been part Jamaican, part Chinese, or part Caucasian and part Indian, he hadn't the faintest idea. He was an orphan and he knew nothing of his parents, but thanks to the spirit entity that shared his mind and body with him, he knew who he was descended from. He was possessed by the astral spirit of his ancestor, Merlin Ambrosius, the legendary archmage, who took the whole idea of being immortal far too literally for Billy's taste. All he needed now was for the *other* one to come awake as well.

He glanced down at the ancient ring he wore, a fire opal runestone set in a heavy gold band with intricate cabalistic carvings. But the fire opal runestone wasn't glowing, which meant that the spirit entity within it was quiescent for the moment.

Well, at least that was something, Billy thought, as he went out into the living room. His great-great-grandfather, some twenty-seven times removed or something like that, he could never remember exactly, was generally a royal pain in the ass, but Merlin didn't bother him half as much as Gorlois did. Gorlois was scary. Merlin was with him constantly, sharing consciousness with him, often preempting his own will, which caused a lot of arguments between them, but Gorlois manifested himself very rarely. And when he did, it wasn't merely a manifestation of another personality using Billy's body. It was complete physical transformation, entailing magic that was even more powerful than Merlin's. For as powerful as Merlin was, he was still part human—a halfbreed. His father, Gorlois, was a full-blooded Immortal, the last of the Old Ones and the sole surviving member of the Council of the White.

At least, that was how Billy thought of him, though perhaps to use the word "surviving" in his case wasn't strictly accurate. Just as Merlin had experienced mortal death in his battle with the Dark Ones, so Gorlois had died when, as the Duke of Cornwall, he had been slain by Uther Pendragon, the father of King Arthur. Thinking that he was doing combat with nothing more than a mere mortal, Gorlois had disdained to use his magic powers. In a rage, he had been intent on killing Uther only with his sword. Only by the time Gorlois discovered that Uther was magically warded and his fighting skills enhanced by sorcery, it was far too late. Uther had given him a mortal blow, and as he died, Gorlois had used his last ounce of strength and will to insure the survival of his spirit. He had projected his astral self into the fire opal runestone in his ring, a ring that then passed to his daughter, the sorceress Morgan Le Fay, becoming the source of much of her power. And, through her, Gorlois had revenged himself upon his only son.

Merlin had used Uther to kill Gorlois so that he could avenge his mortal mother, whom the immortal Gorlois had abandoned when she began to age. And Gorlois had used his daughter by his second mortal wife to even up the score. Now their descendant, Billy, was the repository of both their spirits. It was an uneasy coexistence. Not that there was any real conflict. Gorlois had yet to speak to either of them. Even when he manifested himself, as he had done on only a couple of occasions, when the body they all shared was in the gravest danger, he did not utter a sound. But from time to time, he gave them dreams. Unsettling, frightening dreams. The most recurrent one was a dream in which he was being hacked to death by Uther. He seemed to take a perverse satisfaction in making his son, Merlin—and consequently, Billy, too—experience his mortal death.

Given half a chance, Billy would have taken off the ring and tossed it in the river, but from the moment it came into his possession—before he realized what it was—he had been unable to remove it. So there he was, a fifteen-year-old cockney punk from the back alleys of London, possessed by the spirits of two archmages thousands of years old, with no love lost between them.

"Why me?" he grumbled as he crossed the living room, heading toward the bar. "Why the 'ell'd they 'avta pick on *me*?"

He knew why. Because he was descended from Merlin and Nimue, the De Dannan witch who had seduced Merlin, and that made Billy both spiritually and thaumaturgically compatible with them. But personally, he did not feel very compatible at all.

"Where are you going?" Merlin said.

"To get a bloody drink."

His body turned suddenly, of its own accord, and started heading for the kitchen.

"What you need is a nice warm glass of milk," said Merlin.

Billy stopped himself with an effort and turned resolutely back toward the bar.

"*Milk?* Christ, that stuff's bloody disgustin'. I need a whiskey."

He took another step and came to an abrupt halt once again.

"You shouldn't be drinking at your age."

"Sod off!"

"Listen, you impertinent young whelp—"

"*Sod off,* I said!"

He stood there in the center of the living room, doing what appeared to be a bizarre little two-step shuffle; one step forward, two steps back, two steps forward, one step back. . . .

"Get *out* of it, ya bleedin' wanker! Lemme *go!*"

"That's a catchy step," said a voice from behind him. "But I suspect it would work better with music."

Billy turned to see Modred leaning against the door frame of his bedroom. The last survivor of Camelot was dressed in black silk pajamas and a black silk robe, both exquisitely tailored. He was wearing tinted, gold-rimmed aviator glasses, his blond hair was combed back at the sides, and his beard was neatly trimmed. He appeared to be in his forties, but was in fact several thousand years older, the bastard son of King Arthur Pendragon and his half-sister, the sorceress, Morgan Le Fay. Like Merlin, he had the blood of the immortal Old Ones flowing through his veins, but since he was part human, he would not live forever. He aged, although at a rate far slower than ordinary men.

"Now see what you've done?" said Merlin. "I told you to keep your voice down!"

"Don't blame the boy, Ambrosius," said Modred, coming into the room. "I was awake already." He went over to the bar and poured himself and Billy a couple of Scotches. Giving booze to a minor was the least of his long list of sins, though Billy had been drinking hard liquor since he was ten. "I had a rather unsettling nightmare."

"About giant snakes?" said Kira. She and Wyrdrune came out of their bedroom into the living room of the penthouse they all shared, on the Upper West Side of New York, overlooking Central Park.

Modred glanced at her sharply.

She was slim and feral pretty, with dark eyes and jet-black hair worn short, in a geometric style, swept back at the sides and down over her forehead in the front. She was barefoot and dressed only in panties and a dark blue T-shirt.

"We both had the same dream," said Wyrdrune.

He had thrown on a blue terry-cloth bathrobe. His dusty blond hair was long and curly, worn to the shoulders in the style of an adept. It was disheveled, and between some strands that hung down over his eyes, there was the soft gleam of an emerald runestone set into his forehead. There was a faint blond stubble on his cheeks and chin.

"So did I," said Billy. "But it wasn't a snake in my dream. More like a giant lizard."

"Or a dragon?" Modred said, raising his eyebrows.

For a moment none of them said anything.

"Last time something like this happened," Wyrdrune said, "it was the Dark Ones."

Kira sat down on the couch and gazed at the sapphire set into the center of her right palm. "My runestone isn't glowing," she said. She glanced at Wyrdrune. "Neither is yours."

"Nor mine," said Modred, referring to the enchanted ruby set into his chest, over his heart. "But that could only mean that they're not close."

"What was your dream?" asked Merlin, speaking through Billy.

"A man being crushed in the coils of a giant snake," said Kira. She glanced at Modred. "Yours?"

"Similar," said Modred, "only I had the vision that he was changing into a dragon."

"An' I had one about a giant lizard comin' up outta some bloke's back," said Billy.

"Was he Oriental?" Modred asked.

"Yeah, come to think of it, 'e was."

"With long hair," added Wyrdrune. "Like an adept."

"That's right," said Kira.

"Sound like anyone you know?" asked Modred.

She shook her head. "Not me."

"Me, neither," Wyrdrune said.

"Ain't never seen 'im before," said Billy.

"Ambrosius?"

"No, not I." He paused. "He was Japanese."

"Not Chinese?" said Kira.

"No, Japanese," insisted Merlin. "I'm sure of it."

"I think Chinese," said Kira. "Yeah, definitely Chinese."

"*Chinese?*" a new voice broke in. "What, the middle of the night and you're gonna send out for *Chinese*? Somebody pregnant here or what?"

An old straw broom swept in from the kitchen, shuffling toward them on its bristles and gesturing with spindly, rubbery arms that had three fingers on each hand. Perched on the end of its broom handle was a red cotton nightcap.

"What, nobody sleeps around here anymore?" the broom said in a matronly voice that was thick with a New York Jewish accent.

It was the same voice and accent, in fact, as that of Wyrdrune's mother, the late Mrs. Stella Karpinsky, who had named her only child Melvin, which was the chief reason why Wyrdrune used only his magename. When he had left to attend the School of Thaumaturgy in Cambridge, Massachusetts, he had cast a spell to animate the broom, in order that his mother might have some help and company around the apartment while he was gone. Unfortunately, he had overreached himself, as usual, and the spell had not come off quite the way he had expected.

The broom turned out to be a bit *too* animated and once it was alive, there was no returning it to the inanimate object it had been before. And, in his mother's constant company, it had become impressed with her personality and mannerisms. Now that she was gone, Wyrdrune had "inherited" the broom, perhaps the oddest familiar in all of thaumaturgic history.

Mrs. Karpinsky had dearly loved the broom and always used to take it with her to the automat, where she had tea and Danish with her friends and Broom learned the timeless art of *kibbitzing*. While on her deathbed, she had asked the broom to take care of her son and now nothing could dissuade it from its adopted maternal role. Nor could Wyrdrune come up with any spell to silence or control it.

He wasn't even sure exactly how he had animated the damn thing in the first place. It had no mouth, and yet it spoke. It had no nose, yet it could sniff in the same disapproving manner as his mother had, and it certainly had no hips, but that did not prevent it from standing with its arms akimbo and seeming to cast an irritated gaze at them, though, of course, it had no eyes, yet somehow it could "see."

"Nobody's sending for Chinese, Broom," said Wyrdrune wearily. "We were just talking about someone who *was* Chinese."

"Japanese," corrected Merlin.

"Japanese, schmapanese," said Broom. "It's four o'clock in the morning! Decent, normal people oughtta be in bed at this hour, not having a meshuga cocktail party."

"Actually, I could go for some Chinese," said Kira. "Anybody hungry?"

"You go eating Chinese at this time of the night, you'll get more gas than the Hindenburg," said Broom.

"What's the Hindenburg?" asked Kira, puzzled.

"A dirigible," said Modred. "It blew up."

"Which is what you'll do with Chinese in the middle of the night. Go back to bed, already." Broom turned to Modred, still behind the bar. "Are those my good glasses?"

"I'm sorry, Broom, I couldn't seem to find the jam jars," Modred said with a bemused smile. It was, after all, his wealth, accumulated over the centuries, that supported them all.

"Listen to Mister Smarty-pants, standing there in his fancy-schmancy dressing gown like he was Ronald Colman," said the broom with a sniff.

"Ronald Colman?" Kira said.

"Before your time," said Modred. "Before anybody's time, for that matter, except mine. A rather mannered British actor in old pre-Collapse films."

"I never should've bought that VCR," said Wyrdrune.

"Sure, take it back, already," said Broom. "Why should *I* get any enjoyment around here? I should be cooking, cleaning, and chasing down the roaches, not watching old movies all day long."

"Broom, we don't *have* any roaches," Wyrdrune said patiently.

"Small wonder, with me watching movies all the time. No, Modred's absolutely right. Take it back. I shouldn't be so selfish. Sweep and dust, sweep and dust, that's my role around here. An old broom's got to earn its keep—"

"An old broom's gonna go flying off the balcony in about another second if it doesn't shut the hell up," snapped Kira.

"You hear this? That's the thanks I get for trying to keep a decent house! Fine, go ahead then, *throw* me off the balcony! I've already got half my bristles in the grave! I'm just a useless old broom, only taking up space—"

"Where's my knife?" said Kira. "I'm gonna whittle myself a toothpick."

"Will you two *stop*?" said Wyrdrune. "Broom, we have to talk about something important, okay? Why don't you go and make some coffee?"

"Coffee, he wants. Four o'clock in the morning and he wants coffee. What is this, a truck stop?"

"Please, Broom," said Modred. "It really is important. I

don't think we'll be going back to sleep. Some coffee would be very much appreciated.''

The broom sniffed. "Well . . . long as I'm up, I suppose I might as well make breakfast. No point you should all get acid stomach. I'll whip up some French toast with cinnamon and maple syrup. May as well make myself useful, so nobody should think that all I do around this place is sit around and watch old movies. . . .''

Wyrdrune rolled his eyes as the broom shuffled back into the kitchen. "I *had* to animate that stupid thing. I could have given Mom a kitten or a puppy to keep her company, but *noooo*. . . .''

"It serves you right for casting spells beyond your level,'' Merlin said. "Though I must admit, it was a first-rate piece of conjuring. How you managed it, I'll never know.''

"Thanks,'' said Wyndrune sourly.

"Well,'' said Kira, "now that we're all up, what do we do about this dream? You can't tell me it was just coincidence.''

"No, I don't believe it was,'' said Modred, nodding agreement. "However, it's possible that it might have been a side effect of the bond the runestones forged between us. One of us might have simply had an ordinary nightmare and its intensity might have triggered a telepathic communication of the dream to the rest of us.''

"I suppose that's possible,'' said Wyrdrune, "but nothing like that has ever happened before. Except that time Kira and I shared the same dream when that necromancer took you prisoner in England.''

"If only there was some way we could communicate directly with the runestones,'' Modred said.

Except for Billy, who would have dearly loved not having to share consciousness with Merlin's spirit, it was a frustration they'd all felt many times before. The runestones had become a part of them, had changed their lives irrevocably, and yet in many ways they still remained a mystery.

It was a spell as old as time itself, dating back to the days of prehistory, when another race of beings had ruled the earth. They were called the Old Ones. The very fact that they existed was known only to a small handful of people, as they were similar enough to humans that their remains were indistinguishable from those of humans. There was, however, one essential biological difference. The Old Ones were immortal. Unlike humans, there was apparently no limit to how many times their cell lines could divide. They could be killed, but their immune systems were far superior to those of humans and they did not age.

The Old Ones had been magic-users. They had enslaved primitive humans, using them to perform labor and as a source of life energy to empower their spells. Yet as the humans evolved, the Old Ones gradually ceased to look upon them as anything more than beasts and many of them came to feel that it was cruel and wasteful to destroy them in order to cast their spells. Under the leadership of their ruling elders, the Council of the White, they began to practice conservation of the human thaumaturgic resource, casting their spells in such a manner that they did not totally consume the life energies of humans, but allowed them to recuperate. It was the beginning of white magic.

Yet, white magic was a much slower and more careful process. In order to accomplish the same results, it took more time and concentration. And there were those among the Old Ones who did not wish to give up the old ways of necromancy, which could provide power far more quickly and which could enable them to consume the life energies of humans in order to replenish their own. They rebelled against the Council of the White and continued to practice necromancy. They became known as the Dark Ones. And their rebellion led to mage war.

The conflict between them survived in history as the legend of the *Ragnarok*, the *Götterdämmerung*—the Twilight of the Gods. The population of the Old Ones was decimated by their war and at the end the necromancers were defeated. To punish the surviving Dark Ones, the Council of the White entombed them for all time in a deep subterranean pit in the Euphrates Valley, giving up their own lives to empower the incantation that would hold them.

The keys to the spell the mages of the Council cast were three enchanted runestones, a ruby, a sapphire, and an emerald. Once the spell was cast, the surviving members of the Council of the White infused their own life energies into the stones, to hold the Dark Ones entombed for all time. Only one of them was left alive, the youngest of the mages—Gorlois. It was his duty to place the stones inside a small chest above the pit and then seal up the chamber, after which he cast off his sorcerer's robes and went out into the world to live among the humans, whom the war had left the dominant race on earth.

And that new dominant race proceeded to take fierce vengeance on those who had once ruled them. The surviving Old Ones were hunted down relentlessly and killed. Those who escaped managed to do so only by hiding their true nature. They interbred with humans, as did Gorlois, and their descendants inherited some of their abilities, though with each succeeding generation, their longevity decreased and their abilities became diluted. But even long after the Old Ones were no more, the hatred that the humans had for them persisted, fueled by superstition and tradition. The persecution of witchcraft through the ages, the fear of anyone who seemed somehow "different," the legends of vampires, evil spirits, demons, shapechangers, and werewolves, all had their origin with the Old Ones.

Modred had seen it all. He had lived through all those times of persecution. He was just a boy when he met his father, Arthur, on the field of battle and they engaged in mortal struggle. Arthur had been killed, but though Modred was impaled on his father's spear and left for dead, he had survived. His wounds had healed and he left England, to pursue life as a mercenary for the next two thousand years. He had lived in many different nations under many different names, the most recent and infamous of which was Morpheus, an international assassin wanted by the law enforcement agencies of almost every country in the world. He had accumulated a vast fortune, carefully concealed, widely distributed, and managed by a legion of confederates, most of whom had no idea who they were really working for. A sorcerer himself, he had disdained to use his powers except on very rare occasions, relying on his strength and wits instead. And it was not until two thousand years had passed that he found something to believe in, something greater than himself, something that was now embodied by the ruby runestone that was magically embedded in his flesh, over his heart.

Wyrdrune and Kira had much briefer histories. They were both still young, only in their twenties. As a student warlock who had studied under Merlin, Wyrdrune was too naturally talented for his own good, capable of spells far above his level, but lacking the discipline to properly control them. It was that lack of discipline that led to his expulsion before he could be certified as an adept. His mother had died while he was still away at school and he returned to New York City, alone and almost penniless, determined to somehow raise the money that would allow him to complete his thaumaturgic education. While scanning the newspaper one day, he chanced upon an article about the upcoming auction of some artifacts unearthed in the Euphrates Valley and, inexplicably, he became seized with the compulsion to steal a particular item that was up for bid. A small bronze chest that held three enchanted runestones.

At the same time, Kira, an orphan who had grown up on the streets of New York City and made her living as a cat burglar, became seized by a similar compulsion. Yet neither of them knew that they were already in the grip of forces far greater than they could understand. Although they didn't know it at the time, they were descended after many generations from two of Gorlois's daughters, Elaine and Morgause. And it was for their descent from the last surviving member of the Council of the White that they had been chosen by the living runestones.

When Modred, Kira, and Wyrdrune, the descendants of the three daughters of Gorlois, finally met, the runestones magically became a part of them and their destiny was changed forever. Separately, they were no more than what they'd been before, but together, they could unite to form the Living Triangle, calling forth the full power of the runestones and the spirits of the Council of the White. And that power was needed now, because once the runestones had been removed from the chamber where the Dark Ones slept, the necromancers were able to escape. They had scattered throughout the world and now the only way to stop them was to hunt them down, before they could come into their full power.

"We're forgetting one thing," said Kira. "The last time Wyrdrune and I shared a telepathic dream, it wasn't the runestones' doing. It was the necromancer who had captured you, trying to make us think the contact was coming from you."

"You think one of the Dark Ones is casting spells against us?" Wyrdrune said.

"It's entirely possible," said Modred. "So long as we're alive and have the runestones, we remain a threat to them. One of them, or perhaps more, may be trying to lure us somewhere."

"Or away from 'ere," said Billy.

"Yes, good point," Modred agreed. "Things have been relatively quiet since we returned from Paris. There's been no sign that any of the Dark Ones have been active."

"At least, none that we know of," Wyrdrune said. "That's what really worries me. We simply don't have enough information. There are all sorts of half-forgotten corners of the world where the Dark Ones could have holed up and started to build up their powers. Even with your network of informants, there's still a lot of places they can't cover. How would we ever know?"

"That's been something I've been giving a great deal of thought to recently," said Modred. "I sorely miss Apollonius."

"Who's Apollonius?" asked Billy.

"Not who, what," said Modred. "Although, in a sense, Apollonius was alive. It was a sentient, hyperdimensional matrix computer containing a fortune in thaumaturgically etched and animated chips."

"Wait a minute, I heard something about that," said Kira. "It was in all the papers a few years back. This was some super computer that was supposed to be delivered to the C.I.A. in Langley, only it was hijacked en route. They were calling it the heist of the century."

"Hyperbole," said Modred. "However, it was a rather neat job, if I say so myself."

"You never told us anything about that!"

"It wasn't intentional, I assure you," he replied. "Force of habit, I suppose. After so many years spent as a lawbreaker, I've developed a tendency to keep things to myself. Apollonius was my great secret. It enabled me to run rings around the I.T.C. They never could figure out how I was always able to stay several steps ahead of them. It was because Apollonius had raided their data banks. It was the most sophisticated computer ever built, easily capable of breaking into any data bank anywhere in the world, no matter how secure. It enhanced my fortune considerably. I was never terribly computer literate, but Apollonius took to computer crime like a duck takes to water. To Apollonius, it was merely one big game.''

"What happened to it?" Wyrdrune asked.

"Al'Hassan," said Modred with a grimace. "I had the misfortune to illegally access the data banks at the College of Sorcerers in Cambridge at the precise moment that Al'Hassan was doing the same thing. We were both looking for you, as a matter of fact."

Wyrdrune shifted on the couch, uneasily. It was hard to believe now, but when he and Modred had first met, Modred, in his identity of Morpheus, had been hired to kill him. And if it hadn't been for the fact that Al'Hassan had been after him as well, he might well have succeeded. The only thing that saved him was the fact that Modred had decided that if one of the world's most powerful mages was after him as well, then whatever he had or knew must have been worth a great deal more than Modred had been offered.

Of course, that had been before they realized the true nature of the runestones and the truth of their relationship. Morpheus was no longer a professional assassin, but it was sometimes difficult to remember that the elegant and charming man who stood before them now, a man who had become closer than a brother to both him and Kira, was a ruthless and cold-blooded killer.

"Al'Hassan had been using an astral projection spell to access the school's records, trying to find a clue to your identity. A risky business, but he evidently felt secure enough in his power to chance it. He was already inside the system when I accessed it through Apollonius. He detected it, locked on, traced the break-in to its source, and used some sort of explosive fire spell that not only obliterated Apollonius, but burned down my entire penthouse, as well. As a result, I not only lost Apollonius and some irreplaceable works of art, but the authorities cracked my alias as John Roderick and I was forced to abandon it. Altogether, it was quite an inconvenience.''

Wyrdrune glanced at Kira. An attack by one of the most powerful mages in the world, and he dismissed it as "an inconvenience." Al'Hassan had almost succeeded in killing them all, but in the end, thanks to the power of the runestones, Modred had destroyed him. It was a grim reminder of what their lives had now become. And the fact that Modred could be so casual about it all was sobering. But then, he'd been a mercenary for two thousand years. And Wyrdrune had been a devout coward for twenty-five.

"I wish there was some way to replace Apollonius," said Modred.

"Well, you've got to be the richest man in the world," said Kira. "Couldn't you just buy another one?"

Modred chuckled. "If I could have done that, there would have been no need for me to steal it in the first place. Apollonius was assembled by Yamako industries in Tokyo and programmed by General Hyperdynamics in Colorado Springs. The latter only does work for the government and for the I.T.C. and although Yamako industries might be approached, it would be a very complicated matter. There are only a few such computers in existence. The United States government has replaced the one I'd stolen and the I.T.C. also has one now. It's possible, in fact, it's very probable that the Japanese have one, as well, though if they do, they've kept it highly secret. There's certainly no such machine in private hands. Such a contract would be bound to attract a great deal of attention and attention is the one thing we do not need."

"Couldn't you use one of your corporate blinds to purchase one?" asked Wyrdrune.

"I could, but I'd be inviting certain investigation. Still, it's a highly tempting thought. However, that would not solve the entire problem. There would still be the matter of properly programming the machine, which only General Hyperdynamics is equipped to do. And I could hardly approach them openly. None of my aliases or blinds could withstand a detailed government scrutiny."

"What if you didn't approach them openly?" asked Wyrdrune.

"In that case, they would almost certainly penetrate my cover that much sooner."

"I wasn't talking about using a cover," Wyrdrune said. "If they're the ones who programmed Apollonius, they obviously would have had to write the program first. And wouldn't it stand to reason that they'd keep a backup copy on file?"

Modred put down his glass slowly. He suddenly looked very interested. "Go on. What are you getting at?"

"What if we could raid their data banks and steal the backup program?"

"How?"

"We could use Archimedes."

"*Archimedes?*" Modred laughed. "You can't be serious!"

"Why not?" said Wyrdrune defensively. "It's worth a try, isn't it?"

"You don't know what you're suggesting," Modred replied. "The data banks at General Hyperdynamics are protected by one of the most sophisticated, thaumaturgically warded security systems in the world. And Merlin's little toy is nothing more than a playful personal computer. I'll grant you that it's sentient, but it would be no match against their safeguard programs. They'd detect the break-in immediately, lock on, trace the source, and that would be the end of it. Archimedes would be destroyed and, worse still, we would be exposed. No, for a moment there, I thought you might have stumbled onto an idea, but using Archimedes would be out of the question. It's a delightful little unit and it would be a shame to lose it on such a fool's gamble. It's simply not equipped for such a task."

Wyrdrune grimaced, reluctant to give up the idea. "Isn't there any way that Archimedes could be modified to handle it?"

"Again, I'm not expert on computers," Modred said, "but I can't see how."

"Well, what if we were to upgrade its chips or something?"

Modred pursed his lips thoughtfully. "It could be done. State-of-the-art thaumaturgically etched and animated chips are not exactly available over the counter, but they can be obtained far more easily than a complete hyperdimensional matrix unit. But that would only solve part of the problem. There would still be the matter of the programming. Avoiding safeguard programs is an art in itself. In effect, it would be necessary to teach Archimedes how to become the computer equivalent of a master cat burglar. And none of us possess the necessary knowledge to do that.''

"Maybe not," said Kira. "But I might know someone who does."

They all looked at her expectantly.

"I did a job about six years ago, when I was just a kid who didn't know enough not to take those kinds of risks. I didn't really know the details, I was just part of a team some high-roller put together, but it involved a heist of restricted data from a big investment banking firm. My part was pretty small. I had to break into some big wheel's apartment and steal some kinda little black book with information that would tell us what to look for. But the guy who actually cracked the system and hijacked the data was a real whiz. He got the job done and they never even knew they had been hit."

"Who was he?" Wydrone asked.

"Guy named Claude something," she said, frowning. "Weird guy. One of those genius types. They called him Pirate. I can't remember his full name, but I know where I can get a hold of him."

"Just a moment," Merlin said. "Before you take this any further, has it occurred to any of you that Archimedes might have something to say about this?"

Wyrdrune glanced at Billy. "Well . . . why don't we ask him?"

Billy got up and went back into his room. A moment later he came out and behind him came a boxy little computer, waddling comically like a duck. With its built-in screen, it resembled a small portable TV set with short, stubby little legs. In its own way, it was as odd a thaumaturgical creation as the broom, a special gift for Merlin from the faculty of the College of Sorcerers at Cambridge, on the occasion of his being appointed dean emeritus.

Billy bent down and lifted it up onto the coffee table. "Sit down, Archimedes," he said in Merlin's voice. "There's something we would like to ask you."

The little computer squatted down on the coffee table, retracting its blocky legs into its light beige housing. Wyrdrune glanced at Modred.

"Go ahead," said Modred. "It was your idea."

Wyrdrune cleared his throat. "Uhhh, Archimedes...we were thinking...How would you like an upgrade?"

"An upgrade?" said the computer in a voice that sounded like a chipmunk breathing helium. It popped up on its legs again and started bouncing. "Oh, boy! *Really?*"

"Don't beat about the bush," said Merlin.

"Well, you see..." said Wyrdrune, "what we really had in mind was a special upgrade that would allow you to do a certain kind of job."

"What kind of job?" asked Archimedes.

"Well...sort of an *illegal* job," said Wyrdrune. He cleared his throat again. "We need you to raid a data bank for us. A very special data bank. The upgrade would enable you to do it and we think we can get someone to show you how, but it could be very dangerous."

"But I'd get to keep the upgrade?"

"Oh, yes, you'd get to keep the upgrade. But do you understand what we're asking you to do? We're asking you to be a burglar. To commit computer crime."

"But I *would* get to keep the upgrade? What kind of upgrade?"

"State-of-the-art thaumaturgically etched and animated chips," said Wyrdrune, "with increased storage and processing capability. The best money can buy."

"Oh, *boy!*"

"Archimedes," Merlin said. "Did you hear the part about how this could be very dangerous to you?"

"Could I get Magic Warrior?"

"What's Magic Warrior?" asked Wyrdrune, frowning.

Merlin sighed. "It's a computerized role-playing game. Something involving wizards, warriors, and mazelike dungeons. He's been pestering me about it for months."

"You could have any game you like," said Modred. "But I'm not sure you understand the situation. You'd be going up against sophisticated safeguard programs, far more challenging than any game of mazes."

"*Really?* Even better than Magic Warrior?"

"Much better. And far more dangerous."

"Better than Screaming Zombie Ninjas?"

"Screaming Zombie Ninjas?" said Kira.

"Don't ask," said Merlin.

"All right, all right, enough with the *shmoozing* already," said the broom, coming in from the kitchen. "Breakfast is on the table. You want it should get cold?"

"Hey, Broom, I'm gonna be a *burglar!*" said Archimedes, bouncing up and down.

"That's very nice, dear," said the broom. "Now stop jumping on the coffee table. I just waxed."

Wyrdrune sighed and rubbed his temples. "Why do I have the feeling we're getting in way over our heads here?"

"Hey, warlock, it was *your* idea," Kira said.

"I know, I know. . . ."

"Well, don't get anxious," Modred said. "We're not committed to it yet. We need access to that data, but let's take things one step at a time. First, I'll see about obtaining the upgrade components for Archimedes. And those screaming ninjas or whatever." He grimaced. "Meanwhile, I'd like to meet this Pirate person and form my own opinion of him. How soon do you think you could arrange it?"

"I'll get on it right away."

"All right, then. In the meantime, we can discuss our dreams in greater detail over breakfast. Perhaps we might recall something that will give us a clue to what it means."

"I know what it means," said Wyrdrune with a wry look. "Trouble."

CHAPTER
Two

GINZA LIGHTS. A CACOPHONY OF FLASH AND COLOR. A strobing, pulsing, heaving orgasm of steel, glass, and concrete.

Kanno loved the Ginza. He felt more at home here than anywhere else in the entire city. A predator stalking through the neon jungle. In the days prior to the Collapse, Tokyo had grown more than any other city in the world. It seemed to rise up out of the island like a mutant crystal, many faceted and multileveled, throbbing with heavy metal energy. And the Ginza was its power chord, the decadent heart of the leviathan.

Kanno crushed his cigarette under the heel of his black suede boot and stepped off the sidewalk onto the street. He did not look like a sorcerer tonight. He was dressed in sharply creased black slacks, gathered at the ankles, a black shirt, and a black, raw silk jacket with the collar turned up, his long hair tucked underneath. He wore a black fedora with a purple hatband tilted rakishly over his forehead and expensive jewelry—a gold watch, a diamond ring, and a diamond choker. Just another young urban swell, lousy with money, out for a good and dirty time.

Several scooters "breezed" him as he crossed the street, missing him by fractions of an inch as they whined by on either side of him, their riders looking like rock and roll Huns in their renaissance punk chain-mail leathers and glittering, concha-studded lycras, their faces invisible behind insectoid helmets with polarized visors. The sleek little scooters were shrouded in plastic, aerodynamic bodywork, and powered by thaumaturgic batteries, their paint schemes rendered in ultra-bright metallic colors. Kanno didn't flinch. He merely kept walking steadily until he reached the opposite sidewalk.

The Ginza was once Tokyo's most exclusive shopping district, with the city's largest concentration of expensive boutiques, department stores, fancy restaurants, hostess bars, and coffee shops. Its name meant "silver mint," but though there was still a lot of coin being minted here, it was of a rather different color. The Ginza was now Tokyo's combat zone, a multileveled monument to modern decadence. There were theme bars catering to various elements of the pre-Collapse nostalgia craze, where one could enjoy the atmosphere of the American West, complete with floor shows, brawls, and staged gunfights or joints styled after Saigon bistros, where the patrons dressed up like mercenaries and fondled B-girls in slashed skirts. There were tattoo parlors, peep shows, gambling casinos, discos, whorehouses, drug emporiums, in short, something for every jaded taste. Provided one could afford it, of course.

The wealthy businessmen and the upwardly mobile young people tended to frequent the upper levels of the district, where the action was wild, but considerably tamer than the thrills to be found on the lower levels. The ground level was for the real hardcore thrillseekers, those who didn't mind or were enticed by an element of danger. There were police here, but they were by far outnumbered by the street gangs, the whores, the pimps, the pickpockets, the muggers, and the rapists. And there were a lot of dark alleys and corners where the local denizens could ply their trade.

Kanno brushed past several shills who tried to entice him into their emporiums, his gaze sweeping the street. There. On the corner. Leaning against the wall and smoking a cigarette. Showing lots of long, slim leg in a skirt slashed right up to her waist. Red, high-heeled pumps; black dress; snakeskin jacket. Hair down to her waist. Not a day over sixteen. She still looked fresh, not yet used up or burned out by drugs. Perfect. He could almost feel the vibrancy of her life force.

She smiled as he approached. "Hi. Looking for a date?"

The negotiation took no longer than a few seconds. She hooked her arm through his and whispered into his ear that she had a place around the corner and flicked his earlobe with her tongue, pressing herself up against him. She conducted him down a dark alley. Kanno smiled.

The alley ended in a cul-de-sac. As he had known it would.

The footsteps behind him didn't come as a surprise, either.

Three of them. Young toughs, armed with knives and needle guns.

Kanno turned to face them.

He sensed a movement behind him, and without even turning toward the girl, he caught her wrist and twisted it. She gasped and the knife fell to the ground. He flung her aside.

The young toughs fired their needle guns. The slim, silvery projectiles whistled through the air toward him . . . then came to an abrupt halt, hanging motionless in the air, inches in front of his face and chest. Kanno smiled and they tinkled to the ground like slivers of broken glass.

For a moment they stood still, shocked, staring at him, then they realized the grave error they had made. One of them shouted out, "He's an adept!" and they bolted. They didn't get more than half a dozen steps before the alleyway behind them erupted in a sheet of flame, a burning wall of fire ten feet high, cutting off escape.

And through that fire stepped a figure, unscathed by the flames, a woman dressed in a suit of skintight black leather, a woman with coppery-gold skin and hair as bright red as the flames. She smiled as she approached the three young toughs, moving purposefully, majestically, like a tigress stalking her prey. Her eyes began to glow.

One of the toughs yelled and lunged at her with a long, gleaming butterfly knife. She made a sweeping motion with her arm, not even touching him, and he went flying backward through the air to land in a heap at Kanno's feet. Kanno moved toward him, but Leila snapped, "No! They're mine!"

"The girl," said Kanno, swallowing and moistening his lips. "Let me have the girl. Please. . . ."

"Take her."

Kanno turned toward the girl, still cowering on the ground where he had thrown her. She watched in disbelief as the red-haired woman's eyes flared like beacons and she disappeared, along with the three would-be killers. She stared up at Kanno, eyes wide, shaking her head.

"No . . . no, please . . . don't hurt me. . . . I'll do anything . . . *anything*!"

Kanno said nothing. But suddenly his clothes began to bulge outward and move, as if something was writhing inside them. He grunted as if he were about to be sick and bent forward, then something came bursting out of his shirt with a deafening roar.

She screamed . . .

"Third one this week," said Lt. Fugisawa.

Agent Akiro Katayama, of the Nippon Bureau of Thaumaturgy, stood silently, looking down at what remained of the body. He had seen more than his share of dead bodies in his time, but never one like this.

"The others were like this, as well?" he asked.

"More or less."

Akiro glanced at Fugisawa. "What do you mean, more or less?"

The policeman shrugged. "Sometimes there was more of them, sometimes less."

"I'll want a full report. You have photographs, of course."

"Of course. And you can also view the remains, if you wish."

"I don't wish," said Akiro with a grimace, "but I'm afraid I'll have to. You were right to call me in on this."

"Necromancy?" asked Fugisawa softly.

"No question of it. The trace emanations are extremely strong. Has the media had any word of this?"

"No, we've kept it quiet. In the Ginza, that's not hard to do."

"Good. I don't want a word of this to leak out to the press, is that understood? As of this moment, this is a Bureau case."

"You're welcome to it."

Akiro turned away from the bloody mess lying in the alley and took a deep breath. "Damn," he said. "A serial killer is bad enough, but an adept. . . ."

"At least it gives you a narrower field of suspects," said Fugisawa.

"I don't suppose anyone saw or heard anything?"

"In the Ginza?" said Fugisawa wryly.

Akiro grunted.

"What do you think it was?"

"Something with teeth," Akiro said. "A lot of very sharp teeth."

The apartment looked like an electronics warehouse into which someone had tossed a hand grenade. There was hardly anyplace to stand, much less sit. The ratty old couch, the coffee table, the end tables, various wooden crates, shelves, and

almost every inch of floor space were covered with a cornuco-
pia of electronic components, circuit boards, tools, wire spools,
diagrams, notebooks, pens, pencils, calculators, tape recorders,
audio components, guitars, banjos, mandolins, Celtic harps,
harmonicas, synthesizer keyboards, dulcimers, coiled strings,
coils of solder, old bags of popcorn and potato chips, beer
cans, old pre-Collapse record albums and compact discs, tape
cassettes, floppy discs, manuals, reams of computer paper, and
magazines. The walls and ceiling of the apartment were covered with sheets of foam rubber to deaden the mind-shattering
sonic assault of the audio system, with speakers the size of
room dividers blasting forth the elemental power chords of a
classic pre-Collapse band, The Ramones, singing about how
they wanted to be committed.

Orchestrating all this chaos was a slightly chubby, owlish-
looking young man with a mass of curly black hair, a thick and
full black beard that covered most of his face, and somewhat
distracted-looking brown eyes behind a pair of round, wire-
rimmed glasses. He was wearing faded old jeans, well-worn
running shoes, a black T-shirt, and a threadbare, brown cordu-
roy jacket with patches on the elbows. This was Claude Eustace
Warburton, a.k.a. "Pirate." He did not look very piratical. He
looked more like something that pops up from beneath a tree
stump to grant you three wishes.

Modred winced and covered his ears against the din. Pirate
mouthed something that could have been, "Oh, sorry," reached
into the pocket of his jacket, and took out a remote-control
device, which he used to shut off the audio system.

"My *God*," said Modred, "it's a wonder you're not completely
deaf!"

"What?"

"I said, it's a wonder you're not . . ." His voice trailed off as
he saw the grin. "Very funny."

"How're you doin', Pirate?" Kira said. "This is my friend,
Michael Cornwall."

"Pleased to meet you," Pirate said, offering his hand.
"Come in. Have a seat."

"Where?" said Modred.

"Oh. Just a moment." Pirate went over to the couch and carelessly swept everything on it to the floor. "You want a beer?"

"No, thank you," Modred said.

"I'll take one," said Kira.

Pirate went into the kitchen to get it.

"You must be joking," Modred said to her while he was out of the room.

"Don't let appearances fool you," Kira said. "When it comes to hacking, Pirate's one of the best there is."

"He's hardly more than a boy."

"So is Billy. You gonna judge *that* book by its cover?"

"Mmm. Point well taken. But I'll need to be convinced. Are you sure he can be trusted?"

"Pirate's okay," she said. "He's careful and he plays by the rules. He's got a reputation to protect."

Pirate came back in with a couple of beers, one for himself and one for Kira. He handed it to her, looked around distractedly, swept a mess of stuff off one of the end tables, and perched on it.

"Been a few years, Kira," he said. "Whatcha been up to?"

"Oh, little bit of this, little bit of that," Kira replied. "We came to talk to you about a job we're trying to put together."

"Could always use a job," said Pirate, scratching his head. "Whatcha got in mind?"

"You working on anything right now?"

He shrugged. "Always workin' on something. But I haven't got any jobs lined up, if that's what you mean. Things've been a little slow lately. I'm available. What's the job?"

"We want to crack the data banks at General Hyperdynamics," Kira said.

The beer can froze as he was putting it to his lips. He lowered it slowly and glanced from her to Modred and back again.

"Are you serious?"

She nodded.

Pirate whistled softly. "Now that's what I call a job." He glanced at Modred. "You the man behind this?"

"That's right," said Modred, watching his reaction.

"You have any idea what you're getting into?"

"I have an excellent idea," Modred said.

"You remember the Apollonius job?" asked Kira.

"Sure, who doesn't?" Pirate said. "I wish I coulda been the one to pull it off."

"Well, meet the man who did," she said.

Pirate looked at Modred with new respect. "No kidding? Well, shit, if you've got Apollonius, the job'll be a piece of cake. You don't need me."

"I appreciate your candor," Modred said. "However, the problem is we don't have Apollonius. Apollonius was destroyed in a fire."

"That was one expensive fire," Pirate said.

Modred grimaced and nodded. "Yes, it was, rather," he said, thinking more about the priceless paintings and antiques that had gone up with it.

"The deal is, he wants to replace Apollonius," said Kira. "Build a new one."

"Build a hyperdimensional matrix computer?" Pirate said. He snorted and shook his head. "You're way outta my league. No way I could get my hands on the necessary components. There's only one place in the world set up to produce hardware like that. Yamako Industries, in Tokyo. And it would cost a fucking fortune. We're talking *millions* here."

"Obtaining the components does not present a problem," Modred said. "What we need is someone to assemble them and install the program. Kira seemed to feel that you were the right man for the job."

Pirate raised his eyebrows. "I appreciate the vote of confidence," he said. "If you can get the hardware, I could probably put it together for you. But as far as programming something on that level . . . oh, I get it. You're after the backup program G.H. has in their files."

Modred nodded.

"You can actually get the hardware?"

"I think so."

"I'm impressed. I won't ask you how. You've either got

incredible connections or incredible bucks. I figure probably both. Hijacking Apollonius was an amazing piece of work." He looked at Kira. "I always had a feeling you'd wind up with someone heavy." He turned back to Modred. "I don't suppose Cornwall is your real name. Not that it matters. This is starting to sound real interesting."

"So you think you're up to the task?" said Modred.

"If I say no, do I wind up in the river?"

Modred smiled. "No. That would be sloppy and there is no need for that. You will simply be made to forget you ever met us."

Pirate raised his eyebrows. "You're an adept?"

Modred inclined his head slightly.

"Makes sense. It would've taken a wizard to hijack Apollonius. Well, I'll be very straight with you, Mr. Cornwall. It'll be a challenge. One hell of a challenge, all the way around. I might be able to pull it off. But if I can't, I doubt you'll find anyone else who can. I'm the best there is."

"No offense," said Modred, "but if you are, in fact, the best there is—"

"Why am I living like this?" asked Pirate, anticipating him. "How come I'm not working for G.H. or I.T.M. or any of the other big conglomerates, is that it?"

"Precisely," Modred said.

"I did, at one time," Pirate said. "When I was eighteen, I ran the entire product planning division for I.T.M. You can check it out. I wore a suit, had an expense account, my own office and secretary, the whole corporate number. It drove me crazy. You have any idea what it's like, working for people who aren't even as smart as you were when you were ten? Putting up with office politics, corporate cocktail parties, and all that horse manure? I had an ulcer by the time I was twenty. I finally said fuck it and quit. And I've never been happier. I do *what* I want, *when* I want, and *how* I want. I like it on my own. And I've got foreign bank accounts the I.R.S doesn't know anything about, okay? In other words, I'm not exactly hurtin'. Some people like their custom-tailored suits. If that's your thing, that's fine by me. But I'm a beer-and-pretzels kind of guy. And if I don't like somebody, I tell 'em to fuck off. You, I don't know a lot about yet. Maybe I don't wanna know. But I know Kira and Kira is good people. Her word's good enough for me. I'll do this job for you, Mr. Cornwall, because I like a challenge. But you're talkin' about major risk here. It's gonna cost you."

"All right," said Modred. "But I'll want a demonstration of your capabilities. No offense, but I like to be careful. I wouldn't expect something for nothing, needless to say. I'm prepared to pay you."

"That's fair," said Pirate. "You got anything special in mind?"

"As a matter of fact, I do. And it will involve the hardware we're going to use on the General Hyperdynamics job."

"Yeah? What've you got?"

"A Thaumac 10."

Pirate stared at him for a moment, then started to laugh. "A *Thaumac 10?* You're puttin' me on!"

Modred simply stared at him.

Pirate stopped laughing. "My God, you're serious! That's a kid's toy! You're gonna try to break into G.H. with *that*? Man, that's like throwing spitballs at a gorilla. You'll get eaten alive!"

"I thought you liked a challenge," Modred said.

"Hey, a challenge is one thing. Stupidity's another."

"This is a rather special Thaumac 10," said Modred. "I think you might be surprised."

"Look, I thought you said you knew what you were getting into. This is a joke, right? I mean, come on. I've got units right here that are a lot more sophisticated than a Thaumac 10, for Christ's sake! I don't care how much you pay me, if you want me to rob one of the tightest data banks in the world, I'm not about to try it with a fuckin' popgun!"

"As I said, this is no ordinary Thaumac 10," said Modred. "It's rather special. And we're going to make it even more special. You're going to show me what you can do given unlimited resources."

"*Unlimited?*"

"Unlimited."

Pirate shrugged. "Okay. It's your money."

"Good. We'll be in touch."

* * *

Even in a city chock-full of eccentrics, Wyrdrune thought, Dr. Sebastian Makepeace was not the sort of person one would call inconspicuous. He was very large, for one thing, over six feet six inches tall, and he weighed about three hundred pounds. He also made some rather peculiar fashion choices. He habitually wore a beret, either black or dark brown or dark green or deep purple, from beneath which his long white hair cascaded down to his shoulders, framing his clean-shaven, wide, cherubic face. He always wore a long, black leather trench coat that at least three cows must have given up the ghost for, and he wore it regardless of the weather, though Wyrdrune had never seen it buttoned up. Beneath that, he wore seersucker in the summer and tweeds the other three seasons, well-tailored three-piece suits that always somehow made him look like a dirigible dressed up for a grouse hunt. He never wore an ordinary necktie or a choker, but always some sort of colorful silk scarf, either tied in a huge bow in the style of a Flemish painter or draped carelessly around his neck, like a WW I aviator. He resembled a character out of Dickens . . . if Dickens had taken acid.

His official job was professor of pre-Collapse history at New York University, but unofficially, he was some sort of government spy. Exactly what he did or which branch of the government he worked for had never been made entirely clear. Wyrdrune would have written that claim off to fantasy if it hadn't been for the fact that he'd had personal experience of the influence Makepeace had with certain government agencies. He was also one of Modred's most valued agents, one of a legion of contacts and connections that Morpheus had spread throughout the world. And last, but certainly not least . . . he was a fairy.

No, not *that* kind. The magic kind. As in enchanted sprite, with gossamer wings and see-through negligé. Like Tinkerbell. Or, at least, so Makepeace claimed. *Ex*claimed, more often than not, usually at the top of his lungs, anytime someone brought up the incongruity of a six-foot-six, three-hundred-pound fairy. Wyrdrune had once observed that if Makepeace had wings, he must have taken them off a pterodactyl, which had launched Makepeace in a violent tirade against Hans

Christian Andersen, the Brothers Grimm, and especially Walt
Disney, who, he claimed, had foisted upon a gullible public a
totally erroneous image of fairies.

The entire faculty and student body at the university knew of
this peculiarity of his, as did most of the Village bars, restaurants, and coffee shops that Makepeace frequented, and it was
widely regarded as a harmless and amusing aberration, a mild
neurosis of an aging adept en route to senility. No one took it
seriously. And, at first, Wyrdrune hadn't either. Except . . .

There was something very *strange* about the magic Makepeace practiced. Wyrdrune had never known an adept to do the
things that Makepeace did, the way he did them. And as he and
Billy approached the park bench, they saw Makepeace doing
something that seemed entirely out of character for him. He
was sitting on the bench, with a brown paper bag in his lap,
feeding the pigeons.

"Ah, Melvin!" he said, greeting them in a booming voice.
Wyrdrune winced. Makepeace knew he couldn't stand his true
name, and so he called him by nothing else. "And young
William. You're just in time. I was about to repair to Lovecraft's
for a libation."

He emptied out the last of the corn from the bag, crumpled it
up, and tossed it casually, without looking, over his shoulder. It
described a graceful, floating arc in the air and landed in a
wastebasket about twenty-five yards away.

"The department secretary told us we could find you here,"
said Merlin, speaking through Billy. "Don't you ever keep
office hours?"

"What for?" said Makepeace. "If I keep office hours, I'll
only have the students coming in to bug me. It's bad enough
I'm forced to teach those little pismires, the thought of *advising*
them is insufferable."

"I thought you didn't like pigeons," Wyrdrune said.

"I don't," said Makepeace, moving his considerable bulk up
off the bench. "Come on, let's go get a drink."

"Then what . . . ?"

Suddenly Wyrdrune heard a muffled *pop* behind him. Then
another, and another, and another and another and another . . .

He turned and saw the pigeons bounding up into the air and turning somersaults, making sounds like muffled strings of firecrackers going off. Their breasts began to swell until they all looked like inflated, feathered volleyballs, bouncing all over the place.

"What the 'ell . . . ?" said Billy.

"Popcorn?" Wyrdrune said.

"My special recipe. Pops in your gut, not in your pan," Makepeace said. "I thought it would be more filling than breadcrumbs. More filling, get it?" He clackled.

"You're a sick man, Sebastian."

"That'll teach them to mess on my beret," said Makepeace with a scowl. "It's getting so a man can't walk anywhere in this city without being bombarded. Pernicious little creatures . . ."

"Sebastian, we've got a problem. . . ."

"Dragons in the mind, eh?"

Wyrdrune came to a sudden stop. "How did you know?"

"I know all and see all," Makepeace said.

"E's 'ad the same bloody dreams 'imself," said Billy.

"And I've had the same bloody dreams myself," admitted Makepeace. "I've been expecting you to get in touch."

"How did you know we were having the same dreams?" asked Wyrdrune.

"I didn't, really. I surmised it. These are no ordinary nightmares, Melvin. There's something deeply malevolent about them. And I sense a presence behind them. An uncomfortably familiar presence."

Wyrdrune glanced at him sharply. He'd experienced no such sensation. It was yet another example of Makepeace being . . . *different.*

"A familiar presence?" he said.

"Oh, yes, indeed," said Makepeace. "It would seem that we are being toyed with. Teased. A markedly feminine characteristic, teasing."

Wyrdrune stopped again. They had reached the entrance to Lovecraft's.

"Leila?" he said.

"Leila," Makepeace said. "After you, my friends."

He beckoned them through the door. Lovecraft's, on MacDougal

Street, was a basement-level tavern that was popular with students, adepts, and various Village arty types. The lights were dim, the tables were rickety and covered with black cloth, with white ceramic skulls on each table, holding candles. The decor was reminiscent of a mausoleum, and the waiters and waitresses all dressed in black, with black eye shadow all around their eyes, making them look like sepulchral raccoons. The bartender greeted Makepeace by name as they went through and took a table in the back. A slinky, long-haired waitress in a dress so tight that she could barely move glided over to their table and gave Makepeace a dazzling smile, which somehow looked a little disconcerting with the black lipstick she was wearing.

"Hi, Doc. The usual?"

"As ever, Morticia, my dear. And a couple of beers for my friends."

She glanced at Billy and pursed her lips. "He doesn't look old enough to drink," she said. "You got any ID?"

"Oh, bloody 'ell . . ." mumbled Billy.

"What, did you forget it again, William?" Makepeace said. He turned to the waitress. "He looks so young, he's always getting carded. Check your pockets."

"I don't 'ave no—"

"*Check* your pockets."

Billy stuck his hand into his jacket pocket and, with a look of surprise, pulled out a wallet.

"There, you see? You're so damned absentminded. . . ."

Billy showed the waitress his "proof," which she checked dubiously.

"Sebastian . . ." she said reprovingly.

Makepeace looked up at her innocently. "Yes, my dear?"

"Now you *know* I'm not going to fall for this. . . ."

"Just bring a pitcher and two glasses, dear. If the constabulary raids this place, he'll push his glass over to me."

She sighed and rolled her eyes. "Why do I let you talk me into these things?" she said. She tossed the wallet back down onto the table and it promptly disappeared.

"I do believe she has your number, Sebastian," Merlin said.

"That lovely girl can have anything of mine she wants," said Makepeace with a grin.

"What makes you so certain that it's Leila?" Wyrdrune asked. "I thought she was dead."

"Don't count your necromancers till they start moldering," said Makepeace. "We lost her in the Paris catacombs, but we have no certain knowledge that she was killed when the tunnels collapsed."

"But what makes you so certain that it's her?"

"Part logic and part fairy intuition," Makepeace said.

"Let's hear the logic part," said Wyrdrune wryly.

"The Dark Ones know about you," Makepeace said, "because you've all encountered them before, if only briefly, when you attempted to prevent them from escaping the place of their confinement. But the only Dark Ones who could possibly know about *me* are those whose paths had crossed with mine before. And Leila is the only one whose fate remains uncertain to us. So, logically, she must have survived."

Wyrdrune nodded. "I guess that makes sense."

"As for my fairy intuition, Ambrosius will tell you that to someone with the proper sensitivity, magic has a certain idiosyncratic signature. Just as a psychic can hold an article of clothing and discern certain things about the individual whom it belonged to, so spells have a certain aura about them that can identify the one who casts them."

Wyrdrune frowned. "I never knew that. Is that true?"

Billy shrugged as Merlin replied. "I suppose it's possible."

"What do you mean, you suppose it's possible? You mean you don't *know*?"

"Well . . . so I've heard," said Merlin, somewhat awkwardly.

"How the hell can you not know?" asked Wyrdrune, astonished.

"What, you think I know *everything*?" said Merlin irritably.

"Yes, but . . . *you*, of all people!"

"Yes, me of all people!" Merlin snapped. "So there are some things about magic I don't know, all right? So I've got feet of clay. So *sue* me! Besides, I've never had all that much to do with fey creatures like leprechauns and fairies. They've always made me nervous."

"That's only because you're so damned humorless and stuffy," Makepeace said. "You've always been an insufferable elitist, Ambrosius."

"One pitcher, and *two* glasses," Morticia said, setting down the tray.

"Ah, thank you, my dear," Makepeace said. He picked up the pitcher and drank from it as if it were a glass, emptying almost half of it in one gulp. "You'd better bring one for the boys, as well."

She shook her head in resignation and went back to the bar.

"If it *is* Leila, then how is she getting to us?" Wyrdrune asked.

"We're not faced with an ordinary adept," said Merlin. "We've used our powers against her before. If she's survived, as seems very likely, she's become sensitized to us. I should have thought of that myself. I fear I'm starting to manifest Billy's slovenly habits."

"*Ey!* You don't like it, you can bloody well *leave*, y'know!"

"Is there some problem here?" said Morticia, coming back with the second pitcher.

"No problem, my dear, everything's just fine," said Makepeace.

She glanced at Billy dubiously. "This isn't one of your punk bars, kid. Don't go getting rowdy in here."

"Sure thing, Mum. Give us a kiss."

"Billy . . ." Wyrdrune said, shaking his head.

Morticia leaned down suddenly and planted her mouth right on Billy's, her hand cupping the back of his head. After about ten seconds, she straightened up and smiled. "Now you behave yourself, okay?"

She moved away.

Billy simply sat there, stunned, his eyes glazed, his jaw hanging open.

"Billy?" Wyrdrune said.

No answer.

"Professor? Merlin?"

He passed his hand in front of his eyes. Nothing.

Wyrdrune gave a low whistle.

Makepeace chuckled. "Morticia's a bit of a spellbinder herself," he said. He poured a glass for Wyrdrune. "Drink up, Melvin. This could take a while."

CHAPTER
Three

THREE MORE DAYS, THREE MORE BODIES. AND B.O.T. AGENT Akiro Katayama had not made any further progress. All he had was a pattern. Young women were being killed, all hookers presumably, though some of the bodies had been so thoroughly savaged that it was impossible to make any sort of identification at all, beyond the approximate age and sex. That was the hellish part of any investigation in the Ginza. Tokyo was a teeming city, full of people who survived on the fringes of society, people who had no documentation whatsoever. And many of them gravitated to the Ginza. They were born in poverty and squalor and they often spent their lives that way, living and dying in the city's forgotten warrens.

Those fortunate enough to better their lots usually did so through crime, resulting in a constant influx into Japan's criminal classes of people who did not even officially exist. Unless, at some point in their lives, they happened to be arrested, there was no record of them whatsoever. Which meant no way to contact any next of kin, no way to identify dead bodies through such things as dental records, no way to determine who their friends were, who they worked for, or where they lived. And even if the corpse was recognizable, people in the Ginza were not forthcoming when it came to giving information to the cops. Especially a Bureau cop, because that meant that magic was involved and the lower classes were frequently afraid of magic. So how the hell was he supposed to conduct an investigation?

He knew precious little. He knew, without a question of a doubt, that necromancy was behind it. The trace emanations from the corpses were extremely strong. Not many people could detect them, even among magic-users, but the adept agents of the Bureau were selected from among the best graduates of thaumaturgy schools and they were trained extensively, their natural sensitivities polished to a high degree of acuteness. The minimum grade required for acceptance to Bureau training was wizard. And the platinum shield was not awarded to anyone who failed to pass any aspect of the grueling course, which culminated in a series of exams including certification as a sorcerer. Many tried to make the grade. Only a few succeeded. Akiro was one of the best agents on the staff of the Japanese Bureau. He had already put in fifteen years and in another five, he would have the option of either taking his pension and entering the corporate sector or filing an application for acceptance to the I.T.C. His lifelong goal had been the latter, the highest level of government service that an adept could hope to attain, short of actually sitting on the board of the International Thaumaturgical Commission.

Akiro had no illusions about ever being able to rise that far. He simply did not possess enough natural ability, otherwise he would have been accepted to the I.T.C. straight out of thaumaturgy school. That sometimes happened, although it was very rare. Occasionally, a student would come along who would display such a high level of natural ability that he or she would be selected for a special program upon graduation, an accelerated course of study leading to certification as a sorcerer and enrollment in one of the I.T.C.'s specialized training schools in places such as Cambridge, Geneva, Heidelberg, or Rome. But Akiro had realized early on that such was not to be his lot. He had talent and he had ability, but it came at the cost of steady, plodding work. In time, his record with the Bureau would give him a favorable chance of being accepted by the I.T.C., but only in some field office, behind a desk, or as a subordinate field agent. And that was fine. It would be a good job, with outstanding salary and benefits, and with a great deal of prestige. He could want for nothing more. But he would never get it if his Bureau record contained a case that was not closed. And somehow, he would close this one, not only close it, but *solve* it. The only trouble was, how?

He had nothing to go on. No witnesses. No clues. No leads of any kind. All he had were corpses and corpses did not speak. Already, there was talk on the streets about the hideous murders. Within a matter of days, if not mere hours, the media would be certain to pick up on it. And then they would come to him, as the agent in charge of the case. They would focus their cameras upon him and what would they see? A stocky little Bureau agent in his mid-fifties, slightly overweight, with a receding hairline and inexpensive clothes, in other words, the typical shopworn bureaucrat. They would shove their microphones into his face and what would they hear? A man with an unremarkable speaking voice, who chose his words carefully and had a tendency to falter when he knew that he was speaking for the record. A man who was acutely uncomfortable at the thought of being in the public eye and who had gone to great lengths all his life to avoid it. In other words, a man who would come across on camera as a plodding, unimaginative, minor government official of whom great things could certainly not be expected. They would want to know what he had accomplished and why he had not accomplished more. They would want to know what he was *doing* about these awful murders and why wasn't the Bureau bringing "all their resources" to bear, the suggestion being, of course, that he himself was not up to the task.

And sooner or later, it was inevitable, the Bureau would respond to the pressure. They would need a scapegoat and he would be the logical one to choose, because the media would have already chosen him. He'd be taken off the case and some young, good-looking, flamboyant agent would be assigned to it and Akiro's hopes of further advancement would be dashed. Not a disgrace, exactly, but it would follow him around for the rest of his life. Forget about the I.T.C. Forget about the corporate sector. "Aren't you the one who failed to solve the Ginza murders?" No, at that point he might as well take his twenty and retire to support his family on the Bureau's meager pension.

I will *solve* this case, he thought to himself savagely. He hated the killer, hated him with all the passion of his being, not only for the horrible acts he was committing, but for the way he had disgraced and perverted the art of thaumaturgy and for the threat that he presented to himself and to his family's well-being. And it was only the force of that passion in a man who was, at heart, not passionate at all that brought him to the door of a man who, under any other circumstances, he would not have dared approach.

He stood with his hat held awkwardly in his hands and told the imposing-looking housekeeper that he humbly requested an audience with the master, to speak with him concerning an official matter of the gravest urgency. He displayed his shield and identification and bowed respectfully, even though it was only the housekeeper. The housekeeper gave him a long, appraising look, then asked him to wait. Akiro waited, nervously twisting his hat around in his hands. After a few moments the housekeeper returned.

"The master will see you. Please come this way."

Akiro entered the house and took his shoes off. There were several pairs of soft, heelless *surippa* just inside the door. The word was originally adapted in the pre-Collapse days from the English word "slippers," a custom that also came from the West and was easily assimilated into Japan's "shoes-off-at-the-door" life-style. As usual, the Japanese took the custom even further, with the use of seasonal *surippa* for different times of the year and even for different rooms. When one entered a home, the street shoes immediately came off and *surippa* were donned, to be worn in the corridors until one came to a room in which the floors were covered with tatami mats. Then one removed the *surippa*, for no shoes of any kind were worn on the woven mats. In homes that were carpeted, in western fashion, it was customary to ask the individual homeowner whether *surippa* were worn on the carpets or only socks. And if one needed to go to the bathroom, there were usually several pair of *surippa* by the door, to be worn in the bathroom only and in no other room in the house. One simply changed *surippa* at the bathroom door and then, when finished, changed back again.

To most westerners, this all seemed terribly complicated and even a little silly, but there was sound reasoning behind it, as there was behind most Japanese customs that seemed incomprehensible to the uninitiated western mind. For one thing, it helped to keep the house clean and saved wear and tear on the fragile tatami mats. For another, in Japan's extremely congested society, it helped to create the aura of psychological space where physical space was at a premium. A very small room could subtly be made to seem larger by the simple expedient of taking a few extra seconds to remove or put on slippers before crossing it. A small thing, perhaps, seemingly of no significance to those who came from cultures where space was taken pretty much for granted, but small things and insignificant-seeming customs added up to civilization; manners and traditions that were important in preserving order in a society where so many people lived so close together.

Akiro could immediately see upon entering the simple house that Yohaku kept a very traditional Japanese home. It was beautiful and elegant in its simplicity, with great attention paid to the placement of each and every item of furnishing and decoration to achieve a perfect sense of balance in each room. The simple, delicate screens; the impeccable arrangements of flowers; the ink paintings; the subtle scent of incense; the woodblock prints; the *teien*, the landscape garden visible through the open screen door at the back of the small living room, with its painstakingly raked sand and artistically arranged rocks and shrubs; all combined to give the home a profound sense of tranquil harmony. Akiro was deeply moved, both by the privilege of the audience and of seeing this lovely home. Truly, this was the dwelling of a master.

"Welcome to my humble home, Katayama-san."

Akiro was startled. He had not heard the sound of a sliding screen, nor had he heard any footsteps. Suddenly Yohaku was simply there, an old man in his eighties, dressed in a simple white kimono and sash, his long, fine hair the color of freshly fallen snow, cascading down past his shoulders and looking like a No player's wig. His face was deeply lined, with skin that looked like fragile parchment, yet the deeply sunken eyes were alert and bright, the startling color of cornflowers. He had never seen such eyes on a Japanese. And though the old man was almost painfully thin and slightly stoop-shouldered, there was somehow an aura of great power and grace about him. A man truly centered and at peace with life. Akiro bowed deeply and presented his card.

"*Ohayo gozaimasu*, Yohaku-sama," Akiro said. "Thank you for seeing me."

"Please," said Yohaku, his voice as soft as a caress, "the *sama* is entirely unnecessary. While I appreciate the graciousness of your address, I would much prefer it if you simply called me by my name. Or if that makes you uncomfortable, *sensei* will do."

"Thank you, Sensei," said Akiro, bowing once again and feeling entirely inadequate.

Yohaku smiled. "Please," he said, indicating the living room with his outstretched hand, "come in and sit down. Allow me the pleasure of offering you some tea."

"No, thank you very much, Sensei. Please do not go to any trouble."

"I insist. Besides, it is no trouble whatsoever. Observe."

He made a small, spare, and graceful movement of his hand, merely a turning upward of the palm, and a tea service appeared on the low, black-lacquered table. Akiro held his breath. There had been no dramatic gestures, no spoken incantation, not even a whisper, no sign of concentration whatsoever. It was all done with an utter economy of motion and with no apparent effort. It was all the more impressive for that than any flamboyant demonstration he had ever witnessed by thaumaturgic entertainers.

"I am honored, Sensei."

They both sat down on the floor, across from each other at the table. Akiro lowered himself with some awkwardness, but Yohaku, easily forty years his senior, seemed to glide down to the floor with all the grace of a falling leaf. Akiro said nothing until Yohaku had served them and they drank their first sips of tea from the exquisite, fragile little cups.

"Delicious," said Akiro.

Yohaku smiled and inclined his head slightly.

Akiro cleared his throat uneasily.

"Please, Katayama-san, feel at ease to tell me how I may be of assistance to the Bureau. I presume this is an official call."

"Yes, Sensei." For a brief moment Akiro debated how to begin, then decided to simply let the evidence speak for itself. "If I may be permitted..." He withdrew a manila envelope from inside his jacket, opened it, and took out the photographs, laying them upon the table. "I apologize for disturbing the harmony of your home with such material, but I could think of no better way to state the nature of my problem."

Yohaku glanced down at the photographs, spreading them out on the table before him. His brow furrowed and he let out a soft sigh. Then he looked up at Akiro, a stricken expression in his eyes, but also a question.

Akiro moistened his lips nervously. "I am sorry to have to show such things to you," he said. "But, as you can see, these are no ordinary murders."

"Necromancy?" said Yohaku, his voice barely audible.

Akiro nodded once. "The trace emanations from the corpses were extremely strong. The strongest I have yet encountered. There is great power at work behind this. Very great power."

"And you have no... what do you call them? Leads?"

"None whatsoever, Sensei. There were no witnesses. No one has yet come forth who can supply any information. I am deeply, deeply troubled by this. To date, all the killings have taken place on the Ginza. The victims were all young women and, so far as we know, prostitutes. Nothing more is known about them. Each day brings a new murder. Each corpse looks similar. Brutally savaged, partially consumed. No man could have done this. Certainly, no ordinary man. As yet, no word of these killings has reached the media. We have tried to keep it from them, but there is already talk on the streets and within a day or two at most, it will most certainly be made public and I fear that there will be a panic."

Yohaku nodded gravely.

"I am sorry to trouble you with this, Sensei, but—"

"No, it is quite all right," Yohaku interrupted him. "I completely understand your position. You have done the right thing. Necromancy is a very serious matter." He glanced down at the photographs again, then gathered them together and handed them back to Akiro. "Is it possible for me to see the actual remains?"

"Yes, Sensei, of course. I can arrange it at your convenience."

"In the face of such a thing as this, there can be no thought for convenience," said Yohaku, rising smoothly to his feet. "We will leave at once."

The luxurious and thoroughly western atmosphere of the office was a marked contrast to the stark beauty and simplicity of Yohaku's dwelling, but then Fugisawa was not calling on a venerable mage. The man whom he was calling on was venerated, but in a different way and by an entirely different class of people.

Although Akiro had officially taken over the case for the Bureau, Fugisawa was reluctant to let go, in spite of his laconic comments to the agent about the Bureau being welcome to it. He had tried to tell himself that it was one headache that he didn't need and he'd be better off letting the Bureau handle it, but whatever else he might be, Katayama was not a cop. He was not streetwise. That much had become clear to him almost immediately. He was a bureaucrat, accustomed to investigations dealing with the use of thaumaturgy in such things as corporate crime, not murder. Perhaps, in his rather plodding way, he was even an efficient field agent, but he was not a street cop. And this case required a street cop. There were no witnesses, no leads, no clues. In the absence of such things, a good street cop did not simply wait for them to materialize. He went looking for them. And if he didn't know where to look or how, he went to the people who did. The killings had all taken place on Fugisawa's turf and he was deeply affronted by them. They had also taken place on this man's turf, as well, and Fugisawa suspected that he would be equally affronted.

The office was large and spacious, carpeted in deep brown shag and paneled in teak. There was a large wet bar; several expensive-looking modern expressionist paintings; a black leather-upholstered sofa and matching chairs; no windows and a massive mahogany desk big enough to sleep on. Two sober-faced Japanese men in dark suits flanked the desk and there were two more behind him, near the door. Fugisawa's trained eye picked up the faint, telltale bulge of shoulder holsters, though the suits were tailored so that no one but an experienced cop would have spotted them.

The man sitting behind the desk was in his early fifties, though he looked younger. He was dressed in an elegant dark suit and white shirt with a touch of lace at the throat. He wore an expensive gold watch and a tasteful diamond on the little finger of his right hand. The little finger of his left hand was missing. He was Don Teruyuki Kobayashi, the godfather of the Yakuza.

"Don Kobayashi," Fugisawa said, not bowing, but inclining his head slightly.

"Lt. Fugisawa." Kobayashi smiled faintly. "Please, sit down." He indicated a black leather chair in front of the desk. Fugisawa sat. "Can I offer you a drink? Or don't you drink on duty?"

"Scotch, neat," said Fugisawa.

Kobayashi glanced at one of the men beside the desk and he immediately went to the bar and poured two glasses of an expensive, single-malt whiskey.

"Cheers," said Kobayashi, raising his glass.

"First today," said Fugisawa, and took a drink. "Very nice."

"I'm glad you appreciate it. I assume you've come about the Ginza murders."

"You're well informed, as usual."

"And you suspect the Yakuza?"

"No, I don't."

"Indeed? How refreshing. Am I to take it, then, that your visit is in an unofficial capacity?" Meaning, of course, that he realized it was official, but strictly off the record.

"That's right. This is a bad one. I need some help, Don Kobayashi."

"What's in it for me?"

"Depends on how much help I get," Fugisawa replied. "You'll be serving your own interests, as well, but I'm sure we can work something out. Within reasonable limits, of course."

"Of course. What have you got so far?"

"Practically nothing," Fugisawa said, taking another sip of Scotch. "You probably know as much as I do. Maybe more. Someone or some*thing* is killing hookers and apparently consuming parts of their bodies. And that's about all we've got. Officially, it's not even my case. The Bureau's on it."

"So the rumors are true, then. It *is* necromancy?"

"That's about the only thing we know for certain," Fugisawa said. "The agent handling the case, a man named Katayama, has determined that the trace emanations are extremely strong. He suspects either an entity of some sort or a sorcerer who shapechanges."

"A *sorcerer?* What makes you suspect a sorcerer?"

"Katayama believes it's a very high level of power that's involved. He doesn't believe it's a wizard or a lower-grade adept."

"And what do *you* believe?"

"I believe he's right."

Fugisawa reached inside his jacket. The two men on either side of the desk immediately put their hands inside theirs. Fugisawa froze, then very slowly took out an envelope and held it up. One of the men came around the desk and took it from him, opened it, examined the contents briefly, then gave it to Kobayashi. Kobayashi examined the photographs.

"I thought the reports were exaggerated," he said after a moment. "I see that they were not."

He handed the photographs back to the man at his side, who replaced them in the envelope and gave it back to Fugisawa.

"We cannot have this sort of thing," Kobayashi said. "It's bad for business. What, precisely, do you wish to do about this?"

"I want to stop the son of a bitch."

"As do I. It would serve both our interests. But are you particular about how it should be done?"

"No. I'm not."

"I merely want to make sure we understand each other."

"I think we do."

"I can appreciate your attitude, but I doubt the Bureau would."

"The Bureau doesn't have to know. If Katayama solves the

case, I'm not going to complain,'' said Fugisawa. ''But I've got a feeling about this one. I don't think an arrest is in the cards. You don't just handcuff a necromancer and haul him off to jail. I think Katayama is out of his depth this time. I just want that sick, murdering bastard off my streets.'' Fugisawa paused and smiled. ''*Our* streets. Permanently.''

''I will want a full exchange of information,'' Kobayashi said.

Fugisawa nodded. ''You'll get it. Within reasonable limits, of course. I want to make sure we understand each other, too. I'm not proposing any sort of permanent arrangement here. As you said, cooperation on this particular case serves both our interests. This particular case *only*. You try using this to lean on me later and I'll lean back. Hard.''

Kobayashi smiled and nodded. ''A limited, closed-end partnership, then. With the understanding that you will owe a favor for a favor.''

''Within *reasonable* limits.''

''And what if we cannot agree on what is and isn't reasonable?''

''If any of your people off a citizen or something like that and get nailed cold, I'm not going to be able to get them off for you and I won't even try. Nor will I compromise any police investigation. But if it's something where I can look the other way, we can certainly discuss it. You're a businessman, Don Kobayashi. You understand about such things. And as you yourself admit, this isn't a case where I'm getting something for nothing. We will both benefit by this.''

Kobayashi nodded. ''Very well. In that case, it would be best if we were not to meet here again. If my people need to get in touch with you, you will receive a message that your uncle called. You know the Paradise Club?''

''Of course.''

''If you receive such a message, go to the Paradise Club and ask for the manager. Do not identify yourself as a police officer. Say merely that your uncle sent you. And if you should need to get in touch with me, you may use the same procedure.''

''All right.''

''Thank you for stopping by, Lt. Fugisawa.''

''Thank you for seeing me, Don Kobayashi.''

He stood, inclined his head slightly, and left.

"That's the first time I've ever heard of a cop putting out a contract," said one of the men at Kobayashi's side.

"He's done no such thing," said Kobayashi. "And you'd be wise to remember that."

"I don't understand. Didn't he just say—"

"Lt. Fugisawa may not seem like a subtle man, Shiro," said Kobayashi to his eldest son, "but that appearance is deceptive. What he has done was recognize that sooner or later, we would have to do something about this situation. Stories about an adept serial killer in our district are very bad for business. He has merely come to tell us that if we chose to do something about it, he would not interfere and would, in fact, be willing to cooperate."

"But he promised to give a favor for a favor," Shiro protested. "If that wasn't—"

"That was very gracious of him," said Kobayashi. "We both knew that he did not have to do that."

"But then . . . why?"

"To allow me to save face," said Kobayashi. "Lt. Fugisawa is a most perceptive and understanding man. Such men are rare, Shiro, and useful to know."

"I see. Forgive me, Father. I wasn't thinking."

Kobayashi nodded.

"The question is," said Kobayashi's lieutenant, the man who had handed him the envelope, "how do we go about it? We're not talking about a routine hit. Who do we get to fulfill a contract on a necromancer?"

"We must get the best there is, Takeo," said Kobayashi.

"That would be Tanaka."

"Yes, Tanaka is very good," said Kobayashi, "but he is not the best there is." He pursed his lips and thought a moment. "There was someone once . . . I don't know if he is still in business. Or even alive, for that matter. He would be expensive, but nothing compared to the loss of revenue we would incur if there was a panic and people stopped coming to the Ginza."

"You mean an independent?" said Takeo.

"*The* independent," Kobayashi replied. "The man who calls himself Morpheus."

CHAPTER
Four

"ALL RIGHT," SAID PIRATE, LEANING BACK IN HIS CHAIR AND scratching his unruly head, "I give up. What the hell did you do to it?"

His tools were spread out all over his cluttered work desk. Archimedes sat before him, its casing removed. Pirate had worked with the little computer for about half an hour while they watched, growing more and more impressed as he went along. Then he removed the casing and examined the interior. Now he sat there, staring at it, looking faintly puzzled.

"I thought you were the expert," Modred said with amusement.

"Not on magic, I'm not," said Pirate, shaking his head. "I know what thaumaturgically etched and animated chips can do, but don't ask me how the hell they do it. I'm no adept. I can see where you replaced the standard board with a TM-1000 up-grade and increased the storage capabilities, but that still doesn't explain what this little guy can do. He's got the capabilities of a far more sophisticated unit, only his hardware doesn't bear that out. So the only possible explanation is that you used some kind of enchantment to further enhance the chips. Only I don't know anybody capable of doing work like that."

"Pretty neat, huh?" said Archimedes.

"Yeah, pretty neat," said Pirate. "Who worked on you, little guy? Who gave you the boost?"

The little computer hesitated.

"Go ahead and tell him, Archimedes," Modred said.

"Merlin did," said the little unit proudly.

"Merlin? Merlin Ambrosius? *That* Merlin?"

"The very same," said Modred.

Pirate gave a low whistle. "God damn. I didn't know Ambrosius was a hacker."

"He wasn't," said Modred, deciding that there was no point in telling Pirate that Merlin Ambrosius was standing right behind him, beside Kira, in the body of a teenage boy.

"He *wasn't*? Then . . . what the hell did he *do*?"

"He augmented the built-in thaumaturgic animation with an animation spell of his own," replied Modred.

"What, you mean he just waggled his fingers at this thing and said hocus-pocus?"

"Something like that," said Modred with a smile. "This was his personal computer."

"Well, I'll be damned." Pirate shook his head wonderingly. "I'm impressed as hell. There's no way this little unit is supposed to do what it can do. It's a real little sleeper. I've never seen anything like it."

"See what you can get it to do with these," said Modred, handing him a small package bearing the label of Yamako Industries, in both English and Japanese. It had taken a lot of string pulling, but he'd had it flown in direct from Tokyo the previous night.

Pirate saw the label and glanced at him questioningly, then opened the package.

"Ho-ly shit," he said softly. He took out the plastic-wrapped components, handling them with reverence. "YTM Mark 50s! I'm not even gonna *ask* where you got these."

"Actually, I bought them."

"You *bought* them?" He whistled. "Boy, when you said unlimited resources, you weren't kidding, were you? These things cost a goddamn fortune. I'd kill for some of these!"

"There's another package just like it," Modred said. "You get us that backup program from General Hyperdynamics and they're yours."

Pirate's jaw dropped. "Mister, you just gave me the keys to Heaven!" He patted Archimedes. "Little guy, you're about to grow up into the baddest motherfucker on the block."

"How long will it take you to install them?" Kira asked.

"Come back tomorrow. I could probably get it done tonight, but you don't want to rush with these puppies. Jesus, I never thought I'd get to work with anything like *this*!"

He was fairly bubbling over with excitement.

"We'll leave you to it, then," said Modred. They left the cluttered apartment and headed back home. Wyrdrune and Sebastian were waiting for them in the penthouse. Makepeace was on the phone.

"How's it going?" Wyrdrune asked.

Kira grinned. "I think Modred just made a friend for life."

"He seems to know what he's doing," Modred said. "We'll soon see."

Makepeace hung up the receiver.

"Anything?" said Modred.

Makepeace shook his head. "I still have a few more calls to make. All we can do at this point is get the word out to our network and wait."

"Meanwhile, people keep on dying," Kira said grimly.

The dreams were coming to them every night now. And they no longer had any illusions about what they meant or who they were coming from.

"There's nothing to be done about that," Modred said. "Leila is not the only Dark One out there. You can be sure that the others are doubtless doing the same thing, trying to build up their power for the inevitable confrontation."

"That's just my point," said Wyrdrune. "We've already beaten her once, why doesn't she just lay low like the others and wait till she thinks she's strong enough to take us on again? Or join up with the others? Why send us the dreams? Why tell us what she's doing?"

"Psychological warfare," Modred said. "She doesn't have to tell us what she's doing, we already know. What she's doing is rubbing our noses in it. She's trying to make us feel frustrated and powerless to stop her."

"She's succeeding, too," Kira mumbled.

"Only if you let her," Modred replied.

"What's *that* supposed to mean? None of us can block her out. The damn nightmares are relentless! It's gotten so that I can't stand the thought of going to sleep. I know that every time I close my eyes, I'm going to see some horrible vision of somebody getting torn to pieces.''

''You mustn't let it get to you.''

''It's *already* gotten to me! What the hell am I supposed to do? Tell myself it's just a dream? It would be bad enough if they were only nightmares, but we know they're really happening! Every night, we're seeing somebody getting horribly murdered! It's driving me crazy! And the runestones are no goddamn help at all!''

''Get a hold of yourself,'' said Modred. ''We all know exactly what you're going through. We're all having the same dreams.''

''Doesn't it even *bother* you?'' she said.

''No, it doesn't,'' Modred said flatly. ''I don't let it. I don't like it, but I've seen more than my share of death. I've learned to live with it.''

''Well, *I* haven't!''

''You must. We are at war. There are no battle lines, no boundaries, and we can't see the enemy, but we are at war just the same. And you must *not* give the enemy the psychological advantage over you.''

He paused. ''I once served with a mercenary unit in the Belgian Congo. It was back in 1964. We were up against the tribes of the Maniema district, who had a long history of violence, cannibalism, and witchcraft. Their elite, communist-backed troops were called the Simbas, a word that meant lion in Swahili. They went into battle dressed half like soldiers, half like savage cannibals, wearing bits of uniform, feathers, and animal skins, brandishing automatic weapons, spears, and panga knives, led by their prancing witch doctors and chanting the 'Mai Mulele.' Their witch doctors gave them all small vials of water to drink, which they had 'blessed' and which were supposed to render them immune to bullets. It did not, of course, but the point was the Simbas believed it would, so they were fearless. Those who were killed died not because their 'sacred water' failed, but because their faith in it was not strong enough, you see. And so fearsome was their appearance, and so unnerving was their chanting as they charged, that trained troops of the Congolese Army simply threw down their weapons and ran at the mere sight of them. Psychological warfare had defeated them before there was even an engagement.

"We mercenaries knew it was all a lot of nonsense, of course," he continued, "and so we stood our ground and engaged them. But they simply kept on coming, straight into our gunfire. Many of them fell, mortally wounded, and continued chanting till they died. Others simply stopped and stood there, staring at us like zombies, what they called 'throwing their eyes' at the enemy. They were doped up and entranced with killer frenzy. Psyched, as we used to say. It was really quite unnerving. We eventually beat them, but only because we did not allow them to frighten us. And they were easily some of the most frightening warriors I've ever faced in all my life.

"My point is that psychological warfare is a sword that cuts both ways," he concluded. "You can get yourself psyched and allow it to work for you, or you can allow the enemy to psych you, in which case you've already given him—or, in this case, her—half the battle. Leila knows that she's no match against the combined power of the runestones, but separately, she's more than a match for any of us. And she will play upon our weaknesses—our *human* weaknesses. Always remember that that is her advantage. She is not human. To her, we are an inferior species. I am only part Immortal myself, and it's the human part of me that has the greatest vulnerability. The part that is capable of feeling pity and compassion."

"*Can* you feel pity and compassion?" Kira said bitterly.

Wyrdrune kept silent. He knew, as Modred did not, that there was more to this than the stress Kira was under from the dreams. They were all under that stress, but Kira had other emotional conflicts that she had never quite been able to resolve. She was in love with Modred.

Their own relationship had been rocky right from the beginning. From the first time that they met, on that fateful day when they had independently both tried to steal the runestones from the auction at the Christie Gallery, they hadn't liked each other. Kira had grabbed the runestones while Wyrdrune had effected their escape, and they found themselves forced into an uneasy partnership, a partnership that both of them had sincerely hoped would be extremely temporary, lasting just long enough for them to fence the stones. The only trouble was, the stones would not stay fenced. They kept returning to them. And not only were they unable to get rid of the stones, they were unable to get rid of each other. Consequently, they were both very much surprised when they found themselves becoming emotionally involved. To this day, Wyrdrune did not know if that involvement had come naturally or had been triggered by the runestones, exerting their magical influence over them. But they had been together ever since, and regardless of what was responsible for what they came to feel toward each other, Wyrdrune knew that it was more than magic now. It was magic, in a sense, but a very human brand of magic that came from somewhere deep within the soul. He loved her and he knew that she loved him. But he also knew that love was capable of infinite complexities. She also loved Modred, though she kept trying to deny that to herself.

The runestones had forged a powerful bond between them. Perhaps that was partly the reason for what she felt for him. But there was more to it than that. Kira had a very powerful chemical attraction to Modred, the kind that defied all rational explanation. And it tormented her. Wyrdrune knew that it tormented her because of their own relationship. She didn't love him any the less for what she felt for Modred. But she could not reconcile those feelings. They were all descended from the immortal Gorlois, but Modred's descent was much more direct than theirs, undiluted by the centuries, as theirs had been. And he was also a cold, ruthless, and utterly remorseless killer. A hard and pitiless man who had plied the trade of the assassin for centuries. Kira could not understand how she was capable of feeling love for such a man. And yet, she did.

True, since they had bonded with the runestones, Modred had changed. The dreaded Morpheus had gone into retirement, although they still made use of his extensive criminal network, and living together as they did, united in a common cause, it was often easy to forget what he had been. Or where the money they were living on had come from. Except for times like now, when it was forcibly brought home to them. In some ways, Modred hadn't really changed at all. And never would.

"Pity?" Modred said, raising his eyebrows. "Compassion?" He smiled faintly. "Would it surprise you if I admitted that I was capable of those emotions? I am, you know. But being capable of feeling such emotions is not the same as being ruled by them."

"Well, I'm sorry, but I haven't had two thousand years in which to learn how to turn my emotions on and off at will," said Kira. "And I haven't had much practice in killing people, either."

Modred looked at her curiously. Billy and Makepeace watched them both, looking ill at ease.

"Kira..." Wyrdrune said gently. "Lighten up, okay?"

She met his eyes for a moment, then looked away guiltily.

"I'm sorry," she said softly.

"We're all under a great deal of stress," said Merlin.

Kira sat hunched over, staring at the runestone in her palm. "Sometimes I *hate* these damn things," she said savagely. "Why aren't they *doing* anything? Why the hell can't they tell us..."

Her voice trailed off. She got up suddenly and went into the bedroom, slamming the door behind her. Modred stared after her, a slight frown on his face.

"Sometimes I forget how young she really is," he said.

Makepeace raised his eyebrows. "You think it's just her youth?"

Wyrdrune shot him a warning glance. He suddenly realized that Makepeace knew. He didn't know how, but he knew. Makepeace caught the look.

"What, then?" asked Modred, missing their exchange of glances.

Makepeace simply shrugged. "Women can be very complicated," he said, and let it go at that.

Modred frowned and was about to say something in response when the phone rang. He picked it up.

"Yes?" He listened a moment. "Yes, I recognize your voice.... Yes, it has been a long time. I'm well, thank you. Yourself?... Yes, of course, this line is safe.... Oh, I see. No, I'm retired now and I don't... Who?... That's what I thought

you said. But why me? Surely they have enough people of their
own who are quite capable . . . *What*?''

His entire manner suddenly changed.

"Are you absolutely *certain*? . . . What details can you give
me?''

He listened intently for a few minutes, then said, "I
see. . . . Yes. . . . Yes. No, that changes things. . . . Yes. Tell him
that out of respect for his position and his reputation, I'm
coming out of retirement. That will put him in the position of
having to be extremely obliging. . . . Yes, a man like that could
be very useful. . . . The usual arrangements, yes. Only in this
case, you remember the fee I charged for the last contract that
you brokered? . . . Yes, that one. Triple it. . . . Yes, that's right, I
said triple it. He can certainly afford it. It should impress him
with the significance of this contract and my professional
standing.'' He chuckled. "Yes, that's what I think, too. It's
important to establish these things right away when dealing
with such people. . . . Yes, quite. . . . I'll be leaving first thing in
the morning. And tell him that—no, on second thought, I'll tell
him myself when I get there. . . . Yes, I'll let you know. . . . Yes,
right. I'll be in touch.''

He hung up the phone. Before he could say anything,
Wyrdrune spoke.

"Was that what I *think* it was?''

Modred smiled. "Morpheus has just come out of retirement.''

"Good God! You can't be serious!'' said Merlin.

"Oh, but I am,'' said Modred with a smile. "I've just
accepted a contract. An extremely lucrative one, I might add.''

"Are you out of your mind?'' said Merlin.

"It isn't what you think,'' said Modred. "That is, I *have*
accepted a contract. Only the circumstances are somewhat
unique. It's a contract on a necromancer.''

Wyrdrune stared at him, astonished. *"What?''*

"That call came from Tokyo,'' said Modred. "There's a
serial killer on the loose in the Ginza district. Both the police
and the Bureau seem to be at a total loss. The victims are all
young prostitutes. And the bodies show signs of having been
savaged by some sort of magical creature.''

"Jesus Christ,'' said Wyrdrune softly. "Leila?''

"Yes, Leila! We've found her! She's in Japan!"

"Wait a minute," Wyrdrune said. "Who's paying for this contract?"

Modred smiled. "The client is Don Teruyuki Kobayashi, the godfather of the Yakuza."

"The Yakuza?" said Wyrdrune. "The Japanese Mafia? How the hell do *they* fit into it?"

"The Ginza is Kobayashi's district," Modred explained. "It's Tokyo's combat zone. And a serial killer, especially a necromancer, could be very bad for business. Kobayashi is concerned about loss of revenue from his gambling and prostitution operations. He doesn't want his customers scared off by a psychotic on the loose. So he's hiring me to find the killer and remove him. Or, in this case, *her*."

"I don't understand," said Merlin. "Why must we become involved with gangsters? There was no need for you to accept that contract. You certainly don't need the money. Now that we know where she is, why couldn't you simply turn them down?"

"Logistics, Ambrosius," said Modred. "I am not without connections in Japan, but we'll be going into an area controlled by organized crime. By accepting Kobayashi's contract, I've just enlisted the support of the Yakuza."

"I can see your reasoning," said Merlin sourly, "but I don't like it. We should not be involved with such people. It will invite trouble with both the police and the Bureau."

"In case it's slipped your mind, Ambrosius," Modred said wryly, "I am already in trouble with both the police and Bureau. I'm still a wanted man, remember? However, we are not without friends in the Bureau. And in this case, I'm led to believe that we can even expect a certain amount of cooperation from the police. It seems that Kobayashi has some sort of an arrangement with them."

"So we leave in the morning?" asked Makepeace.

"Not you, Sebastian," Modred said. "I'll need you here. Have you forgotten our young computer criminal? I'll need you to stay here and keep an eye on Pirate while he completes his work. I'll call him and let him know that you'll be taking charge."

"You mean you're going to go ahead with it?" asked Wyrdrune.

"Of course," Modred replied. "Kobayashi was a stroke of luck. We're still crippled without access to proper data. In order to find the other Dark Ones, we'll need the ability to access police and Bureau databases throughout the world. And Archimedes is simply not up to that task. His new storage capabilities will accept the G.H. program, but he is simply not sophisticated enough to operate it properly. We need a hyperdimensional matrix unit." He paused. "And come to think of it, as luck would have it, the problem of obtaining the necessary components has just been rather neatly solved."

"How?" asked Wyrdrune.

"Simple," Modred said with a smile. "In lieu of my fee, I'll have Kobayashi get them for us."

"Steal them, you mean," said Merlin.

"How he does it isn't my concern," said Modred. "But he will do it."

"What makes you so sure?" asked Wyrdrune.

"I spent some time in Japan," Modred said. "In many ways, the Japanese are a very admirable people. Quite possibly the most civilized people on the planet. Their social structure is complex and their customs are often intricate and fascinating. They make rituals and ceremonies out of such things as drinking tea and arranging flowers. It sounds rather peculiar to someone who grew up in the West, but after you've been there for some time, you come to appreciate and understand these things. You see, the Japanese still have something most of the world has lost. They have culture.

"Take a man like Kobayashi, for example," he continued. "An American in his position would be very rich and would tend to flaunt his wealth in a vulgar manner. He would tend to swagger and throw his weight around to show what an important man he was. He would, as they say, lack culture. Yet, despite never having met Mr. Kobayashi, I can infer certain things about him merely by knowing that he has attained the position that he has and is a Japanese. He will be an understated man, one who dresses tastefully, but not ostentatiously. He will not wear much in the way of jewelry. A gold watch, perhaps a small diamond. But it will be a very fine watch and a flawless diamond. He will be well groomed and his manner will be subdued. He will have an appreciation for fine wines and art. He will not own many works of art, but the ones he does own will be among the most highly prized. He will have a hobby that he will pursue with a studied devotion, and it will be the sort of hobby that reflects favorably upon his standing and his personality. Something in which he can take enormous pride. He will be charming and soft-spoken, a gracious host, and you would never suspect that he is a high-ranking don in one of the most powerful crime organizations in the world. Rather, you would think he was a chief executive officer of some important corporation—which, in effect, he is. But as charming and gracious and elegant as he might seem, he will also be cold, ruthless, and utterly deadly.''

"Rather like someone we all know,'' said Merlin dryly.

Modred chose to ignore the comment. "He will get the components for me because to refuse to do so would mean either that he was unwilling, which would put him in a bad light after I've so graciously agreed to come out of retirement out of respect for him, or that he was unable to do it. Either way, he would lose face. He will do it, if for no other reason than to show me that he can.''

"He's still a gangster. You make him sound like Lancelot, for God's sake,'' Merlin said irritably.

"In some ways, he is,'' said Modred. "In his own way, Kobayashi lives by a code not unlike that of chivalry. But there is one essential difference. Lancelot was stupid. Kobayashi isn't.''

CHAPTER
Five

"SIR, THERE ARE SOME REPORTERS WAITING TO SEE YOU,'' his secretary said.

Akiro looked pained. "Outside? In the office?"

"No, sir, down in the lobby."

"Newspaper reporters? Or television?"

"Both, I think. Should I tell them that you're out?"

"Yes, please do," said Akiro, relieved that whoever was on duty at the desk downstairs had not allowed them to come up. If they'd been in the outer office, he would have had to use a teleportation spell to duck them and he didn't like to do that. Teleportation spells required a great deal of energy and they took a lot out of him. They always left him feeling tired and somewhat nauseated.

"Tell them they just missed me. I've gone out to pursue the investigation and you don't know when I'll be back. You know the sort of thing. On second thought, no, wait. Perhaps it would be better if someone more official were to speak with them. Is Morio in his office?"

"Yes, sir, I believe he is."

"Would you ask him to step in for a moment, please? And then you might as well go to lunch."

He had known that this was coming. It was inevitable, of course. There would be no way to keep the story quiet now, but he simply wasn't up to facing them. Newspaper reporters were bad enough, with their badgering questions, but the television people were even worse. There was a technique that television reporters frequently used. They would ask a question, and if the answer that you gave them was too short or didn't satisfy them, instead of going on to another question, they would simply stand there, with the microphone pointing at your face, waiting silently while the camera rolled on. It was a way of trying to make the subject talk more. If he didn't, it had the effect of making him look uncomfortable, incompetent, or uncooperative, as if he had something to hide. Few people could stand up to the silent pressure of that implacable camera lens. Akiro knew full well that they'd do it to him and he'd only wind up fumbling for words and looking foolish, or simply standing there and looking uncomfortable, which would be just as bad.

Moments later there was a knock at his office door and Morio Suzuki entered. Suzuki was deputy commissioner of public affairs for the Bureau, which was a fancy way of saying that he was a P.R. man. He was not an adept. He was a civil servant. He was young, in his early thirties, good-looking, and extremely personable. He looked great on camera and he was not uncomfortable around reporters. He spoke easily, fielding awkward questions smoothly and glibly. He was also politically very deft, with good connections through his family. He would, someday, have an outstanding future in politics. Right now, he was paying his dues, but he was not impatient and resentful, as a lot of wealthy, well-connected young men in his position might have been. Akiro, who understood the political infrastructure far better than he could function within it, had marked him from the start as a highly capable and responsible young man.

"You wanted to see me?"

"Yes. Please sit down, Morio."

Morio took the indicated chair, sitting erect and in an attentive posture.

"I've got a problem, Morio."

"The press downstairs?"

"Oh, you know already."

"You want me to talk to them?"

"I would be grateful if you would. You handle that sort of thing so much better than I do."

"Do I give them the standard line or do you want me to actually tell them something?"

Akiro smiled. "I'm not sure how much you could tell them that they don't already know, or else they wouldn't be here."

"It's about the Ginza murders, of course."

"Yes, I'm afraid it is. I'll be very honest with you, Morio. I don't want to talk to them. I'm no good at handling the press, I'd only come off looking like a bumbling incompetent."

"I think you're being a bit hard on yourself."

"No, no, it's true. I get positively flustered whenever I have to look into a camera. And I look terrible on television. You, on the other hand, handle such things very well."

"Thank you, sir."

"The thing is," Akiro continued, "I really haven't got anything for you to tell them. We haven't made much progress on this thing." He grimaced. "Hell, we haven't made *any* progress."

"It might be helpful if I told them that Master Yohaku has agreed to assist us in our investigation."

"You know about that?"

"I try to make it my business to know about what goes on in this building," Morio said. "I know he came by with you to look at the bodies and examine the reports."

"Yes," Akiro said. He pursed his lips thoughtfully. "But I do not know if mentioning that would be wise. It would tell them that we're in trouble on this investigation and it would essentially confirm that we are dealing with a necromancer."

"The media have their sources here," said Morio. "They probably already know that Master Yohaku has been consulted. That's not the sort of thing you could keep quiet."

"No, I suppose not. So you think we should go ahead and mention it before they do?"

"I would strongly advise it. It would at least make it appear as if we're doing something and it would tell them that we're treating this case very seriously."

"Yes," Akiro said, nodding, "I suppose that would be best. There probably isn't much else we can do right now."

"I'll take care of it," said Morio. "I'll tell them that Lt. Fugisawa is handling the case and the Bureau is working with him closely in an advisory capacity."

Akiro knew what he was saying. Let Fugisawa take the heat. He was tempted to go ahead and let him do that, but that would be cowardly and it would not be fair to Fugisawa. And if they knew that Yohaku had been consulted, they'd want to know why the Bureau had not officially stepped in and taken charge. No, much as he wished he could, he could not avoid taking responsibility.

"I wouldn't phrase it quite that way," he said. "Officially, this is a Bureau case and the responsibility is mine. If they insist on speaking with me, tell them I'm out of the office, pursuing the investigation. Tell them we're following some leads and we'll have a full statement for them shortly, you know the sort of thing."

"That won't keep them satisfied for long."

"Just buy me some time, Morio. At least until I've got something I can tell them."

"All right. I'll do my best."

"Thank you. I appreciate it."

"Just doing my job."

"I know, but thank you just the same."

Morio got up to leave. As he walked out, a man dressed in dark green sorcerer's robes appeared at the door. He wore a simple black tunic suit beneath the open robes and his long black hair fell to his shoulders. He was slim and good-looking, in his early to mid-forties. He did not have the manner of a Bureau official.

"Inspector Katayama?"

Akiro stood respectfully. "Yes, I am Katayama. How may I help you?"

The sorcerer gave him a small bow. "My name is Kanno. I was a pupil of Master Yokahu's. He told me that you might be in need of some assistance."

Akiro knew who he was now, but that knowledge gave him little comfort. The man was a highly respected adept, but he was a thaumagenetic artisan who specialized in creating beautiful and highly prized magenes for wealthy socialites and prominent figures in the business sector. He could not see how the man could possibly be of any help in a criminal investigation. So much for expecting any assistance from Yohaku, he thought wryly. The old master had delegated the task to one of his former pupils. He probably should have expected something like that. The problem was, now he'd be stuck with him. There was no way to refuse the offer of assistance without offending them both.

"Please, sit down," Akiro said, indicating a chair. "My secretary has gone out to lunch, I'm afraid, but may I offer you some tea? Or something stronger, perhaps?"

"No, thank you," Kanno said. "I hope my coming here does not place you in an awkward position."

"No, no, of course not," Akiro hastened to reassure him. "I very much appreciate your coming. It was most considerate of you."

"Yet you are undoubtedly wondering how a man who spends

his time designing expensive magenes for the amusement of the
wealthy can possibly be of any help to you in your investigation."

Akiro blushed. "Yes, well . . . no, that is . . ."

Kanno smiled. "Forgive me, Inspector. I did not mean to
embarrass you. Believe me, I appreciate your position. But the
master has requested me to offer you my assistance and I could
hardly refuse. However, if you think that I would only be
getting in the way—"

"No, no, of course not," Akiro said. "I can certainly use all
the help I can get."

"My specialty, of course, is thaumagenetic engineering,"
Kanno said, "but I am well versed in other forms of magic.
Perhaps I could be of some assistance in detecting clues.
Master Yohaku tells me that these murders appear to have been
accomplished by some sort of magical entity. And I do have
some small experience with thaumaturgically animated life
forms."

Yes, there was that, Akiro thought. Perhaps the man could be
of some use, after all.

"Would you care to see the reports?" he asked.

"Thank you," Kanno said, "but I'd prefer to see the
victims' remains first, if that is possible. I would like to get a
first impression uncolored by the theories or conclusions of
others."

Sound thinking, thought Akiro. Perhaps the man might be
useful, after all, though he didn't want to get his hopes up.
"Certainly. We'll have to go down to the police pathology lab.
If you would follow me?"

If he expected a shocked reaction from the sorcerer, Akiro
was disappointed. He hadn't really known what to expect, but
when the body of the first victim—or what was left of it—was
pulled out, Kanno merely frowned slightly and bent over it,
studying it carefully. He examined it intently for several minutes, then wordlessly proceeded to the next one.

It was a marked contrast to the manner in which Yohaku had
examined the bodies. Even though he had already seen the
photographs, which were nothing if not graphic, the mage had
reacted with shock and pain at the sight of the actual corpses.
And he had been visibly shaken by the strength of the thauma-

turgic trace emanations that he had detected, even though they were no longer fresh and had already started fading. Kanno exhibited no emotion whatsoever as he went from one body to the next, saying nothing, his features betraying no emotion except for a slight frown of concentration. When he was through, he straightened up and nodded to the pathology attendant, who pushed the tray holding the remains of the last victim back into its compartment.

"I would like to see the autopsy reports," he said, "but I have a feeling that they will not tell me anything I do not already know. What about the victims' clothing?"

Akiro nodded to the attendant and they were brought. There wasn't much left of the clothing they had worn, either. They were torn and soaked in blood. Kanno had them spread out on a lab table, then he stood over them, his hands outstretched, palms down over the table. He closed his eyes. Akiro watched, fascinated, as the sorcerer moved his hands over each individual item of clothing, his head moving from one to the other, as if he were seeing them, though his eyes were tightly shut. Then, at the last item of clothing, he hesitated.

His frown of concentration deepened. He opened his eyes and stared down at the blood-soaked, tattered swatch of garment before him, all that was left of a girl's blouse. He dropped his left arm to his side and bent over the table, holding his right hand, palm cupped and facing downward, over the garment. He spread his fingers out slightly and his lips moved, though he didn't say anything out loud. He slowly raised his hand . . . and something came floating up from the piece of blood-soaked cloth.

Akiro could not even see what it was at first. He strained, squinting, but there didn't seem to be anything there. And then, something floating in the air before Kanno caught the light and shimmered faintly.

"Tweezers, please," said Kanno.

The attendant went over to the drawer and took out a pair of tweezers. He handed them to the sorcerer. Kanno took them in his left hand and gently plucked something very small out of the air.

"What is it?" Akiro asked.

Kanno held it up to the light. It seemed to be a thin flake of some sort, no larger than a fingernail, iridescent and almost translucent.

"A scale," Kanno said.

"A scale? You mean, like on a fish?"

"No. A reptile."

The attendant handed him a small plastic bag. Kanno deposited the scale inside.

"You mean a snake?" asked Akiro with a frown.

"No. A serpent."

"A serpent? What's the difference?"

"In this case, the difference is considerable," said Kanno. "I had already suspected it from the wounds on the bodies. The punctures were inflicted by large fangs and the serrated wounds by multiple rows of teeth, such as those of a shark. There were also clawmarks, where it seized its victims. The shark fastens onto its prey, then shakes it, tearing the flesh. However, unlike a shark, this creature possesses small, powerful arms with sharp claws, which it sinks into its prey. It then wraps itself around the victim, as indicated by the bruising on the bodies, and holds them while it tears at them with its jaws."

"How big *is* it?" asked Akiro.

"Difficult to judge precisely," Kanno replied, "but I would guess it is somewhere between five and six feet in length. It would be immensely powerful and possibly capable of flight. In any case, it is not a creature that occurs in nature."

Akiro exhaled heavily. "You mean that someone *made* this thing?"

"There are three distinct possibilities," said Kanno. "Either it was thaumagenetically engineered, by a specialist at least as skilled as myself, or it was conjured up somehow."

"You mean like a demonic entity?"

"Precisely."

"And the third possibility?"

"A shapechanger," Kanno said. "Which would indicate a sorcerer of immense skills who literally transforms himself into the creature."

"What sort of creature is it?" Akiro asked, holding his breath.

"A dragon."

"A dragon!" Akiro exhaled heavily. "And you say it can *fly*?"

"I do not know. It's possible."

"The media will turn this into a circus," Akiro said.

"I have no doubt of that," said Kanno. "But at least you now have something you can tell them."

Akiro shook his head. "I'm not sure what's worse," he said. "Telling them nothing or telling them that there's a dragon on the loose somewhere in the Ginza."

"There have been no witnesses?" asked Kanno.

"None."

"Interesting," said Kanno.

"What do you mean?"

"Well, at the risk of sounding immodest," Kanno said, "I know of no one in Japan, with the exception of myself, whose skills at thaumagenetic engineering would be sufficient to create such a creature. And if it was 'on the loose,' as you put it, it would seem unlikely, in a district as crowded as the Ginza, that no one should have caught a glimpse of it. Consequently, it would seem more probable that the creature is not, in a manner of speaking, on the loose, but that it appears and disappears during the times that the killings actually take place."

"Which would suggest that the necromancer must be present on the scene," Akiro said.

"Exactly."

"I see," Akiro said. "Well, at least that's something. I had already suspected the possibility of a shapechanger. Your conclusions seem to reinforce that."

Kanno smiled to himself. This was going to be even easier than he had expected. It was a stroke of luck that this Bureau agent had gone to Yohaku for help. Anxious to do as much as he could to help, the frail old man had asked his favorite pupil to render his assistance, never suspecting that Kanno himself was the killer. And it had taken so little to impress this bumbling investigator. The discovery of a minute clue that everyone else had missed. The scale on the blouse, which, of course, had not been there before. It would be a simple matter to mislead them.

They would now be looking for a shapechanger, which suited Kanno's purposes perfectly. He was becoming more and more adept at controlling the dragon. He could animate the tattoo and release it, then, if necessary, arrange to be somewhere else, among witnesses, when the murders actually occurred, thereby giving himself an ironclad alibi. It was perfect. The fools would never catch him. And that left him with only one thing to be concerned about.

Leila.

He had never suspected the existence of anyone like Leila. And where there was one, there would probably be others. The Dark Ones. Who *were* they? What did they *want*? Power, yes, that much was certain. His own powers had increased immeasurably since he had met her, but her powers were growing at a far greater rate. And she was already the most powerful adept he had ever encountered. There had been many more killings than those the police and the Bureau knew about. Unlike the dragon, Leila did not leave behind any trace of her victims. She transported them to his sanctuary beneath his shop, in the underground mall where she now lived. Her victims simply disappeared. And they were usually people who would not be missed.

He, too, could have easily killed without a trace, but that was not what Leila wanted. He knew why. It was to cover for her own activities. So long as the authorities were occupied with the dramatic Ginza murders, they would not pay as much attention to the disappearances, if they even noticed them. Missing persons would be a much lower priority in the face of a flamboyant serial killer case. Only what would happen when Leila no longer had a use for him? That time would surely come and as the only one who knew about her, Kanno realized that he presented a potential threat. And he knew he was no match for her. He was far less concerned about the police and the Bureau than he was about what she might do. He had to find a way to protect himself. She had to have a weakness. Somehow, he would have to find it. To do so would require great care and patience. It would be the greatest challenge he had ever faced. But the years had taught him patience. He only hoped that she would give him enough time.

* * *

It was a long flight and they were all tired when the plane landed at New Tokyo International Airport in Narita, about forty miles out of Tokyo. Fourteen hours in the air had taken their toll. They were anxious to check into their suites at the Imperial Hotel, get some much needed sleep and adjust themselves to the new time zone. As always, Modred insisted upon going first class and he had arranged for a chauffeured limo to meet them at the airport.

The Imperial was one of Tokyo's oldest hotels, located across from Hibiya park, within walking distance of the Ginza. It had been renovated after the Collapse and another thirty floors had been added to its tower, affording guests a magnificent view of the city through the floor-to-ceiling bay windows in the rooms. It was a hotel catering primarily to well-heeled foreigners and businessmen on large expense accounts. The atmosphere was subdued and dignified, with the accent on service. Modred had reserved adjoining suites, with connecting doors, on the top floor of the tower, with the windows looking out over the Ginza and the harbor.

The hotel staff did not quite know what to make of their newly arrived guests. Modred, elegantly dressed, as always, was no surprise to them, but eyebrows were raised when they saw Wyrdrune in his brown warlock's cassock and running shoes, Kira in her black leather jacket, skintight lycra breeches, and high boots, and Billy, with his unusual haircut and renaissance punk clothes. Try as he might, there was nothing Merlin could do to induce him to change his appearance in any way. And jaws positively dropped when they saw Broom. However, they were impressed with Modred's fluency in Japanese and if the elegant westerner chose to travel with such an unusual entourage, that was certainly his privilege. Besides, he was taking not one, but two of their most expensive suites, so if there was any disapproval, the hotel staff did not display it. Even Broom, which always found something to complain about, could not fault the service or their accommodations.

The first thing they did after settling in and washing up was to order dinner sent up to their rooms. Modred also had them bring some newspapers. When they arrived, he found what he was looking for. The Ginza murders were prominently featured. There had been another killing the previous night, bringing the total up to ten.

Wyrdrune came in from the suite he shared with Kira. Billy was sharing Modred's suite and, with the exception of Modred, who had changed into a black silk dressing gown, they had put on the cotton kimonos supplied by the hotel. All but Billy, who had simply changed back into his clothes. He was never without his tatterdemalion, fringed, patchwork leather jacket, but at least he'd taken off his fingerless leather gloves before sitting down to dinner.

"Gor', I'm starved," he said, attacking the food.

Modred glanced at him with amusement. "All the money we've got, and you insist on dressing like a cross between an urban commando and a garbage picker."

"Well, I'd look bloody ridiculous in one o' them things," Billy said, indicating Modred's silk dressing gown with a jerk of his head.

"Yes, I suppose you would, at that."

"As if he doesn't look ridiculous enough already," Merlin said.

"Ey, 'at'll be enough outta *you*!" snapped Billy.

"Now you listen here, you impertinent young whelp—"

"If you two are going to insist on arguing," said Modred, "at least have the grace not to do it with your mouth full."

"What's the paper say?" asked Kira.

"There was another killing last night," said Modred.

"As if we didn't know," said Kira. They'd had the nightmares on the flight over, causing some minor consternation among some of their fellow passengers and the stewardesses.

"According to the newspapers," Modred said, "the Bureau has enlisted the aid of a mage named Yohaku."

"I know him," Merlin said. "He was one of my students many years ago. One of my best pupils. But he must be quite old by now."

"Perhaps we should go see him," Wyrdrune said.

"I would advise against it," Modred said.

"Why?" asked Kira.

"Need I remind you that I am here as a contract assassin?"

Modred replied. "Which, in a sense, makes all of you my confederates. If we were to have any contact with the authorities, it would make our position very awkward, to say the least. It would involve some very complicated explanations. Besides, I am quite sure that Don Kobayashi will be able to keep us informed of whatever the authorities discover."

"I'm sure that Yohaku can be trusted to remain discreet about our contact with him," Merlin said. "I had planned on contacting him as soon as I learned we were going to Japan." Billy's face scowled. "What's so amusing?"

Modred was grinning. "Forgive me, Ambrosius. It's your table manners."

Billy had been wolfing down the food like a fraternity pledge at a toga party, but every time Merlin "took over," he would immediately stop and straighten up in his chair to speak or sedately sip his tea. And then Billy would once more resume attacking the food before him, bending over the table and snatching at things as if he hadn't eaten in months. The abrupt switches back and forth were comical. Even as Modred spoke, Billy was cramming his mouth with food.

"Well, I'm bloody famished!" he said, his mouth full of steamed dumplings ducked in sauce. He wasn't bothering with either the chopsticks or the silverware. He was simply picking them up with his fingers and dunking them, then stuffing them into his mouth. Abruptly he sat up in his chair again and finished chewing, then carefully wiped his dripping mouth.

"The way you're assaulting this somewhat questionable food," said Merlin disapprovingly, "you'll give us a case of indigestion. Now slow down, for goodness sake, and leave some for the others."

"Bugger off!"

Billy reached for another dumpling with his right hand and then suddenly picked up a fork with his left hand and stabbed himself in the right hand with it.

"Ow! Bloody 'ell!"

"If it wasn't a physical impossibility," said Merlin, "I'd turn you over my knee and give you a sound thrashing."

Modred and the others laughed.

"Behave yourself!" said Merlin. "Now, as I was saying, I

think it would be a mistake for us not to approach Yohaku. He is, after all, the most powerful adept in Japan, with enormous influence, and I personally know him to be a man of extremely good character. He could be of great help to us.''

"I don't doubt your word," said Modred. "However, I still don't think that it would be a good idea. At any rate, it would be premature. I would prefer to find out exactly how things stand first. Besides, though I have the highest respect for your judgment, I do not know the man.''

"You don't know this Kobayashi, either," Merlin said. "And I can't believe that you would sooner accept help from a gangster than from one of the most highly respected adepts in the world!''

"I may not know Kobayashi," Modred said, "but I know what to expect from him. And our dealing with a man like Kobayashi would not attract as much attention as would our seeing a man as celebrated as your former pupil. Not that I doubt for a moment that Yohaku would be discreet, but to a man like Kobayashi, discretion is the soul of his profession. Aside from that, there is another consideration that you seem to have overlooked. When was the last time you saw your former pupil?''

Billy's face frowned. "Well . . . it's been years. But what does that have to do with it? He will certainly remember me. If you think my being in Billy's body will—''

"Billy has nothing to do with it," said Modred. "I have no doubt that Yohaku will accept you for who you are. But can we accept Yohaku for who *he* is?''

"What do you mean?" Then Billy's eyes grew wide as Merlin realized what Modred meant. "Surely, you don't believe—''

"At this point, I don't believe anything," said Modred. "But I *suspect* everything. And everyone.''

"I can't believe it!" Merlin said.

"Even a mage would not be invulnerable to Leila's influence," said Modred.

"But if Yohaku was Leila's acolyte, the runestones would reveal that to us immediately," said Wyrdrune.

"True," said Modred, "but that would also force our hand

and reveal our presence here to Leila. We failed to stop her once before. This time, I want no mistakes. I want us to be sure of our ground. I want us to have every advantage.''

"But then Kobayashi could be under Leila's influence, as well," said Kira. "This whole thing might have been a trap to lure us here."

"Possibly," Modred agreed, "but I think the odds are very much against it."

"Why?"

"Because it would be too obvious. If Kobayashi were her acolyte, then the moment we met with him, he would be revealed. After the last time, she would hardly seek such a direct confrontation. She will pick her time and place very carefully. And she would not waste her energy in empowering a man like Kobayashi. She would choose an adept."

"You can't be sure of that," said Wyrdrune.

"Oh, I think I can," said Modred. "I think I understand the way she thinks. In many ways, she reminds me of someone."

"Who?" asked Kira, puzzled.

"My mother," Modred said softly.

Having the dead woman around made Kanno feel uncomfortable. Ever since Leila had brought her back to life, she had kept her in the sanctuary as her servant. Kanno had never known her name. She was simply one of the whores he had kidnapped to sacrifice in his rituals. He had thought nothing of her. But now, her presence preyed on his mind constantly.

There was something wrong with her. Well, what was wrong with her, thought Kanno, was that she was *dead*. A reanimated corpse. She never spoke, and for all Kanno knew, she couldn't speak. Her skin had a ghastly pallor and her eyes were extremely disconcerting. She breathed and perhaps, somewhere deep within her mind, something resembling thought occurred, but there was no evidence of it. She was like some sort of automaton, a zombie moving with abrupt and jerky motions, like a marionette whose strings were tangled. Beneath her white gown, there was a gaping, gory hole in her chest where Kanno had torn out her heart. He didn't like to think about that nebulous *something* that now pulsed in the place where her heart had been, but every time he saw her, he could not help but think about it. It unnerved him. And that, he thought, was the sole reason for her existence. To keep him on edge. She was a constant, walking dead reminder of the extent of Leila's power.

Not that he required reminding. Leila had transformed the sanctuary. His crude sacrificial altar on the pedestal of the old fountain was gone. In its place, there was now an intricately carved slab of solid gold, gleaming in the phosphorescent glow of the bubbling pool that surrounded it. It bathed the area around it in an eerie green light. Pungent incense burned in the bronze braziers placed around the underground mall. The dusty, ruined shops and restaurants, once filled with rats and rubble, were now palatial chambers, elegantly furnished, hung with tapestries and lit with torches, with sculpted columns that depicted unspeakable perversions and acts of grotesque brutality, like the carvings in the ancient temples of the cult of Kali. That was what the sanctuary had become—a temple. A temple for a dark goddess. It looked like some vision out of the Arabian Nights.

The dead woman, her skin as pale as the underbelly of a slug, set a tray down on the low table before them. The tray had a decanter of wine on it and two crystal goblets. She brushed against Kanno as she moved away and his skin crawled. Leila was reclining on a Roman-style couch. She was barefoot and wearing a robe of dark green velvet, which clung to the lush contours of her body in a way that made it obvious she was wearing nothing underneath. One long, exquisitely shaped leg was exposed almost to her waist.

"Pour the wine, Kanno," she said.

He complied. Her fingers brushed his as she took the goblet.

"You've done well," she said. "I'm pleased with you."

"Thank you, Mistress."

"Have you not wondered what my purpose is?" she asked.

"I have, of course, but I knew that you would tell me if you thought it was appropriate."

She smiled. "Are you afraid of me, Kanno?"

"No, Mistress."

She raised her eyebrows. "No?"

"From the moment you appeared, my fate was in your hands," he said. "I have no illusions that I shall outlive my usefulness."

"And that does not frighten you?"

"There is little point in fearing the inevitable."

"So you have resigned yourself to death, then?"

"No. I have merely accepted it. I shall endeavor to survive, but I know that I must die eventually. And most men know nothing of what death holds in store for them. I already know two things. When it comes, it shall come from you. And when I die, it shall be at the height of my power, power far greater than anything I could have dreamed of. What man could ask for more?"

"Many might hope for immortality," she said.

Kanno smiled slightly. "Why wish for something that I cannot have?"

"And if I could give it to you?"

Kanno glanced toward the dead woman, standing against the wall like some wax statue, staring vacantly into space.

"Like that?" he said. "No, thank you."

"No, not like that. That is not life. You were right. No one can restore life once it has fled. But to restore life is not the same as to prolong it. I could teach you how to do that."

"But, Mistress, I already know."

She looked at him with surprise. "You do?"

"Of course. The spell itself is not so difficult, only the cost in energy is very high. One kills to gain the power to prolong one's life, only the spell consumes so much life energy that one must kill again to replenish the power that has been lost. And then that power must once again be consumed to fuel the spell, and it must be once more replenished, and so on and so on, in a never-ending cycle. Only each time, more power is needed to effect the spell, so that one becomes like a drug addict, addicted to life, yet never able to obtain a dose that's strong enough. Life is prolonged, somewhat, but at what cost? Eventually, one must still die. There is no way for a mortal to become immortal. I am much less concerned with the quantity of life than with its quality."

Leila gave him a long, appraising look. "I keep underestimating you. And I keep forgetting that you are a sorcerer of unusual skill. A human of unusual perception. You really are different from the others.''

Kanno inclined his head in a slight bow.

She smiled. ''Perhaps *I* should be afraid of *you*.''

Kanno smiled. ''What threat could I possibly present to you?''

''That is a question you will have to answer for yourself,'' she said. ''And you will try, won't you? You will try very, very hard.''

He said nothing.

''Won't you?'' she repeated, her voice low.

''Of course,'' said Kanno.

Her eyes glittered. ''Come here.''

He moved across to her couch and bent over her. Her arms went around his neck and pulled his face down to hers. His hands slipped inside her robe, slowly moving across the taut, silky contours of her body as her tongue slipped into his mouth and she reached down for him. The game was in the open now. They fully understood each other. And as their bodies meshed upon the couch, Kanno wondered which of them would win.

CHAPTER
Six

THE MEETING WAS TO BE IN THE EAST GARDEN OF THE OLD Imperial Palace, near the Nijubashi Bridge. Once the home of Japan's imperial family, the palace had been built on the site where Edo Castle used to stand in the days of the shoguns. Dating back to the 1600s, Edo Castle had once been the largest castle in the world, towering 168 feet above its foundations and having an outer perimeter of ten miles. Now, all that was left of it were crumbled fragments of the foundation. There was nothing left of the original Imperial Palace, either. The first one, completed in 1888, had been reduced to rubble during the air raids of World War II. The second, rebuilt in 1968, was burned down during the riots of the Collapse. The present palace was the third incarnation, a replica of the original. It no longer housed the imperial family, as there was no longer an imperial family. Now, it was merely a museum, visited by tourists and by local Japanese who enjoyed a leisurely walk through its gardens or a jog along the cherry tree-lined paths.

On this occasion, the garden was deserted, for it was after hours. It was close to sunset and the grounds had been closed for the day. But no one attempted to stop Lt. Fugisawa as he went through the gate and made his way along the deserted paths toward the bridge. He was fairly sure that he was being watched, but he saw no sign of it until four men suddenly stepped out on the path before him. Fugisawa recognized two of them. They had been at Kobayashi's office that day. The first man had been one of those standing by the door. Fugisawa didn't know him. The second was Kobayashi's eldest son.

"It's all right," Shiro Kobayashi said to the others as they moved to block Fugisawa's way. "Let him pass."

One of the men stepped forward and started to reach for Fugisawa's gun inside its shoulder holster. Fugisawa caught his wrist. They locked eyes. The others quickly reached inside their jackets, all except Shiro.

"I didn't say to frisk him. I said to let him pass."

There was icy finality in the young man's voice. The others relaxed, taking their hands away from their jackets. Fugisawa released the man's hand.

"*Sumimasen*," the man said, apologizing with a slight bow.

Fugisawa said nothing. His eyes met Shiro's and they exchanged brief nods. Then the men stepped aside and allowed him to continue down the path.

Kobayashi was waiting for him on the bridge. He was wearing a well-tailored gray flannel suit with a light overcoat thrown over his shoulders.

"Good evening, Lt. Fugisawa," he said as he leaned against

the railing of the bridge, tossing flower petals over the side into the water.

"Don Kobayashi."

"This has always been my favorite spot in the city," Kobayashi said, looking out at the reddening sky. "One stands here and seems to hear the echoes of his ancestors."

"It's pleasant," said Fugisawa curtly.

"You don't appreciate it?" said Kobayashi.

"Not the way you seem to," the policeman replied with a shrug. "I don't really have the luxury for walks in the park."

"Ah, you must make the time, Lieutenant," Kobayashi said. "A man must take the time to achieve proper harmony and balance in his life."

"You misunderstand me. I didn't say I didn't have the time. I said I didn't have the luxury. There's a difference. It takes a lot more than a pretty garden and some cherry blossoms to balance off what I see out there every night." He indicated the Ginza with a motion of his head. What he left unsaid, but clearly understood, was that much of what he saw on the streets of the Ginza every night was the sole responsibility of Kobayashi. "Looking at flowers and tending bonsai just won't cut it."

"I see," said Kobayashi evenly. "What will?"

"Seeing justice done," Fugisawa said.

Kobayashi smiled. "You're an idealist, Fugisawa. And here I thought you were a practical man."

"That, too," said Fugisawa, "otherwise I wouldn't be here. What do you know about a sorcerer named Kanno?"

Kobayashi looked at him with surprise. "Surely, you're joking. You mean to tell me that you don't know who he is?"

"I know who he is," said Fugisawa irritably. "I just want to know what *you* know about him."

"Ah. I see. Implying that there is something a man in my unique position would know about him that others might not?"

"More or less."

"Well, I'm sorry to disappoint you. Insofar as I know, Kanno is perfectly respectable. A genius. A brilliant thaumaturgic artist who is extremely well thought of in society. I myself am fortunate to keep two of his magenes at my home. Extraordinary creatures. Living works of art. I take great pride and joy in them.''

''So when you're saying he's respectable, you're saying . . .''

''That, to my knowledge, he has no vices. He is not known to use drugs or drink or gamble. He is unmarried, yet he has no personal involvements that anyone knows of. If he has a sex life, he is admirably discreet about it. To the best of my knowledge, his art is his life and he lives like some sort of contemplative, albeit very comfortably. His work is in extremely great demand among the cognoscente. In all ways, he is a man who would seem to be above reproach. Why do you ask?''

''He seems to be advising the Bureau on the case.''

''Ah. Well, nothing could be simpler. He was a pupil of the great Yohaku himself. When the Bureau approached him, the master obviously asked Kanno to render his assistance. Yohaku is a very old man, after all.''

''So what you're saying is that there is no reason, that you know of, to suspect him?''

Kobayashi raised his eyebrows. ''Of what? You don't mean the killings, surely?''

''I don't know. Of anything.''

Kobayashi smiled. ''You're not a very trusting man, Fugisawa. You're looking a gift horse in the mouth.''

''The Trojans didn't and look where it got them,'' said Fugisawa.

Kobayashi shook his head and chuckled. ''I like you, Fugisawa. If the police department should ever fail to appreciate your talents, you can always come to work for me.''

''I appreciate the spirit, if not the substance, of the offer.''

Kobayashi chuckled again. ''That was as graceful an insult as I've ever heard. Well, so has Kanno managed to come up with anything?''

''He says the killer is a dragon.''

''A *dragon*?''

''He found a small scale on one of the victims' clothing. I don't know how the hell forensics missed it. I would've raked them over the coals for it, but Katayama apparently just let it slide.''

"I gather you don't approve of the way he's conducting the investigation."

"No, I don't. He's too damn passive. But it's really not his fault. He has no experience in dealing with homicide. He just doesn't know what he's doing."

"Mmmm. That must make things rather awkward between you."

"Not really. He doesn't even know I'm still involved. As far as he knows, I've officially turned the case over to the Bureau and washed my hands of it."

"Ah. So then you're not getting your information directly from him."

"No, I'm not."

Kobayashi nodded. "It is useful to have one's sources."

"Yes. I guess you'd know all about that."

Kobayashi held up his hand. "Truce, Fugisawa. We are, at least for the moment, on the same side. To which end, I have already taken steps to achieve a solution to this problem that would work to our mutual advantage."

"You mean you've put out a contract on the killer?"

Kobayashi smiled. "Truce is not the same as trust. I have not forgotten to whom I am speaking, Lieutenant."

"You want to check me for a wire?"

"Why, are you wearing one?"

"No."

"Then I will take you at your word. But I am not responsible for any assumptions you might make."

"Well, then I will go ahead and make them. Assuming you made any arrangements regarding our mutual problem, should I assume you followed your usual procedures?"

"This is an unusual situation."

"I see. An independent, then."

"As I said, I am not responsible for your assumptions."

"Come on, Kobayashi, give me a hint. I'm already much farther out on a limb than you are. It might help if I knew whom not to bother."

"It might, but then, we're talking about assumptions and hypothetical situations, aren't we?"

"Yes, we are."

"Then let's hypothesize, purely for the sake of argument, of course, that I might not know, specifically."

Fugisawa frowned. "How the hell can you make any business arrangements if you don't know who you're dealing with?"

"Some people are very careful," Kobayashi said evenly. "Even more careful than I am. They take great pains to remain unknown. In fact, there are some people who rise to the very top of their professions without anyone being aware of their true identity."

"The very top of their professions?"

"Oh, yes. The *very* top."

Fugisawa stared at him for a long moment. "Are we talking about who I *think* we're talking about?"

"I have no idea what you mean, Lieutenant."

Fugisawa exhaled heavily. "You hired *Morpheus*?"

Kobayashi glanced at him and raised his eyebrows. "Who?"

"I heard he was dead."

"I have no idea who you're talking about, Lieutenant."

That clinched it. There was no way a man like Kobayashi wouldn't know who Morpheus was. No way whatsoever. It would be like an adept not knowing who Merlin was.

"Sorry. My mistake."

Kobayashi shrugged. "Was there anything else, Lieutenant?"

"Yes. I'd like to ask a favor."

"Ask."

"I'd like Kanno watched. Discreetly. But I'm not in a position to assign any department personnel to do it."

Kobayashi nodded. "I think that would be a waste of time. But if you wish, it will be taken care of."

"Thank you."

"You're welcome, Lieutenant." Kobayashi smiled. "As a concerned citizen, I'm always anxious to assist the police in any way I can."

"I'm sure," said Fugisawa with a grimace. "You're liable to assist me right into jail."

Kobayashi chuckled. "Good night, Lieutenant."

"Good night, Don Kobayashi."

* * *

Wyrdrune couldn't sleep. He was tired, but he simply couldn't close his eyes. He looked at Kira, lying in bed beside him. His eyes lingered lovingly on her naked body. She always tossed the covers off them when she slept. There was nothing he could do about it. No matter how many times he pulled the covers back over them, she'd just toss them off again in her sleep. He had simply gotten used to it; one of the many little compromises one had to make in a relationship. Like getting used to her throwing her underwear on the floor and leaving it there, always squeezing the toothpaste tube in the middle, and never cleaning up the hair she left in the bathroom sink. He always liked to line up his shoes carefully in the closet. She simply tossed her boots in. He always hung up the bath towels. She always left them on the floor. They were the sort of things that he hadn't really noticed at the start of their relationship, because the chemistry was still high and he was still drunk on the novelty of it, but eventually they began to get to him. But he never said anything about it. He kept telling himself that if you can't simply accept a person as they are, without trying to change them, then the downslide starts. The little things become bones of contention and they gradually develop into bigger things and then you start drifting apart. If you really loved someone, you had to take them as they were, warts and all. And you also had to realize that you probably did things that drove them crazy, too.

They had made love earlier that night. And, as always, it had been wonderful. Every time they made love, Wyrdrune felt as if the roof fell in on him. He reveled in her touch; in the taut, silky feel of her firmly muscled body; the electric softness of her skin; the warmth and fullness of her lips. He loved her so much he ached. He had never thought that he would feel that way about anybody. And he wondered if she felt the same way about him. Sometimes he didn't think she did.

It always seemed to him as if she was holding something back. It was nothing he could put his finger on, but it was there, just the same. It made him feel foolish and a little guilty, but there was no avoiding it. It was nothing that she said or did, but somehow he always felt that even in bed, Modred came between them. He wondered, and he hated himself for it, if she ever thought of Modred when they made love.

He could not complete with Modred. Modred was everything he wasn't. Modred was mature, sophisticated, handsome. Modred was self-assured and confident, with the build of an Adonis and a powerful, magnetic personality. And Modred was dangerous. A killer. And though he knew that Kira was deeply disturbed by that, he also knew that she was perversely fascinated by it. She was drawn to him in spite of herself. She had always been a danger junkie. It was one of the things that had made her a successful cat burglar. She got off on risk, on taking chances. And there was nothing risky about himself, Wyrdrune thought. He was safe and eminently predictable.

He had no doubt that Kira loved him. He was the one she shared her bed with, not Modred. Modred seemed completely oblivious of her feelings toward him. It seemed incredible that he could be unaware of how she felt about him. The way she sometimes looked at him, the subtle clues in her manner and tone of voice and body language, it was all there, plain as day. How could he fail to see it? Maybe he simply chose not to notice.

Wyrdrune sighed and got out of bed. He looked down at Kira. She was lying on her side, her legs slightly bent, her hands tucked beneath her check. She looked so vulnerable lying there, like a beautiful child-woman. She always tried to cultivate a toughness, a streetwise, aggressive manner that was part of her survival instincts, born of years of fending for herself. She always tried to look tough, dress tough, act tough, but at night he saw her as she really was. His gaze lingered on the graceful curves of her back and buttocks, on her long, exquisitely shaped legs, on the delicate arch of her feet. He loved to watch her while she slept and he felt desire stirring within him. He bent over and gently kissed her naked thigh. She moaned and shifted slightly in her sleep.

He was starting to get a headache. He went into the bathroom and opened up the medicine cabinet, looking for the bottle of aspirin he always packed anytime they went anywhere. He was prone to anxiety headaches. A by-product of his constant worrying. He couldn't help it. He always worried. He shook out a couple of pills and ran some water in the sink. He took the pills, put the bottle back, and closed the medicine cabinet door. He saw his reflection in the mirror. The emerald runestone in his forehead was glowing faintly.

"Damn," he said.

He went back into the bedroom. Kira was thrashing and moaning in her sleep, her head jerking from side to side on the pillow. She was damp with sweat. The runestone in her palm was emitting a soft blue glow. It was happening again. Someone out there was dying.

He ran over to the bed and bent over her, holding her by the shoulders.

"Kira! Kira, wake up! Kira!"

He couldn't wake her.

"Kira!"

He shook her. She still did not wake up. She continued to cry out and twist in his grasp.

"Kira! Wake up!"

He shook her as hard as he could, lifting her up and slamming her back down against the bed repeatedly. Her eyes opened abruptly as she awoke with a gasp.

"Jesus," he said. "Are you okay?"

She was breathing hard. "Yeah, I think so."

He ran out of the bedroom and through the connecting door, into Modred and Billy's suite. Modred was sitting on the couch, a drink in front of him. He was cleaning his 10-mm semiautomatic Colt. He looked up as Wyrdrune came rushing in.

"What is it?"

"You weren't asleep?"

"No. I had a headache and I thought I'd clean my gun and take my mind off things for a while."

"Kira just had another nightmare! I almost couldn't wake her up."

Modred glanced toward the door of Billy's bedroom. He got up quickly and they both went to the door. They could hear Billy in there, groaning and crying out in his sleep.

They went inside. Billy was thrashing around in bed, all tangled up in the covers. They were all bunched together and rolled up. He had entwined himself in them and he was struggling to break free . . . as if from the coils of a serpent.

"Billy!" Modred said.

Billy kept on struggling against the tangled sheets.

"Billy!"

Wyrdrune bent over him and grabbed his shoulders, shaking him. "Billy! Billy, *wake up*!"

No response.

Wyrdrune shook him harder. *"Billy! Billy, wake up, God damn it!"*

He couldn't rouse him.

Wyrdrune felt Modred's hand on his shoulder, pulling him away. Then Modred bent over Billy and slapped him hard across the face. Once. Twice. Three times.

"Aaaah!" Billy's eyes snapped open, staring wildly.

"Is he all right?"

Kira was behind them in the doorway of the bedroom. She had thrown on a cotton kimono.

"Gor', what a bleedin' 'orror," said Billy, breathing hard.

His hair was matted and his thin chest was covered with a sheen of sweat.

"It's getting worse," said Wyrdrune. "It's got to stop."

"It's because we're close now," Modred said.

"Can't we *do* something?"

"We are doing something," Modred replied. "Calm down."

"Calm down? *Calm down?* Jesus, you had to hit him three times to snap him out of it! Why the hell aren't the runestones doing anything?"

"Because they probably don't choose to."

"Why?"

"They have a life force of their own. They will do what needs to be done, when it needs to be done. And not before."

"Blimey, I need a drink," said Billy.

"For a change, I won't object," said Merlin. "I need one, too."

They went back out into the living room. Billy and Kira went over to the bar. Modred went back to the coffee table and reassembled his pistol. He inserted the magazine and racked the slide, chambering a round. Then he put on the safety, leaving the pistol "cocked and locked," and put it back in its shoulder holster.

"This can't go on," said Wyrdrune. "We've got to *do* something. She's getting stronger."

"I already told you," Modred said, "we *are* doing something. You must be patient."

"Patient! Christ, people are *dying*!"

Modred glanced up at him. "People always die. And many more will die before we've seen an end of this. You might as well accept that."

"I can't."

"You have no choice."

Modred went over to the window and looked out at the Ginza.

"She's close," he said. "Very close."

She was waiting for him when he got back to the sanctuary. Kanno knew she had just killed. There was fresh blood on the altar, but no other evidence of any of her victims. She had evidently already disposed of the bodies. He knew what would be expected of him now. Each time, after she killed, she wanted to have sex. It could hardly be called making love. She wanted something, he supplied it. It was as simple as that.

He did not delude himself that she had any feeling for him. He certainly had none for her, though he pretended that he did. Leila was an insatiably carnal creature, but to her, sex was merely another way of exercising power. To Kanno, sex meant absolutely nothing. It was a biological function, nothing more. He did not find having sex with her repulsive. Quite the contrary. She was an extraordinarily accomplished lover. She was beautiful and intensely desirable. Kanno had no trouble performing with her and he could take pleasure in her body, but he did not for one moment allow that to cloud his judgment. He was a man of discipline.

Already, his patience had been rewarded. He had discovered that she was not infallible. She believed that he was slavishly devoted to her, that he worshiped her. She had a monumental ego. It wasn't much, but it was something that he might be able to use against her when the time came. It was a weakness. In time, he was sure she would reveal others.

She was waiting for him in her chambers, along with her ever-present attendant, the animated corpse. Kanno could not understand how she could bear to be near that creature. There was something profoundly repellent about her. In life, she had not been unattractive. A young Eurasian whore, perhaps seventeen or eighteen years old, with a sultry, pouty face, long black hair, a slim, long-legged body, and full, slightly upturned breasts. But now, she was like an empty, soulless husk. The long black hair hung lank and snarled upon her shoulders. The skin had taken on a deathly pallor. It was drawn and almost translucent. Ghostly. And the face had no expression whatsoever. The eyes were dark, empty pools. She shuffled about, barefoot, moving with that curious, marionettelike gait. Her long, filmy white gown was soiled and dingy. Dust clung to her. Just looking at her made Kanno's stomach turn.

"Come in, Kanno," Leila said. "I've been waiting for you."

She was reclining on the couch, dressed in a long, black, silky gown slashed deeply up the side, exposing her perfect legs. It had a plunging neckline that left nothing to the imagination. Her thick red hair cascaded down her shoulders and her coppery skin seemed to gleam in the torchlight. She was a vision that would have excited any normal man to lust and Kanno was not entirely immune to it, but he prided himself on his control. He was the master, not the slave of his emotions.

"How did matters go with the police?" she asked, smiling.

"They are fools," said Kanno. "They suspect nothing."

"And our work, it is receiving much attention? It is generating fear?"

"The media is making a great deal of it," Kanno replied. "All Japan knows of it by now."

"Good," she said. "We must make them properly receptive."

Kanno frowned slightly. Receptive for what? She had still not revealed her plans to him. Perhaps now would be the time.

"You have been a faithful acolyte, Kanno. I am pleased with

you. And when the time comes, your loyalty will be rewarded. I will make you my high priest.''

"Thank you, Mistress." High priest? What was she talking about?

"But there is still work left to be done before we can assume our rightful place," she said. "Before the others can arrive."

The others? His stomach tightened involuntarily. She was talking about others like herself, he realized. The Dark Ones. How many of them were there? And *where* were they?

"We have waited a long time," she said, partly to herself. "A very long time. These islands, with their teeming population, will make an excellent beginning."

And he suddenly realized what she meant. It was with an enormous effort that he kept the impact of that realization from showing on his face. She was talking about subjugating the entire population of Japan! And that was only a *beginning*?

"But you need not be concerned," she continued. "You will be rewarded for your faithful service. When the time comes, we will require acolytes. And it is only fitting that you should be their high priest. You will see power such as you have never dreamed of. That should satisfy even your ambition.'' She smiled. "And speaking of being satisfied . . .''

She made a languid motion with her hand and suddenly he stood before her, naked, the brilliant coils of the dragon tattoo winding around his body. She gazed at him with a smoldering look and leaned back on the couch. He trembled, involuntarily, and she took it as a sign of excitement, but it was really fear, coursing through his body like the icy waters of the River Styx. His mistress was Death incarnate.

As he lay beside her and felt the warmth of her body, he felt himself starting to respond, despite the cold feeling in the pit of his stomach. His fear of his inhuman lover was working as an aphrodisiac and he abandoned himself to it. As she lay beneath him, moaning softly, he moved against her and concentrated on giving her the pleasure she demanded from him. And it occurred to him that a moment such as this would be the ideal time to kill her. But one thought kept nagging at him like a dog worrying a bone. What if he failed?

What if she would not die?

* * *

The two long black limos pulled up to the curb in front of the small shop in the Shinjuku district. A sign over the door said "House of Nihonto," the house of the sword. The shop was well known throughout all of Tokyo for supplying the finest Japanese swords and knives in the entire country, perhaps the finest steel in the entire world. The swordsmiths of Nihonto were unquestioned masters of their art, producing blades vastly superior to any ever produced in Toledo or Damascus. The legendary sword of the Samurai was a prized possession in the proper Japanese household, embodying as it did an aesthetic ideal of beauty through simplicity and purity. A sword produced by the House of Nihonto was the ultimate in symbols of status. Only the very wealthy could easily afford them, though many Japanese businessmen of the middle class saved for years or borrowed on their homes to purchase one, so that they could proudly display it in their homes.

Don Kobayashi was well familiar with the House of Nihonto. He owned a number of blades crafted by their master swordsmiths. The sword possessed added significance to the members of the Yakuza. To them, it was more than an aesthetic symbol, a work of art. It was also a totem of their power and, sometimes, a tool of their profession. Each and every one of them was a devoted student of kendo and the elite soldiers of the Yakuza were like modern samurai, proficient not only in the use of firearms, but also in the martial arts, especially the way of the sword. The House of Nihonto, therefore, was well known to all of them and it was with a considerable amount of surprise that Don Kobayashi learned that this was the place chosen by Morpheus for their meeting.

He had not quite known what to expect. He had been told he would be contacted, but he had fully expected that contact to come by phone. Morpheus was known for being immensely secretive. No one of Kobayashi's acquaintance had any idea who he really was or what he looked like. But his reputation was well known in certain international circles. He was the consummate assassin. A modern ninja, it was said, in every sense of the word. He had never failed in a contract and he was wanted by the law enforcement agencies of almost every country in the world. Both the Bureau and the I.T.C. had extensive dossiers on "hits" attributed to Morpheus, but not even they had succeeded in running him to ground.

The original Morpheus, Kobayashi knew, was long dead. There had been stories about Morpheus since before the time of his father. Obviously, the tradition was being carried on by a successor. Kobayashi wondered if it was a family business. The idea of a dynasty of mysterious, professional assassins appealed to him. From time to time, an imposter would appear, claiming to be Morpheus, but the real Morpheus—whoever he or they might be at any given time—had always been fiercely protective of his reputation. Invariably, these imposters turned up dead, shot between the eyes with a 10-mm semiautomatic.

For several years now there had been no word of Morpheus and it was thought that the most recent holder of the name had either died or gone into retirement. Kobayashi himself had not known which was true, but when he had made inquiries, through channels known to certain trusted individuals, he had learned that the latter was the case. Many lucrative contracts had been turned down. But now this Morpheus, whoever he might be, had come out of retirement, specifically out of respect for him. Kobayashi felt very surprised and flattered. And he was even more surprised and flattered when the call came and he learned that he was actually going to meet with Morpheus face-to-face.

He was also surprised at the choice of the location. He might have expected some out of the way bar or sex emporium in the Ginza, someplace that might be more conducive to a secret meeting, someplace where two people might talk in a manner that would not allow them to actually see each other, but he had not expected this and he realized now that the choice had been inspired. It demonstrated a unique knowledge and an understanding on the part of the mysterious assassin. The House of Nihonto was a very respectable establishment, catering as it did to some of Japan's finest and most influential citizens. It was also one of the few places that was regarded as "neutral ground" by the various families of the Yakuza, which were often in competition. It would be unthinkable for any acts of hostility to occur here. It would be regarded as a desecration.

Just the same, Takeo had insisted on their not taking any chances. Kobayashi remained in the car while Shiro and Takeo got out and walked across to the entrance of the shop. The doors of the car behind them opened and four men got out. Two of them followed Takeo and Shiro into the shop, while the other two remained on the sidewalk, close by Kobayashi's car, scanning the street around them alertly.

The small shop was almost empty when Takeo, Shiro, and the two men entered. There were glass display cabinets to the left and in front of them, as well as one in the center of the shop, square-shaped and about waist high. They held a glittering array of steel, not common cutlery, but exquisitely crafted custom knives of every size, shape, and description. There were ceremonial seppuku knives and fighting *tantos*, as well as variations on the traditional American fighting knife, devised centuries ago by Rezin Bowie and made famous by his brother, James. Some had traditional grips, others were of ivory, horn, micarta, and beautiful laminated and exotic woods. There were elegant Fairburn-Sykes British commando knives, Gurkhas, Filipino butterfly knives, Italian stilettos, Scottish dirks, and a dazzling variety of folding blades, all handcrafted with unique perfection. And the walls behind the cabinets were hung with swords of every description.

The swordsmiths of the House of Nihonto prided themselves on being masters not only of the traditional Japanese sword, though they were, of course, most famous for that, but of every type of sword that had ever been in existence, from the Roman gladius to medieval broadswords to Florentine blades and Saracen scimitars. They catered to some of the wealthiest collectors in the world and regarded no task as too great or too small, providing they could bring to it their usual high standards of quality. But most expensive and highly prized were the Japanese swords, such as those in the central display case— gleaming blades with graceful curves and painstakingly wrapped hilts, they were lovingly polished and honed to such a razor sharpness that if a silk scarf were dropped upon the blade, it would be sliced in two.

There were only two customers in the shop, young people, Americans or Europeans, by the look of them. One was a girl of about twenty or so, dressed in tight maroon lycras, high boots, and a leather and chain-mail jacket of the sort favored by style-conscious youths. The other was a young boy, in his early teens, scruffy-looking, with bloused, multipocketed military trousers and paratroopers boots, and a fringed and zippered leather coat that looked as if it had been sewn together from remnants. He had an outrageous hairstyle, short on the sides and thick and full in the center, a crest rather like a horse's mane, cascading down to the middle of his back. One of those punks, thought Shiro, with distaste. Tourists, undoubtedly. There was no question of them being able to afford anything in the shop except, perhaps, one of the small sharpening stones that were sold in special little wooden boxes labeled with the shop's name as inexpensive souvenirs. Nonetheless, the boy was eagerly examining some knives, asking the salesman to take out one after another from the display case. British, Shiro thought, hearing his crude accent. The salesman was being exceedingly polite to them, even though they were quite obviously wasting his time.

To the right of the shop were several small cubicles, little rooms where the more serious customers (the better class of people) could be waited on in comfortable privacy while they partook of a little tea or saki. There were three cubicles in all. The doors to two of them were open. The door to the third was closed. Shiro was just about to open it when a very well-dressed salesman approached him.

"May I be of service, Mr. Kobayashi?"

He was, of course, known in this establishment.

"Who's in there?"

"A young gentleman, a warlock," said the salesman. "I believe he's waiting to speak with one of the masters about an apprenticeship."

Takeo opened the door, Shiro and the two others close behind him, their hands inside their jackets. Sitting on the floor, on a cushion placed behind a low table, was a young Occidental with shoulder-length, curly blond hair. He was wearing a brown warlock's cassock and a headband, with his hair worn outside it. Some sort of fashion statement, Shiro thought wryly. What was the point of wearing a headband if you didn't use it to hold down your hair? He was mildly surprised to see a western youth seeking apprenticeship with the House of Nihonto. He looked American. A student at the university, most likely. He was aware that some westerners were Japanophiles, often displaying a far greater interest in the Japanese traditions than many of the local young people, who seemed to be obsessed with anything that was American. The young man looked up at them questioningly. He started to rise.

"Don't bother getting up," said Takeo. He motioned one of the men behind him to remain in the display room of the shop, then had the other follow him across the small cubicle and through a curtain in the back. They came out into a short hallway that extended to the front of the building, with curtained doorways leading into the other two cubicles to the right. He checked them once again to make sure they were still empty, then went down the hall, which led out into the back workroom of the shop, where several of the masters and their apprentices were at work. They looked up at him briefly, then went back to their tasks. The salesman came up behind him once again.

"Is there something I can help you with, Mr. Kobayashi?"

"We were supposed to meet someone here," said Shiro.

"Ah. I see. Perhaps you and your associates would care to wait in one of the cubicles? I could offer you some tea, if you like, or saki?"

Shiro pursed his lips as his gaze swept across the immaculate workroom. "No, thank you. Perhaps in a moment." He turned to one of the men. "Stay here."

The man nodded and took up a post just inside the small hallway, where no one could come in without passing him. Takeo and Shiro went back through the cubicle, past the faintly puzzled-looking young warlock and out into the main room of the shop. The two young people were still looking at the knives. Shiro debated whether or not to order them out, then decided not to bother. A couple of kids were no threat and the salesman would doubtless lose his patience with them soon and they would leave. He went to the door and signaled the men outside.

One of them opened the limo door and Don Kobayashi

stepped out. The others fell in step beside him as he walked across the sidewalk and entered the shop.

"He isn't here," Shiro told his father.

Don Kobayashi glanced at his expensive watch. "We'll wait five minutes," he said.

The salesman approached and bowed respectfully. "*Konnichi wa*, Don Kobayashi-san. We are honored with your presence. How may we serve you?"

"I am to meet someone here," said Kobayashi.

"Ah, yes, of course. Please, come this way." He directed Kobayashi to the middle cubicle. "May I offer you some refreshment while you wait?"

"Thank you. Some tea would be very nice."

"Certainly. I will see to it."

"And I do not wish to be disturbed."

"Of course."

Kobayashi entered the small cubicle, closed the door behind him, unbuttoned his jacket, and sat down on the cushion behind the low table. Shiro, Takeo, and the others took up position outside. He glanced at his watch again. When he looked up, he was startled to see a man standing in the room, just inside the curtain. He was holding a small tray with a tea service on it.

"Good afternoon, Don Kobayashi," he said in impeccable, unaccented Japanese. "I am Morpheus."

The man looked to be in his early to mid-forties, blond, with a neatly trimmed beard and tinted, gold-rimmed glasses. He was about five-ten or five-eleven, a hundred and ninety pounds or so, well built and with good bearing. He was dressed in a dark, elegantly tailored, neo-Edwardian suit with a modest touch of lace at the throat and cuffs.

"May I offer you some tea?" he said, setting down the tray and sitting down across the table from him.

"Please," said Kobayashi, looking at him with interest.

Modred poured for them.

"I did not even hear you come in," Kobayashi said.

Modred smiled. "Forgive me if I startled you. I did not want to keep a man like yourself waiting."

"I must confess that I am somewhat surprised to see you. I

was under the impression that you were a most secretive man. I did not expect to actually meet you face-to-face."

"In certain rare cases, I make exceptions to my usual procedure," Modred said. "I did not wish to show disrespect by asking you to deal with intermediaries."

"I'm flattered. However, how can I be certain that you are not, yourself, an intermediary? No offense intended, but I find it hard to believe that Morpheus would actually risk such a meeting."

"None taken. You have one man stationed outside, in the hallway, and several others in the shop. It's understandable that you would wish to take security measures. Why don't you call out to them?"

Kobayashi raised his eyebrows. Then he called out, "Shiro!" There was no response.

Kobayashi frowned. He called out again. "Shiro! Takeo!"

"What could be keeping them?" asked Modred, raising his eyebrows.

Kobayashi stared at him. Then he got to his feet, went to the door, and opened it.

It was dark inside the shop. The curtains were pulled down over the front windows and the front door was locked, as if the shop were closed. The salesmen, the two young tourists, Shiro, Takeo, and the others were all standing in the darkened shop, frozen like statues. Kobayashi stared at them with astonishment, then walked up to his son. Shiro's eyes were open, but he didn't seem to see him.

"Shiro!"

They all just stood there, motionless.

Kobayashi reached out to touch his son, then pulled his hand back. His mouth tightened. He went back into the cubicle.

"What have you done to them?"

"They are quite all right, I assure you," Modred said. "When our meeting is concluded, they will be as they were before. They will be unharmed, but they will remember nothing. They will not even be aware that any time has passed."

"You're an adept!" said Kobayashi.

Modred inclined his head slightly. "I have some small skill."

Kobayashi nodded. "That explains a great deal. It appears that I have come to the right man."

Modred smiled and indicated the cushion. "Please, sit down. We have much to talk about."

CHAPTER
Seven

AKIRO SUPPOSED IT WAS INEVITABLE. THE REPORTERS HAD not been satisfied with Morio. They would not be put off by a spokesman, they wanted the investigating agent and they had staked him out, catching him as he was leaving the building. They had descended upon him with their cameras and microphones and notepads, surrounding him and peppering him with rapid-fire questions. He knew that it had not gone well, but as he sat in his apartment and morosely watched the evening news, he saw that it had gone even worse than he had thought.

They had gone with the story as their lead. The anchorman had started off by reciting the mounting toll of heinous murders and then they cut to the interview, showing him leaving the building furtively, his hat pulled low over his eyes, visibly recoiling as the reporters descended upon him, wincing as their microphones were pointed at his face. He hesitated, he stammered, he floundered, he looked like a man caught doing something wrong. He cringed as he watched the interview. He looked awful on camera. He looked nervous. He looked incompetent. He looked stupid. Worse, he looked guilty. His answers to their questions were lame and sounded exactly like the sort of rote things people said when they were trying to avoid saying anything. It was painful to watch. His worst fears had been realized.

To make matters even worse, they had also interviewed

Kanno, apparently having caught him earlier in the day, and they ran that segment immediately after they ran his. It made for a sharp contrast. On camera, Kanno looked much better than he did. He was good-looking and well spoken, totally unruffled. He confirmed that he was "assisting the Bureau on the investigation in an advisory capacity" at the request of his old sensei, Master Yohaku, to whom the Bureau had appealed for help. Under questioning, he confirmed that necromancy was involved, that the murders were the work of some sort of "creature," and when pressed for details, he outlined what he had deduced about it from viewing the remains of its victims, which left the impression that both the police and the Bureau could have easily deduced the same things, but had either failed to do so or would not admit what they had learned.

He mentioned the discovery of the scale, which clearly implied that the Bureau had somehow overlooked it—and they had, damn it, though Akiro couldn't imagine how—and when pressed for details about that, he was forced to admit that it was a reptilian scale. He hesitated to comment further, but under pressure, he revealed that he had "reason to believe" that "the monster" (which sounded much worse than "the creature") was probably a dragon. And then they pressed him about that and he was forced to elaborate, giving his guesses as to its size and nature and his belief that what they were faced with was a shapechanger.

They ate it up. And when they cut back to the anchorman, there was a graphic on the rear projection screen behind him, an artist's conception of "the monster," which resembled some sort of slathering, prehistoric beast straight out of a science fiction movie, with a shadowy human figure behind it and the legend, "Ginza Monster" superimposed over it in dripping red letters. And the anchorman had closed with the statement that the authorities seemed helpless while "the monster's reign of terror" continued unabated.

Akiro groaned and shut off the TV. His wife came up and set a martini down before him. She sat down on the couch beside him. He looked at her gratefully and downed half of the drink in one gulp.

"Is it that bad?" she asked.

He shook his head with resignation. "It's an absolute disaster," he said.

"The media always exaggerates. You'll solve it, I know you will," she said supportively.

He grimaced. "I'm no closer to solving this case than I was the day I took it."

"A break will come. It always does."

He took her hand and squeezed it. "Perhaps, Keiko," he said, "but even if it does, it will come too late for me. The damage has already been done. Because of me, the Bureau has been made to look bad. In the morning, I will almost certainly be taken off the case. And that will end any chances I have of being accepted by the I.T.C."

"But you have an outstanding record," his wife said. "You've put in fifteen years of service and you've never failed to close a case. Surely, that must stand for something."

"You're only as good as your last case," Akiro said with a sigh. "The competition for positions in the I.T.C. is among the most intense." He shook his head. "No, any hope I had of that is gone now."

She was silent for a moment. "I know it's something that you wanted very much," she said, "but is it really so terrible if you don't work for the I.T.C.?"

"What else is there?" he asked. "The corporate sector? I can forget that, too. I'll be the man who failed to solve 'the Ginza Monster case.' Nobody wants to employ a failure, Keiko."

"That wasn't what I meant," she said. "You could retire."

"Retire?"

"We don't really need the money," she said. "I've managed to put some away over the years and I still have my job. Another three years and I'll be able to take my pension. And you'll have yours. We'll manage."

He looked at her and smiled. "I was hoping that we could do more than merely 'manage.' The children are getting older and they'll need our help. And you deserve so much more than what I've been able to give you."

She squeezed his hand. "I don't need expensive clothes or fancy jewelry," she said. "All I ever wanted was to be with you. To spend more time with you. We're not getting any younger, you know.''

He leaned over and kissed her. "What did I ever do to get a wife like you?''

"You made me pregnant, remember? But I would have married you anyway.''

He chuckled. "I thought your father would have a stroke. He never did like me.''

"I like you. And that's all that counts.''

He sighed and nestled his head against her shoulder while she stroked his thinning hair. "You were always good for me. Perhaps you're right. We've both been working very hard for a long time. And we're not as young as we used to be. But still . . .''

"I know. You wanted to go out a winner. But it isn't over yet.''

"By tomorrow, it probably will be. Watanabe will take me off the case. He'll probably turn it over to Sakahara. He's young, he's bright, and he's hungry.''

"And he's inexperienced," said Keiko.

"There's nothing like on-the-job training. This case will either make him or break him. As it's broken me.''

"Stop it! Stop it right now!''

She pushed him away and Akiro looked at her with surprise, taken aback by her vehemence.

"I won't have you sitting here and wallowing in self-pity, feeling sorry for yourself!'' she snapped. "Watanabe hasn't taken you off the case yet. And even if he does, that doesn't mean you have to drop it. You can ask for some time off. You've certainly got it coming and if Watanabe takes you off the case, he'll hardly be in a position to deny you. It would be like kicking someone when he's down. You'll be able to work on it on your own time, like you used to do when *you* were young and hungry. You want to go out a winner? Then get off your fat ass and *do* something about it! I didn't marry a quitter!''

He stared at her for a moment, a bit stunned by her outburst, then he smiled. "I love you.''

She stared into his eyes. "You can do something about that, too."

He gulped down the rest of his drink, took her by the hand, and led her to the bedroom.

Don Ito Nishikawa did not like the young man sitting across the table from him. He had nothing but contempt for him, but the young man was useful and Nishikawa was not a man who would allow his personal feelings to get in the way of business. A dapper man in his mid-forties, he controlled the Roppongi district for the Yakuza and he was anxious to move up in the organization. The Ginza was a plum he'd had his eye on for a long time, but there was an obstacle in his way. That obstacle was Don Teruyuki Kobayashi. And the young man sitting across the table from him in the private back room of the bar was going to give him the means to overcome that obstacle.

Nishikawa could not think of a more despicable creature than a son who would turn against his own father, but he concealed his distaste from Yoshiro Kobayashi. This rather spoiled young man had been privileged to occupy an important position in his father's organization and this was how he showed his gratitude. By selling out his own father. He was not, however, selling him out cheaply. Shiro was well aware of his value to Nishikawa and he had made no bones about it. He had come to him with a proposition, a proposition he had known that Nishikawa would be unable to turn down.

Shiro did not wish to follow in his father's footsteps. He wanted no part of the Yakuza. He had taken degrees in economics and business administration and what he really wanted was to leave Japan, go to America, and become an investment banker. There was, in fact, nothing to prevent him from doing this, but he apparently lacked the courage to make an open break with his father and he did not wish to be disinherited. Don Kobayashi possessed a considerable personal fortune and Shiro obviously intended to receive his share when his father died. Moreover, he was not above hastening the time when that would happen. He believed that running the family's operations on the Ginza was beneath him. He wanted to do his stealing in more congenial surroundings. And he wanted to make the move in comfort. The present situation had provided him with the ideal opportunity.

The Ginza murders were making Kobayashi look bad. They had caused a drastic falling off in business and had brought a great deal of unwanted attention to the area. Under ordinary circumstances, the police were not really concerned about the vice and gambling operations there. Technically, such things were illegal, but in the Ginza, they were cheerfully ignored by both the population and the authorities alike. But murder was something else again. A serial killer could not be ignored, especially when he was a necromancer. Necromancy was a capital offense in every country in the world and it was so rare, and the nature of the murders so grisly, that it had become the biggest story in the country.

The media was crawling all over the Ginza, as were the police and the agents of the Bureau. The latest word had it that a special I.T.C. investigator was going to be brought in and all this resulted in a giant headache for Kobayashi. The police could not be seen to be looking the other way with so much attention directed at them. The whores, already suffering from fewer customers and fear of being the next victim of the killer, were being swept off the streets and taken away in large vans, so that the media could at least see that the police were doing something. The drug emporiums were being shut down and the gambling casinos were being raided. Lacking the ability to apprehend the killer, the police were doing everything they could to appear busy and conscientious. And Kobayashi was coming in for some severe criticism from his superiors in the organization for not being able to take care of "the problem" on his turf.

In an effort to save face, he had confided to the council that he had already taken steps to remedy the situation by putting out a contract on the killer. He had his people pursuing their own investigation and he had gone to great trouble and expense to convince the legendary Morpheus to come out of retirement and take on the job. That had impressed the council favorably and bought him some more time, but if he did not achieve some results soon, his position would be very precarious indeed. Nishikawa was determined to make it as precarious as possible.

To that end, much as he detested the young man, Nishikawa found Shiro Kobayashi a godsend. For a price, he was willing to help bring down his father. It was a high price, but it was well worth it. Nishikawa sorted through the photographs he had just taken from the manila envelope that Shiro passed across the table. They were pictures taken at the East Garden of the Imperial Palace, on the Nijubashi Bridge. They showed Don Teruyuki Kobayashi having a secret meeting with Lt. Fugisawa, of the Tokyo Police. In light of all the recent police activity in the Ginza, Nishikawa thought that the members of the council would find these photographs very remarkable, indeed.

"I thought you would find those interesting," said Shiro Kobayashi smugly.

"Who took these?"

"If you mean does anybody else know about them, no. I took them myself."

Nishikawa slipped the photographs back into the envelope and gave them to one of his aides, standing behind him at the table.

"That's very good," he said. "But at the moment, I am more concerned with your father's dealings with this man Morpheus. He is said to be the best there is. To my knowledge, he has never failed to deliver on a contract. Is it really true he's hired him?"

"It's true," said Shiro. "They had a meeting earlier today."

"He actually met with Morpheus face-to-face?" said Nishikawa with surprise.

"He says he did. I was there, along with some of our people, but we saw nothing."

"What do you mean, you saw nothing?"

"The meeting took place in one of the private showrooms at the House of Nihonto. My father met with Morpheus alone. However, we saw no one either come into or leave that room. We had been placed under a spell."

"A spell? Morpheus employed a wizard?"

"Perhaps. Or maybe he did it himself. My father said he told him that he had, in his own words, 'some small skill' as an adept.''

"That's very interesting," said Nishikawa. "It would go a long way toward explaining how he's been so successful. However, in this case, it is important that he *not* be so successful."

"Finding the killer will not be easy, even for a man like Morpheus. But if you're worried, perhaps you could provide him with some incentive not to do his job so well," suggested Shiro.

Nishikawa frowned. It was typical of this turncoat to believe that everybody had a price. "From what I know of Morpheus, trying to buy him off would be a waste of time. He has an enviable reputation. He is the complete professional. Once he's accepted a contract, he always sticks by its terms, regardless of the circumstances."

"It's worth a try," said Shiro.

"Then let the offer come from you," said Nishikawa dryly. "If he accepts, which I very much doubt he will, I will supply the money. But it is more likely that, having accepted a commission from your father, he will report the offer to him. If you wish to take that chance, it's up to you. I have no desire to have my name come out in this matter."

Shiro considered the possibility. "He would be foolish to turn down a greater sum. Especially since he would not have to do anything to earn it."

"Then make the offer. But my name had better be kept out of it. If my hand in this matter is revealed, I can promise you that you will never see America."

"You don't have to make threats, Don Nishikawa. I fully understand the risks I'm taking. And I might add that I'm taking them on your behalf."

Nishikawa grimaced with distaste. "Spare me your hypocrisy. You're doing this for yourself and no one else."

"Perhaps, but you stand to profit the most from it. Otherwise we wouldn't be here, would we? I can see to it that Morpheus is approached discreetly. He doesn't need to know who is behind it. And if he refuses, he can always be eliminated."

"*You?* Eliminate Morpheus?" Nishikawa chuckled. "That is something I would like to see."

"I would not do it personally, of course," said Shiro. "I am not a fool. The man is a professional assassin. I am not. But he is still only a man. He is not immortal."

"Judging by his reputation, he is the next best thing," said Nishikawa.

"According to what my father told me about him," replied Shiro, "he is relatively young. In his mid-forties. That would make it impossible for him to have carried off the contracts on which his reputation largely rests. Clearly, this is another Morpheus, a son, perhaps, or someone who has been trained by the one who has retired to carry on in the tradition. Doubtless, he has accomplished some contracts of his own, but he is living on the reputation of his predecessor. And I have my own people in my father's organization, people I've brought in whose first loyalty is to me and not my father. They are very capable professionals in their own right. Once this new Morpheus is located, eliminating him will not be difficult."

Nishikawa thought this over. What young Kobayashi said made sense. He was a loathesome creature, but he was clearly not a fool. He knew what he was doing. He was nowhere near the man his father was, but he had an aptitude for devious double-dealing. He would, thought Nishikawa, make a very successful investment banker. And he would also have to be watched carefully. His very presence here demonstrated that he was clearly not a man to be trusted. He could be trusted to serve his own best interest, nothing more.

"How will you manage to locate him if you've never even seen him?" asked Nishikawa.

"I have a good description of him from my father," Shiro replied. "And I believe that he is here with some accomplices. There were three people in the shop at the time the meeting took place. A young American warlock, perhaps the one who was responsible for the spell, and two others. When we recovered from the spell we had been placed under, all three of them were gone. They were rather distinctive in appearance. They should not prove too difficult to find."

"If you were caught, it could be very inconvenient for me," said Nishikawa, weighing the possibilities.

"I've told you, I'm not a fool. I have no intention of coming anywhere near Morpheus myself."

"Yes, but I do not know your people. They could lead him right to you, and you would be able to lead him directly to me. I would prefer to avoid that risk."

"There are risks in any undertaking of this sort," said Shiro in a condescending manner that made Nishikawa want to strike him. But he restrained himself. There was no reason to abuse a tool that could be useful.

"Quite true," he said, after taking a moment to compose himself. "But it would be foolish not to minimize those risks. If your people are able to locate Morpheus, go ahead and approach him with your offer. One never knows, it's just possible that he might accept it. If not, then you are to keep careful track of him and report to me at once. If it is necessary for him to be eliminated, I would prefer to use my own people. People who can be trusted not to talk. And people whose capabilities I am more certain of."

Shiro seemed not even to perceive the insult. He merely shrugged. "As you wish."

"If your father has any further meetings with Lt. Fugisawa, do what you can to get evidence of those, as well. It would serve to make our case stronger with the council."

"No problem. My father trusts me."

Nishikawa smiled wryly. "How unfortunate for him."

"You don't like me very much, do you?"

"Whatever gave you that idea?"

"It makes no difference to me. I could care less. Just as long as you live up to your part of the bargain."

"Of course," said Nishikawa. He snapped his fingers and the man behind him handed him a white business envelope, which Nishikawa passed across the table. "Your thirty pieces of silver," he said dryly.

Shiro smiled. "I am not Judas and my father is certainly not Christ. Besides, there is one very significant difference between Judas and myself. I have no intention of hanging myself."

"Given enough rope, you just may," said Nishikawa. "*Oyasumi nasai*, Yoshiro."

"Good night to you, too, Don Nishikawa. When this is finished, I'll send you a postcard from New York."

He got up and left the table.

Nishikawa spoke softly to his aide, without turning around. "When this is finished, kill him."

There was a soft knock at the door. Thinking it was room service, Billy went to open it. It was not room service. It was a slim Japanese man in his late forties with closely cropped, salt-and-pepper hair and a deadpan expression on his face. He was wearing a shabby dark suit that was several years out of fashion and looked as if he'd slept in it. He looked at Billy and his eyes widened slightly.

"Who the 'ell are you?" said Billy.

"Lt. Fugisawa, Tokyo Police." He held up the little leather folder holding his shield and ID.

Billy's eyes narrowed suspiciously. "Somethin' wrong?"

"I'm looking for Mr. Michael Cornwall."

"What for?"

"Do you mind if I come in?"

"Why?"

"I'd like to ask him a few questions, if I may."

"Bout what?"

"May I come in?"

"Let the gentleman come in, Billy," Modred said from behind him.

Billy hesitated a moment, then stood aside as Fugisawa entered. Fugisawa smiled at Billy and said, "Thank you," thinking, this one's had run-ins with the law before. He could always tell. In this case, it was particularly obvious, even if it wasn't for the young punk's street-tough appearance. The moment he saw the shield, his manner became instantly and aggressively defensive. Fugisawa glanced at the other man inside the suite. Tall, well-muscled, blond, with a neatly trimmed beard and tinted, gold-rimmed, aviator-style glasses. He was wearing a pair of gray slacks, embroidered velvet slippers, and a black silk dressing gown. The moment he saw him, Fugisawa knew. A thrill went through him.

"You would be Mr. Michael Cornwall?" he said.

Modred looked at him for a long moment, then smiled faintly. "I think you already know who I am, Lieutenant."

Fugisawa tensed. "Do I?"

He reached up casually and made a motion as if to adjust his trousers. And suddenly, he found himself looking into the barrel of a big, black semiautomatic Colt 10-mm with a silencer attached. He froze.

"Be so kind as to remove it with two fingers, Lieutenant, and then hand it to my friend."

Fugisawa moistened his lips. "Don't be foolish. You don't think I came without backup, do you?"

Modred smiled. "Why don't you call them, then?"

Fugisawa's lips tightened into a grimace, then he slowly took out his 9-mm and handed it to Billy.

"Be sure to get the one in his ankle holster, Billy," Modred said.

Billy bent down, pulled up Fugisawa's trouser leg, and removed a small .32 semiautomatic from its nylon holster.

"You have a good eye," said Fugisawa wryly. "I didn't think it showed."

Billy patted him down quickly, then said, "E's clean now."

Modred put the gun away. "Sit down, Lieutenant. May I offer you some tea or coffee?"

"I could use something a little stronger."

"Scotch?"

"Please. Straight up."

As Fugisawa sat down at the table, Modred walked over to the bar and poured two drinks. "Ask the others to join us, Billy, won't you?"

Billy went through the connecting door.

"I underestimated you," said Fugisawa. "I was sure you'd brazen it out. What gave me away?"

"A very slight involuntary tension of the facial muscles," Modred said. To Fugisawa's surprise, he spoke in perfect Japanese. "Almost imperceptible. Don't feel badly, Lieutenant. You have a very good poker face."

"Not good enough, apparently," Fugisawa responded in his own language. "Your Japanese is excellent. Far better than my English. You have spent time in Japan before?"

"I lived here once, but it was a long time ago," said Modred with a smile.

The connecting room door opened and Billy came back in, along with Wyrdrune and Kira. And, Fugisawa was astonished to see, an ambulatory broom with thin, rubbery arms that had three digits on each hand.

"This is Lt. Fugisawa of the Tokyo Police Department," Modred said to them, reverting back to English.

"*Oy vey!*" said Broom as Fugisawa's eyes grew even wider. "*Now* what did you do? Are we going to be arrested?"

"Be quiet, Broom," said Wyrdrune.

"I was about to ask Lt. Fugisawa how he found us," Modred said.

Fugisawa hesitated. "What difference does it make?"

"I am trying to be polite," Modred said. "I would prefer if you tell us voluntarily."

"And if I don't, you will politely shoot me in the kneecaps with your pistol? It may be silenced, but I'm afraid that I'm liable to scream. That could tend to disturb the other guests of the hotel."

"It wouldn't be anything quite so dramatic," Modred said. "Merely a simple spell of compulsion."

"I see," said Fugisawa, glancing at Wyrdrune. "Your friend is an adept, of course. A highly skilled one, judging by his unusual familiar. And I suppose that he will teleport my body elsewhere when you're finished?"

"You will not be harmed in any way whatsoever," Modred said.

"We're not murderers, Lieutenant," added Wyrdrune.

"At least one of you is," replied Fugisawa dryly.

"Believe what you choose," said Modred. "But there is no purpose to be served in killing you when you could just as easily be made to forget you've ever seen us."

"I'm beginning to understand how you've managed to elude the authorities for so long," said Fugisawa.

"How did Kobayashi know where we are?" asked Kira.

Fugisawa glanced at her sharply. "So Kobayashi told you about me. Somehow, I didn't think he'd violate our confidential agreement, but I might have guessed."

"As a matter of fact, he didn't," Modred said. "It was a logical deduction. No one except Kobayashi and a few of his trusted men knows I'm in Japan. And we knew that Kobayashi had some sort of an arrangement with the police. You are obviously part of that arrangement."

"It isn't what you think."

"What do I think?"

"That I'm on his payroll. I'm not. I'm a good cop."

"A good cop who has a confidential agreement with the Yakuza?" asked Wyrdrune wryly.

"Not with the Yakuza per se. With Kobayashi," Fugisawa said. "It doesn't involve any money. We both have our own reasons for wanting this necromancer serial killer off the streets. We merely agreed between ourselves to cooperate on that. *Only* on that. And you're wrong about Kobayashi being the only one who knows you're here. He's bragged about it to the council of the Yakuza. Having a serial killer loose in his district is causing him a lot of problems and making him look bad, like he can't keep order on his turf. He tried to save face by telling the council that he's convinced the famous Morpheus to come out of retirement and take on the contract. The word's already on the streets."

Modred's lips compressed into a tight grimace. "That's most unfortunate. However, that still leaves us with the question of how he knew where to find us."

"He didn't," Fugisawa said. "*I* found you. I've had Kobayashi under surveillance and I've been keeping track of everyone he's met with since this whole thing started."

"You saw us leaving the House of Nihonto," Kira said.

"A couple of my men did. They saw Kobayashi and his people go in, then they saw them close the store. They thought that was a bit unusual. They thought it was even more unusual when you came out after a while, so one of them followed you while the other one remained to watch the store. He saw Kobayashi and his people come out a short while later. They looked upset."

"I picked up the tail," Modred said. "I thought it was one of Kobayashi's people, but I was certain that we shook him."

"You did," Fugisawa replied. "He was very upset about that. He's very good, which meant that you were even better. And it also meant that you weren't just ordinary tourists looking at some swords."

"So you checked with the hotels, of course," said Modred.

"It didn't take that long. You're not exactly an inconspicuous-looking group."

"I see I've become quite careless in my old age," said Modred wryly. "We'll have to arrange for other accommodations."

"What, I have to pack *again*?" said Broom.

"Broom, we have some important matters to discuss," said Modred. "Why don't you go into the other room and watch some television?"

"If I wanted to watch television, I could've stayed at home," said Broom, "where at least I could understand what they were saying. I haven't left that room ever since we got here. Some fun trip this is turning out to be!"

"Broom," said Wyrdrune, "this isn't a vacation."

"You're telling me?"

"Broom...."

"All right, all right, already, I'm going!" The broom turned around and shuffled into the other room. "I can see I'm only in the way here. I don't even know why you bother keeping me around. I only seem to get on everybody's nerves. Lord knows, you work your bristles to the nubs, you'd think maybe somebody would show some appreciation, but nooooo...."

Wyrdrune rolled his eyes and slammed the connecting room door shut. "God, what a *yenta*."

"I heard that!"

Fugisawa shook his head in disbelief. "Astonishing. That broom reminds me of my ex-wife's mother."

"Your ex-wife was Jewish?" Wyrdrune said.

"No, Cantonese."

"Must've been a *yachna* in the woodpile somewhere," Wyrdrune said.

"A what?" asked Fugisawa, frowning.

"This conversation is becoming surreal," said Modred.

"Can we get back to the matter at hand, Lieutenant? You went to considerable trouble to find me. And you did not come here with a squad of backup officers. You do not strike me as a stupid man, which leads me to believe that an arrest was not what you had on your mind. So what exactly did you want from me?"

"I wanted to check you out and see if you were who I thought you were."

"And then?"

"Then I was going to have you watched."

"In the hope that I would lead you to the killer?"

"Essentially."

"And then you'd get to make not one, but two very glamorous arrests?"

"Would you believe me if I said no?"

"I don't know. Try me."

"I've never tried to arrest a sorcerer before," said Fugisawa. "Especially a necromancer as powerful as this one seems to be. I don't think jail is the answer in a case like this. You don't muzzle a mad dog. You kill it."

"I see," said Modred with a smile. "So if I tried to kill the necromancer and failed, you'd be there to finish the job while she was occupied with me."

"That was more or less what I had in mind." Fugisawa frowned. "Wait a moment. You said *she*? You think the killer is a woman?"

"Perhaps not the actual killer," Modred said, "but there *is* a woman behind all this. Actually, female would be the correct term, not woman. Leila is not a human being."

Fugisawa stared at him. "Leila? You *know* who it is?"

"Oh, yes. Our paths have crossed before."

"What do you mean she's not a human being?"

"She's one of the Dark Ones."

"The Dark Ones? I don't understand. What is that? Some kind of organization?"

"They're the last of a race of immortal beings who were here when your ancestors were still walking on their knuckles," Wyrdrune said.

Fugisawa stared at them with disbelief. "What kind of

nonsense is this?'' he said angrily. ''I thought you were using a figure of speech. Are you trying to tell me that these Dark Ones are *literally* not human beings? That they're some kind of aliens? Do you take me for a fool?''

''Quite the contrary, Lieutenant,'' said Modred. ''If I thought you were a fool, I would not risk taking you into my confidence, but you have clearly demonstrated that you are not a fool. You said precisely the right thing.''

''And what was that?''

''That you do not muzzle a mad dog, you kill it. And that is precisely what our mission is. To hunt down and kill the Dark Ones before they can grow powerful enough to enslave the human race.''

Fugisawa shook his head. ''I can't believe I'm hearing this. *A mission to hunt down immortal beings who want to enslave the human race?* I've never heard anything so ridiculous in my entire life! What is this 'mission' nonsense? You're working for Kobayashi as a contract assassin. Why are you telling me this drivel? Perhaps you think this is amusing, but—''

''Silence!'' Billy suddenly said, but in a voice and accent totally unlike the voice that Fugisawa heard him use before. It was not the voice of a teenage boy. Startled, he stared at him and saw blue fire dancing in his eyes. ''Young man, you have not the faintest inkling of what you have become involved in. If you wish to retain the power of speech, I strongly suggest that you shut up and listen.''

Fugisawa gaped at him. ''What sort of trick is this?'' He glanced at Modred incredulously. ''He's an adept, too? At *his* age?''

''His chronological age is fifteen,'' said Modred, ''but he is also fifty or sixty years older than myself. I'm not quite sure, exactly. We did not really keep track too carefully, back then.''

''This is too much!'' said Fugisawa, rising angrily. ''I will not be ridiculed like this! I—''

Twin bolts of blue thaumaturgic energy lanced out from Billy's eyes and struck Fugisawa in the chest, hurling him backward over his chair to the floor. It felt like the blow of a sledgehammer. Fugisawa landed on his back and his head struck painfully against the floor. For a moment he was stunned, gasping for breath. A small tendril of smoke rose up from his singed shirt.

"That was unnecessary, Ambrosius," Modred said. "Please try to restrain yourself."

Wyrdrune and Kira rushed over to Fugisawa and helped him up.

"Are you all right?" asked Wyrdrune with concern.

Fugisawa was too dazed to reply.

"I'd keep my mouth shut, if I were you," said Kira softly. "Merlin's got a nasty temper."

"Merlin?" said Fugisawa weakly.

They helped him back to the table, picked up his overturned chair, and eased him down into it. He felt something hard against his arm, where Kira was holding him.

"Sorry 'bout that, guv," said Billy. " 'E gets a bit carried away every now an' then."

Fugisawa put his hand up to his chest. It felt as if he had been burned. He looked at Billy with a mixture of fear and confusion.

"*Sumimasen,* Fugisawa-san," said Modred. Then, in English, he added, "You are a very fortunate man. Few people have felt the wrath of Merlin Ambrosius and lived to tell the tale. Except, of course, that you will not tell this tale to anyone. Because, for one thing, your own reactions stand as proof of how difficult it is to believe. And, for another, once we have explained it to you fully, you will realize the necessity for secrecy. Now then, I trust we have your full attention?"

Fugisawa could only manage a weak nod.

"Good. It is a long and rather complicated story. And it centers around three enchanted runestones."

He opened up his shirt and Fugisawa saw a gleaming ruby embedded in the flesh of his chest. Kira held up her right hand, palm out toward him, showing him the sapphire. And Wyrdrune removed his headband, revealing an emerald set in the center of his forehead.

"Before we begin, however, an introduction is in order. Wyrdrune's, Kira's, and Billy's names you must already know, from your inquiries of the hotel. However, as you have just seen, Billy is a great deal more than he appears to be. And my name, as you might have suspected, is not really Michael Cornwall. I am Modred, son of King Arthur Pendragon and the sorceress Morgan Le Fay. And I have lived for some two thousand years..."

CHAPTER
Eight

TAICHI KAWASHIMA AND FUMIO HATTORI HAD BEEN WATCHING the small shop in the Shinjuku district since noon. Nothing of significance had happened and they were bored. Don Kobayashi's orders were to keep the sorcerer under surveillance and report on everything he did. So far, he had done nothing, but they knew better than to question Don Kobayashi's orders.

The heat was on and all of Kobayashi's operations on the Ginza were suffering as a result. The "Ginza Monster," as the media had dubbed the serial killer, had everybody nervous. This sorcerer, Kanno, was supposed to be assisting the authorities in their investigation, but so far, it seemed he had done nothing. He hadn't even left his shop.

At closing time, the apprentices left and locked up. The sorcerer remained inside. They waited. Four hours passed and he did not come out.

"What the hell is he doing in there?" said Kawashima irritably.

"Who knows?" replied Hattori. "Maybe he's working."

"I'm getting tired of this. I'm hungry. When are Kiyoshi and Yuro supposed to relieve us?"

"Nine o'clock."

Kawashima glanced at his watch. "They're over an hour late, the bastards."

"I know. They'd better have a damn good reason."

"Shit," said Kawashima. "That's him. He's leaving."

"Great."

"What do we do?"

"We follow him. What else is there to do?"

"He's probably just going to go home."

"Yeah? And what if he doesn't?" said Hattori. "What if he does something Don Kobayashi wants to know about? You want to explain to him that we weren't there to see it because we decided to have supper?"

"Wait till I get my hands on those two."

"We'll follow him," said Hattori. "He'll probably go home and then I'll keep watch while you call Takeo and tell him Kiyoshi and Yuro never showed up to relieve us. Let them explain it to Takeo."

"Lousy sons of bitches."

But Kanno did not go home. They followed him to an apartment building several blocks away and watched him go inside.

"What the hell's he doing there?" said Kawashima.

"I don't know. Maybe he's got a girlfriend."

"Want me to go check it out?"

"No," replied Hattori. "Takeo said to be discreet. Just write down the address."

"Great. He's up there getting a piece of ass and we're sitting down here in the street like a couple of morons."

"There's a phone over there. Why don't you go ahead and call in? Tell them where we are."

"Right."

Kawashima went to make the call. He was back in a few minutes.

"Okay, someone's going to show up to relieve us in about half an hour."

"Damn! Isn't that Kanno?"

He was just leaving the building.

"Yeah," said Kawashima. "He's changed clothes. Got his hair tucked up under the hat."

"Shit. Let's go."

"I'd better call back and tell them that we're leaving."

"There's no time," said Hattori. "Come on."

They followed him, at a distance, to the station and saw him board a train heading across town. They got on one car behind him. He got off at the Ginza station.

"This is getting interesting," said Hattori. "Wonder what he's up to in the Ginza?"

"Maybe he'll go somewhere where we can get something to eat."

Kanno did, in fact, enter a bar, but it was not a place that served food. They had to satisfy themselves with drinks and cigarettes, sitting across the room from him while he sipped a martini and watched nude dancers going through seductive motions on the small stages placed around the bar. Several "hostesses" approached him, but he shook his head each time and remained alone at his table, his eyes riveted to the dancers.

"Guess this is how the respected sorcerer gets his kicks," said Kawashima wryly. "He likes to watch naked women."

"Go use the phone over by the rest room and check in. Tell them where we are. It looks like he might be here awhile."

Kanno finished his drink and ordered another. After a couple of minutes, Kawashima came back to the table to join his partner.

"It's going to be a long night," he said with disgust. "We're supposed to stick with him. Fuck. What time is it?"

"About eleven-thirty."

"I'm going to kill those bastards."

"Forget it. We're stuck now. Have another drink. Enjoy the view."

"I'll tell you what I'd like to enjoy right about now," said Kawashima with a grin. "That blonde right over there."

"The one with the big tits? Yeah, I've been watching her."

"She looks American."

"California girl."

"Nice ass, too," said Kawashima. "How much money have you got?"

"Hey, we have a job to do, remember?"

"Come on, let's just call her over to the table when she's finished. Maybe we can set something up for later."

"Forget it," said Hattori. "Kanno's leaving."

"Shit!"

They followed him out of the bar, keeping well back.

"*Now* where the hell's he going?"

They watched him cross the street.

"Let's stay on this side," said Hattori, holding his partner back. "I don't want to get too close."

"You know what? I think the bastard's cruising!"

"So? Adepts gotta get laid too, right?"

"With all his money, he's going to pick up some street whore?"

"Maybe he likes it sleazy. I don't know. He is supposed to be helping out the Bureau. Maybe he's out looking for the killer."

"The way he was eyeing those dancers in the bar?"

Hattori shrugged. "He's a man. I didn't notice you blushing and looking away."

Kanno stopped and started talking to a hooker in a black leather minidress and boots. A moment later she took his arm and they started walking down the street.

"Look at that," said Kawashima. "You figure he's just going to ask her a few questions? Hi, honey, how's tricks? Seen any Ginza Monsters lately?"

His partner did not reply. Kanno and the hooker turned a corner and walked into an alley.

"Hey, I got a funny feeling about this."

"Come on," Hattori said. They trotted across the street. They were almost to the alley entrance when they heard a frenzied scream.

"*Shit!*"

They both pulled out their guns and ran into the alley. At first, they couldn't see anything in the darkness. They proceeded cautiously. The screaming had stopped. And then they heard some movement just ahead of them, behind a dumpster.

"I don't like this," whispered Kawashima. "Let's get the hell out of here."

Suddenly something came hurtling at them over the dumpster with a roar. Something that moved with incredible speed. Something long and sinewy, with leathery wings and claws and gaping jaws. There was the sound of a shot, then a horrified scream and a hideous, snapping, crunching noise as Hattori went down beneath the creature's weight. Kawashima screamed and turned to run.

There was a figure standing in the alley, blocking his way. Kawashima didn't stop, but kept on running full speed, intent only on escaping from that horror that had killed Hattori. The figure's eyes seemed to light up with a bright green glow and suddenly he was falling.

He struck the ground hard and tumbled, then scrambled to his feet . . . only to discover that he wasn't in the alley anymore. He had no idea where he was. He was in some sort of an enclosure, in what looked like an underground plaza. With a sharp intake of breath, he glanced around and saw burning torches, a strangely glowing pool, and some sort of shrine standing in the center of it, on a large pedestal. It looked like it was made of solid gold. Splattered with dried blood. He heard footsteps behind him and spun around.

It was a woman. The most beautiful woman Kawashima had ever seen. She was dressed all in black leather, with high-heeled boots that clicked on the floor as she approached him slowly. She was tall and long-legged and the leather hugged the lush curves of her body. Her fire-red hair fell down past her shoulders and her skin had an incredible coppery-golden hue. Her eyes were a bright, almost phosphorescent shade of green. Under any other circumstances, on finding himself alone with such a woman, he would have been seized with a paroxysm of lust and would not have hesitated to satisfy it on the spot. But the emotion that seized him now was fear. Fear and confusion. For a moment he thought he must be dreaming, but what had happened to Hattori was no dream. It was a nightmare.

He raised his gun and aimed it at her. "Who are you?" he demanded, his voice strained. "Where am I? How did I get here?"

She smiled. Her eyes flared with a hellish green light and the gun in his hand suddenly glowed red with searing heat. He cried out and dropped it, clutching at his hand. The skin on his palm and fingers was charred and blistered. She came closer. Trying to ignore the agonizing pain in his right hand, he reached with his left hand for the small of his back and pulled the butterfly knife out of its sheath. With a quick and practiced motion, he flipped it open and lunged at her.

With a motion that seemed almost languid, yet incredibly fast, she caught his hand by the wrist and squeezed. There was a sharp, crackling sound and he screamed as every bone in his wrist was crushed. He blacked out from the pain.

When he came to, he was lying on his back, naked, and she was standing over him, dressed in long black satin robes. Her eyes seemed unfocused and she was chanting something in a guttural language he couldn't understand. He tried to get up, but discovered that he couldn't move. There didn't seem to be anything holding him down, no restraints of any sort, but no matter how hard he tried, he couldn't move a muscle. He began to whimper.

"Please . . . please, let me go, please, I won't say anything, I won't tell anybody, please. . . ."

She looked down at him and he saw that she was holding a long, curved dagger in her hand. He lost control of his bodily functions. Slowly the dagger came down toward him. His throat-rending scream echoed through the sanctuary.

Akiro had given up on getting a full night's sleep. The call came, as he had known it would, shortly after one A.M. He knew, even before he picked up the phone, that there had been another killing. Keiko had been lying asleep, beside him. He had tried to sleep, needing the rest desperately, but sleep simply would not come. He had been lying awake for hours, staring at the phone on the bedside table, waiting for it to ring. He snatched it up at once.

"Katayama."

"There's been another one, Inspector. Two of them, this time. One male, one female. A unit's already been dispatched to pick you up."

Akiro sighed wearily. "All right. Thank you. I'll be right down."

He hung up the phone.

Keiko was awake.

"Again?" she said softly.

He nodded and got out of bed.

"Two of them, this time. They're sending a car to pick me up. Go back to sleep."

"You haven't had any sleep at all, have you?"

He grimaced and shook his head.

She got up out of bed. "I'll make you some coffee."

"Keiko, there's no time—"

"Don't argue. It will be ready by the time you get dressed."

She went into the kitchen. He sighed and went into the bathroom to comb his hair and throw some cold water on his face. He looked at his face in the bathroom mirror. It looked old. Old and drawn and tired. There were bags under his eyes.

In another few hours, he thought wearily, they'll take me off the case. But meanwhile, I've got to go and look at two more bodies. Or whatever's left of them. I've got to go there and look at them, as if it would make any difference whatsoever, and see if there are any witnesses—there won't be any, of course—and I've got to listen to the reports of the officers who discovered the victims. Then I've got to talk with the forensics people and make my examination of the scene and wait for the medical examiner to show up and somehow keep away from those damned reporters, then go into the office and make out my report and add it to the file. By that time it will be morning. And, with any luck, I may have time to eat something to get my energy up—if, by some miracle, I have any appetite at all—before Watanabe calls me into his office to tell me that I'm being taken off the case.

He'll be very apologetic and he'll tell me that he knows how hard I have been working and he'll say something about how the case being assigned to someone else is no reflection on my performance of my duties, which has always been exemplary, but due to the exigencies of the circumstances and the pressure that the Bureau has been under, etc., etc., and that will be, to all intents and purposes, the end of my career. I can almost hear him now, he thought.

"You look exhausted, Akiro. You've been working on this thing practically around the clock. Why don't you take a few days off and get some rest? You've earned it."

What really hurt was that some young Turk like Sakahara would get to take advantage of all the work he'd done. All the painstaking hours of working with his team of Bureau agents and police, using anyone who could be spared, from deputy field agents down to administrative personnel, to compile B.O.T. records of every adept of the wizard and sorcerer levels in Japan, and obtain from Customs the records of every visiting wizard and sorcerer who had recently entered the country, and checking them against their whereabouts on the nights the murders were committed. It was a slow and exhaustive process, one that required extreme delicacy in making the necessary inquiries, as many such adepts, particularly sorcerers in the corporate sector, were not without powerful social and political connections. Lacking any other hard evidence to go on, there had been no choice but to resort to his tried-and-true, plodding, methodical approach. The list of potential suspects had been long, indeed, and not a few feathers had been ruffled—which could well be another reason why he would be taken off the case—but as a result, the list had already been reduced considerably as suspects were gradually eliminated. Whoever took the case over would get the benefit of that and would receive all the credit when the killer was eventually apprehended, as Akiro had no doubt he would be. It was only a matter of time. Unfortunately, his own time had just about run out.

As he stared at his reflection in the mirror, his eyes grew hard. It doesn't matter, he told himself. Office politics didn't matter. The media didn't matter. His career didn't matter. The only thing that mattered was stopping the killer. Keiko was right. She had not married a quitter. In all his years of service, he had never yet failed to get the job done. He had never given up. He was not about to stop now and wallow in self-pity. They could take him off the case, but they could not control what he did on his own time. And he would have that time. Watanabe would give him leave, if for no other reason than to get him out of the way. But he would not be cut off. He had a lot of friends in the Bureau, people he had worked with for years, people who could keep him posted, unofficially, of developments in the investigation.

"One way or another, you bastard," he mumbled to himself, "I'll get you."

He got dressed quickly and went into the kitchen. Keiko

already had the coffee waiting for him. He had drunk perhaps a third of it when the buzzer sounded from the lobby.

"That will be my ride," he said, pushing himself away from the table.

"Take this with you," said Keiko, handing him a thermos full of coffee. "I put some brandy into it."

He kissed her on the cheek. "I don't know what I'd do without you. I don't deserve you."

"I know," she said with a smile. "My father once told me the same thing. Now go on. They're waiting for you."

The Paradise Club was one of the hottest night spots on the Ginza. And one of the safest, too. Owned and operated by Teruyuki Kobayashi, it was a far cry from most of the sleazy clubs in the district. It boasted the largest multilevel dance floor in the entire city and the most beautiful showgirls in Japan. It featured live bands, a state-of-the-art sound system and spectacular thaumaturgic special effects, orchestrated by adepts stationed in glass booths above the dance floors. It was a popular "in" place with Tokyo's young, well-heeled social set, who came there to mingle, to see and to be seen. Well-dressed, powerfully muscled bouncers with black belts in the martial arts maintained order and kept the riffraff out. Often, there were lines outside on the sidewalk, with armed security guards patrolling the outside of the club to make sure that no one acted up or hassled any of those waiting to get in.

Lately, there had been no long lines outside the Paradise Club. With all the lurid stories in the media about the "Ginza Monster," many of the night owls were finding other places to roost. But there were still those who were confident of safety in numbers and who had no intention of roaming the Ginza streets. They arrived at the door of the Paradise Club each night, coming by cab or train and walking, rather quickly and never alone, the short distance from the station to the club. Then, once safely inside, they could strut their stuff and feel properly adventurous. And when the next story came out about another victim, they could cavalierly tell their friends, "Oh, yeah, I was down there last night."

When confronted by the bouncer at the door, Fugisawa said, "I came to see my uncle."

The man nodded and stood aside, and said, "Yes, sir," respectfully.

Wyrdrune and Kira came in behind him and paid the cover charge. As they entered the club, Fugisawa walked up to the bar while Wyrdrune and Kira, apparently not with him, moved out onto the dance floor.

"I've got a message for my uncle," Fugisawa told the bartender, speaking loudly and leaning close to him, to be heard above the music. The bartender nodded and moved to a phone behind the bar. He picked it up and spoke for a second, then hung it up. He brought Fugisawa a drink, a Scotch, neat, set it down in front of him, and tapped the bartop twice with his knuckles, to indicate that it was on the house. Then he moved away. Fugisawa sat and sipped the Scotch, glancing around at the people in the club.

The floor was fairly crowded, but after a few seconds, he spotted Wyrdrune and Kira, dancing together. He gave no indication that he knew them. They looked like just a couple of ordinary kids out there. Young tourists moving to the music. Looking at them, it was still hard for him to believe what he now knew about them.

The story they had told him was incredible. He had not wanted to believe it, in spite of the evidence. Clearly, it had seemed impossible for someone of Billy's age to possess the kind of power that he had and Wyrdrune was far too advanced an adept for a mere warlock who had never finished school. Kira, it seemed, possessed no thaumaturgic ability whatsoever on her own, but through the runestone in her palm, she could summon up more power than a sorcerer of the highest level. And to think that Morpheus was actually Modred, son of Arthur, King of Britain-a figure out of myth and legend—and that he was part Immortal . . . that alone had seemed beyond credulity. But when they told him of the Dark Ones . . . it was all much more than he cold possibly accept.

Only then Modred brought a phone to him and asked him to check with England's Scotland Yard.

"Make the call yourself," he'd said. "Ask for Chief Inspector Michael Blood. If they tell you that he is not available, say that it's in reference to Operation Runestone. They will reach him wherever he might be and he will call back within moments."

"And then what?"

"Tell him who you are and ask him about a series of grisly murders he investigated that occurred in Whitechapel about two years ago. Murders in which necromancy figured prominently. Then tell him that you seem to have a very similar situation here. Tell him that you've met someone named Michael Cornwall, who's told you a story that seems completely unbelievable and ask for his opinion."

"For all I know," Fugisawa had said, "he could be a corrupt cop on your payroll."

"I suppose he could be," Modred had replied, "except that his father is a British lord and a prominent investment banker. Chief Inspector Blood, while hardly a flamboyant man, has access to more money than he knows how to spend. You could verify that easily. And when you're finished speaking with him, feel free to call the Los Angeles Police Department. Ask for Captain Rebecca Farrell, of the Hollywood Precinct. Follow the same procedure. Ask her about the Sunset Strip slasher. And mention us to her, as well. And if you still have doubts, there is also an inspector of the Paris police I can refer you to. You can ask him about the deaths in the Rue Morgue."

Fugisawa had made those calls right there in front of them. Neither Modred nor any of the others made any move to take the phone and speak to them. And each call produced the same result. Each officer first asked him a few questions, to satisfy themselves he was who he claimed to be and that he had actually spoken to "Mr. Cornwall" and his companions. Then each of them described the cases they had worked on and the incredible events surrounding them, each confirmed the existence of the Dark Ones; and each vouched that everything that "Mr. Cornwall" and his unique companions said and claimed, regardless of how incredible it seemed, was true. And each of them said unequivocally that if there was anything that they could do to provide Fugisawa or "Mr. Cornwall" with assistance, that he was not to hesitate to call, at any time of day or night.

Fugisawa had been shaken when he had completed the calls. And then the remote pager that he carried when he was off duty sounded and he called in to discover that the killer had struck again. Two victims this time. Another hooker. And one man who had been identified as a member of the Yakuza. There had also been a message for him. His uncle had called.

Now, as he sat at the bar of the Paradise Club, his mind was in a turmoil. As a cop, he had always played mostly by the rules, but all the rules suddenly seemed to have changed. He was having secret meetings with a Yakuza don. And he was now cooperating with the world's most wanted professional assassin. Who happened to be about two thousand years old and had retired to hunt immortal necromancers. If he didn't know better, he would have thought he was a character in some weird fantasy novel.

"Excuse me, sir," said a nattily dressed man whose well-cut suit didn't quite hide the bulge of his shoulder holster, "your uncle will see you now."

Fugisawa got up and followed the man. They went around behind the dance floor and through a door marked "Private," which had a bouncer stationed in front of it. The two men nodded at each other and they went through. The moment the door closed behind them, all noise from the club was immediately cut off. They walked down a short, carpeted corridor to a door at the other end. The door was marked, "Manager." The man leading Fugisawa paused at the door and knocked. It was opened from the inside and he stood aside to let Fugisawa enter.

It was a quiet, well-appointed office, very modern furnishings, wet bar, carpeting, dark-stained oak desk, and a bank of video monitors. There were, apparently, surveillance cameras placed all around the inside of the club. The screens all showed different views of the bar, the dance floors, the front entrance, the booths and tables, and even the hallway outside the rest rooms. Don Kobayashi was sitting behind the desk in a high-backed leather swivel chair, flanked by his son, Shiro, and his chief lieutenant, Takeo Itigawa. There were also two men standing just inside the door.

"Come in, Lt. Fugisawa," said Kobayashi. "Please, sit down."

He indicated a leather chair placed in front of the desk. Fugisawa sat down.

"Would you care for a drink?"

"No, thanks. Just had one."

"You have heard the news?"

"I heard. I don't have all the details yet. One of your people, I understand."

Kobayashi pursed his lips and nodded. "Two of my people, to be precise."

Fugisawa frowned. "What, you mean the hooker?"

"No. Not the hooker. There were actually *three* killings. At least, I am reasonably certain there were three. The police are not yet aware of the third. The body has not been found, you see. The man found in the alley was Fumio Hattori. One of my people, as you said. He was with Taichi Kawashima, who has disappeared and who, I presume, is also dead. They were doing a job for me. For *you*, I should say." He paused. "They were following Kanno."

Fugisawa suddenly sat up very straight in his chair. "*Kanno!* Are you sure?"

"I'm not in the habit of stating facts unless I'm sure of them," said Kobayashi. "Although I quite understand your reaction. He is a man of impeccable reputation. A brilliant artist, highly regarded in society, a pupil of the great Yohaku. One of Japan's most highly respected adepts. And yet Kanno is your necromancer."

Fugisawa stared at him with astonishment. This new shock, on top of all the others.

"You're absolutely *certain*? There can be no mistake?"

"Takeo?" said Kobayashi.

"As you asked, we put several people on the sorcerer to watch him," said Tanaka. "Hattori and Kawashima had been watching his shop since noon. He did not leave all day. At closing time, his apprentices locked up the shop and left. Kanno remained inside. That was not unusual. He apparently often worked late into the night. Hattori and Kawashima were due to be relieved, but the two men who were supposed to take over for them did not show up, fortunately for them, as it turns out. So they were about to call in to report that and ask that someone come to relieve them. But before they could make the call, Kanno left the shop on foot and they had no choice but to follow him. This would have been shortly after ten o'clock. They followed him to an apartment building several blocks away and watched him go inside. Here is the address.''

Takeo handed him a slip of paper.

"Kawashima then called in to report. I told him that I would send someone out to that address to relieve them in approximately half an hour. But apparently moments after he made that call, Kanno came out again and they were forced to follow him once more. He had changed his clothes. A snappy black suit, very chic, the sort of thing the customers here at the club wear, and a hat, with his long hair tucked up underneath it. They followed him to the train station, where he got on a crosstown subway. He got off at the Ginza. They followed him for several blocks, until he came to a place called The Honey Pot, a nude show club. . . .''

"I know it," Fugisawa said.

"He went inside and took a booth. He ordered a drink and sat watching the dancers. It appeared that he was going to stay awhile, so Kawashima called in once again from a phone in the club and reported everything that had occurred up to that point. He asked to be relieved once more, but since I had no idea how long Kanno would remain in one place, I gave instructions that he and Hattori should stick with him. And that was the last I heard from them.''

"So you don't actually know for sure that Kanno killed them?" said Fugisawa.

"If you mean do I have proof, no," said Takeo, "but unlike the police, I do not require proof. I knew those men. If I gave them instructions to stick with Kanno, they stuck with Kanno. They were following him when they were killed.''

"But you don't know for certain that Kawashima was killed," said Fugisawa.

"If he were alive, I would have heard from him.''

"What about those two men who were supposed to relieve them?" asked Fugisawa. "I assume you knew them, as well, but they didn't exactly follow your instructions, did they?"

"They were, in fact, following my instructions to the letter," said Takeo, "but their vehicle was struck by a scooter while they were on their way to relieve Kawashima and Hattori. The scooter rider was killed. A police cruiser happened to be on the scene and one of the officers was observant. He detected the bulge of their shoulder holsters underneath their jackets and they were arrested on the spot. Fortunately for them, as it turns out. They are still in custody. However, after hearing what happened to Kawashima and Hattori, they are not complaining."

"Have you got anybody watching Kanno now?"

"I have sent five men to watch his shop, but there has been no sign of him. He may be inside or he may not. I also have five men watching his residence and another five men watching the apartment building Kawashima and Hattori saw him enter. So far, they have not been able to determine which apartment he went into. Up to this point, none of them have seen him. They all have instructions to kill him on sight."

"No, absolutely not," Fugisawa said. "Tell them to maintain surveillance, but I don't want anybody shooting at him."

"You do not give orders here, Fugisawa," said Kobayashi softly. "*I* will determine what course my people take, not you. The moment Kanno shows his face, he's dead."

"But you really don't know for sure it's Kanno," Fugisawa protested. "What if you wind up killing the wrong man?"

"Kanno is the killer."

"But what if he *isn't*?"

Kobayashi merely shrugged. "I very much doubt that. In any case, I am willing to take that chance. There is far too much at stake. The council expects results from me. I have no desire to lose face before them."

"You'll lose a great deal of face if you're arrested."

Kobayashi smiled. "Then arrest me. I'm sure that your superiors would be very interested in hearing the details of our 'arrangement.' How do you think Inspector Katayama of the B.O.T. would respond to that?"

"Don't push me, Kobayashi. I'm not going to be intimidated. I'm warning you, call your people off. Call them off right now."

Kobayashi's eyes narrowed. "Shiro, I think Lt. Fugisawa's leaving."

Shiro snapped his fingers and the two men at the door instantly came to stand on either side of Fugisawa.

"Good night, Lieutenant," said Kobayashi.

Fugisawa glowered at him, then got up and was escorted out the door.

"I fear that he may be a problem," said Kobayashi after Fugisawa left.

"Problems can be eliminated," said Shiro. He glanced up at the video monitors and saw Fugisawa being escorted out of the club.

"Yes, I think that might be best," said Kobayashi.

Shiro was staring at the monitor intently. Fugisawa was just going out the door, but his gaze was on the two young people who were going out after him.

"I'll be right back," he said.

He went outside into the hall and hurried out into the main room of the club. He encountered the two men who had escorted Fugisawa out returning.

"Two people just left here," he said. "A girl in yellow breeches and a black chain-mail leather jacket and a young man in a warlock's cassock, with a headband. Follow them."

The two men hurried out the door.

CHAPTER
Nine

"I'VE MADE A VERY BAD MISTAKE," SAID FUGISAWA AS HE took his seat in the back of the limo. Wyrdrune and Kira got in, as well. The soundproof divider partition was up, so the chauffeur couldn't hear them. "I thought I could control Kobayashi. I should have known better."

He briefly told them what had transpired during the meeting. As he spoke, unknown to any of them, the men sent to follow Wyrdrune and Kira carefully noted the vehicle's license plate and went back into the club to report to Shiro.

"Unless they are fortunate to have the advantage of surprise and manage to kill Kanno right away," said Modred, "the Yakuza assassins won't have a chance against him. Assuming he is the necromancer."

"It certainly looks that way," said Fugisawa, "but Kobayashi could be wrong. Those men of his could just as easily have run across the killer while they were following Kanno. There isn't any proof. But Kobayashi is not concerned with proof."

"Proof isn't a problem," Wyrdrune said. "At least, not for us. Do you know where Kanno's shop is?"

"Yes, of course."

"Why don't we go there and have a look?"

Fugisawa gave them the address in the Shinjuku district and Modred picked up the phone, switched it to intercom, and told the driver where to take them.

"Tell me about the Bureau agent who's in charge of the case," said Modred as the limo headed away from the Ginza toward the Shinjuku district. "What is your assessment of him?"

"Akiro Katayama," Fugisawa said. "A good man, steady, by the book, but he's out of his depth. He's never failed to solve a case before, but then he's always worked with white-collar crimes in the corporate sector. He's never been confronted with a homicide before, much less a serial killer. I have a feeling he won't be on the case much longer. With all the media pressure on the Bureau, they're going to need a fall guy and Akiro's the obvious choice. He'd been ducking the reporters, but they finally caught up with him the other day. I saw the interview. It was pathetic. The poor bastard was totally intimidated. He doesn't know how to handle the media at all. He came off looking like an idiot."

"Is he an idiot?" asked Kira.

"No," said Fugisawa, shaking his head. "He's just a bureaucrat who's in over his head."

"In that case, it would probably be best to keep him out of it," said Modred. "That was my first instinct all along. A man who is easily intimidated by reporters could easily let something slip and public knowledge of the Dark Ones would cause a worldwide panic."

"Katayama is not the type to let things slip. But who'd believe it, anyway?" asked Fugisawa. "I still find the whole thing very difficult to accept."

"That's probably their greatest strength," said Wyrdrune. "It's like the old legends about vampires. All the stories always used to say that the single greatest strength of the vampire was that no one will believe in his existence. And, ironically, all those stories, the folklore about vampires, witches, werewolves, and the like, had their origins with the Dark Ones."

"How many of them do you think there are?" asked Fugisawa.

"Unfortunately, we really have no way of knowing," said Wyrdrune.

"Can't you ask the runestones? You said they were alive."

"In a sense, they are," Wyrdrune replied, "but it's not life the way we understand it. They don't possess discrete personalities and we can't really communicate with them in any traditional sense. The only runestone that actually has what you might call an individual personality is Billy's."

"The enchanted ring?" said Fugisawa, glancing at the fire opal on Billy's finger.

"That's right. And enchanted is the operative term," said Wyrdrune. "The ring contains Gorlois's astral spirit. And there's a lot about the concept of astral spirits that we don't really understand."

"But you can ask Ambrosius, can't you?" said Fugisawa.

"Indeed, they can," said Merlin, speaking through Billy, "but there is still only so much I can tell them."

Fugisawa could not get over the idea that the greatest mage in the entire world was speaking to him through the body of a teenage boy. Billy's voice, his mannerisms, his facial expressions, and the way he held himself all became transformed when Merlin spoke through him. It was decidedly unsettling.

"The freeing of one's astral spirit is one of the most difficult spells there is," continued Merlin. "It requires enormous strength of will and concentration. Prior to my physical death, I had only done it a few times, for very limited periods, and it always left me totally exhausted. Because to free the astral spirit is to flirt with death. The astral spirit—or the soul, if you will—is the animating essence of the body. In the moment of death, it separates from the body and floats free. Sometimes it does not separate completely, such as in cases where people are near death, where they come as close as possible to actually dying and are then brought back. At such times, many people have reported having out-of-body experiences, the sensation of floating somewhere outside of themselves, looking down on their own bodies, or of going through some sort of dark tunnel, being drawn powerfully toward a bright light at the other end. What they were experiencing was the separation of their astral selves, only they were brought back from death before that separation could become complete."

"What happens when the separation does become complete?" asked Fugisawa.

"Well, I am one example," Merlin said, "and Gorlois is another, as are the other runestones. However, I don't think that's really what you're asking. What you're asking is a question that no one could possibly answer, the question that has puzzled and fascinated scientists, philosophers, and theologians for centuries. What happens after we die? The answer is, of course, that no one knows. No astral spirit has ever returned once it has gone completely through that long dark tunnel toward the light. Perhaps the light is God and if you are a religious man, that thought might give you comfort. But I have no idea what it really is. I do not know what lies beyond. I have never made the journey. A highly skilled adept can achieve a voluntary, controlled separation of his astral self—what is known as astral projection—but only at the cost of immense effort.

"Occasionally," he went on, "people die and their astral spirits do not go through the tunnel, or whatever phenomenon it is, instead remaining somehow bound to the temporal plane. Again, no one has ever managed to explain this. I have my own theory. I believe it's possible that those to whom this happens have had, somewhere in their past, an Old One for an ancestor, an Immortal. The Old Ones were extremely powerful adepts. After the Mage War that saw an end of their supremacy on earth, the mighty struggle between the Dark Ones and the Council of the White, the surviving Old Ones went into hiding. They were persecuted by the humans, who greatly outnumbered them. Many of them interbred with humans, and over the years—as is the case with Wyrdrune, Kira, and Billy—the Immortal strain became diluted, though it was never entirely eliminated. There are those who have an inherent, natural aptitude for magic. Wyrdrune, for example, who was always far too naturally talented for his own good.''

''Thanks,'' said Wyrdrune wryly.

''Don't interrupt your elders.''

The statement, coming as it did from the body of a fifteen-year-old, seemed highly incongruous to Fugisawa.

''As I was saying,'' continued Merlin, ''such people who have a natural aptitude for magic, and those who demonstrate what are called paranormal abilities, such as extrasensory perception and so forth, are most likely descended from an interbreeding of a human and an Old One. They possess some subliminal inherited ability, often latent, rarely controlled. Such control requires the discipline of thaumaturgy. Some of these people, particularly those who are neither emotionally nor spiritually prepared to accept death, suffer what I call a 'regressive separation' of the astral spirit when they die. Their astral spirit separates and floats free, but does not go where it is supposed to go—wherever that may be. Call it Heaven, call it Hell, call it Nirvana . . . who knows? As a result, only their physical selves actually die. Their astral selves, their souls, tend to linger on. This explains the phenomenon of hauntings. Ghosts and poltergeists and so forth.

''In my own case,'' Merlin said, ''I achieved a controlled separation of my astral spirit at the moment of my physical death. I was engaged in battle with the Dark Ones, attempting to prevent them from escaping from the pit to which they had been confined. I failed. And, in failing, I was overcome by them and my body fell into the pit. At that moment, I used all my powers to free my astral spirit and I succeeded, but then there was the question of where my astral self was going to go. I felt a powerful force drawing me, yet I resisted with all my might, because I was not yet ready for my soul to go to its final rest. Or, as some present have suggested, to its eternal torment. My work on earth was not yet done. So my spirit remained free, drifting through the ether, aimless. Bodyless. I knew that in order to complete the work I had to do, I had to find a body. But it could not be just any body. I needed the body of an adept or, failing that, of someone who possessed a strong natural aptitude for thaumaturgy. And so my spirit floated free, searching. And, whether by luck or by destiny, I found young Billy, an orphan street urchin in London, of dubious parentage and even more dubious potential.''

"Ey, you could've moved on, y'know,'' Billy suddenly broke in.

"Perhaps I could have,'' Merlin said, and Fugisawa marveled at the way their personalities switched back and forth. "But I was inexplicably, inexorably drawn to you. You pulled at my spirit like a magnet, much to my chagrin, because I could not imagine a more unsuitable vessel to contain my spirit. Only when my spirit merged with yours—''

"They call it possession,'' Wyrdrune said with a smile.

"Call it what you will,'' said Merlin irritably, "but when I became a part of Billy, I realize that it was because he was my own descendant after many generations.''

"But as I recall, your legend does not mention you ever having children,'' Fugisawa said.

"Quite true,'' said Merlin. "Nor was I aware I had any. But when Modred's mother, Morgana, better known as the sorceress Morgan Le Fay, plotted my removal, she chose one of her pupils, a De Dannan witch named Nimue, to seduce me, knowing the powerful attraction I would have to one of the De Dannan tribe—''

"What 'e means is 'e couldn't keep it in 'is pants,'' broke in Billy.

Fugisawa had to grin.

"Well, somewhat crudely put," said Merlin dryly, "but essentially correct. Nimue was a very talented witch and she took me off guard."

"Yeah, I'll bet she did," said Billy.

"Do you mind?"

"No, no, go on, I always like this part."

"No respect," said Merlin gruffly. "No respect at all."

"So she 'ad 'er way with you, you poor innocent old sod, an' when you were lyin' there, all guilty and remorseful like, with a big shit-eatin' smile on your face, she—"

"She placed me under a spell," said Merlin snappishly, "and Morgana immured me within a giant oak tree. Yet what she didn't know was that Nimue had become pregnant with my child. A child that inherited the blood of an Immortal, from Gorlois, through me. And Billy is descended from that child."

"With a few niggers in the woodpile in between," said Billy, referring to his mixed racial background.

"Really, William . . ."

"But if he is able to communicate with you, as you can communicate through him, then why can't you communicate with the runestones in the same manner?" Fugisawa asked.

"Because the process was not the same," said Modred. "The method by which Merlin achieved the separation of his astral self was very different from the spell the mages of the Council of the White used to animate the runestones. We don't know exactly *how* it was different, but it was different, with an entirely different purpose in mind."

"They gave up their own life energies to empower the spell," said Kira. "They didn't free their astral spirits so much as combine them and use them to power an enchantment. A living spell, embodied by the runestones.

"Three stones, three keys to lock the spell,
Three jewels to guard the Gates of Hell.
Three to bind them three in one,
Three to hide them from the sun.
Three to hold them, three to keep,
Three to watch the sleepless sleep."

* * *

"It is, of course, a translation from their ancient language," Merlin said, "an incantation containing the most powerful symbols of thaumaturgy. The number three, six lines to the incantation, the number three occurring nine times in the spell, multiples of three . . . the Living Triangle. There are five small triangles in a pentagram, containing fifteen points, five multiplied by three, and the five larger triangles that make up a pentagram, each adding three more points, for a total of fifteen . . . again five multiplied by three, for a total of ten triangles in a pentagram, thirty points, ten multiplied by three . . . the ten triangles of the pentagram multiplied by the six lines of the incantation and the nine recurrences of the number three, equal three hundred and sixty, the degrees of the Eternal Circle. The Living Triangle, the Warding Pentagram, and the Eternal Circle, as indicated by the strongest of the ancient chains of numerology. A binding spell of incalculable power. The runestones are the keys—the three in one, the Living Triangle. The Warding Pentagram, which surrounded the pit from which the Dark Ones have escaped, was the lock. And the Eternal Circle was the pit itself, the prison. For the binding spell to be secure, the keys must be inside the lock. Only once the keys had been removed, the Eternal Circle could be broken."

"And that was how the Dark Ones escaped?" asked Fugisawa. "Someone removed the keys?"

"One of my best pupils," Merlin said. "And one of my worst failures. Rashid Al'Hassan. He was too ambitious, too greedy, too hungry for power. He was searching for the ancient thaumaturgic secrets of his pharaonic ancestors and he stumbled upon the place where the Dark Ones had been entombed. He became possessed by them and he removed the runestones from within the pentagram, which enabled the Dark Ones to grow strong enough to break free."

"So that was how he died," said Fugisawa.

"He died because I killed him," Modred said. "But I was too late. The Dark Ones had already escaped."

"And the runestones became part of you because you were all descended from the three daughters of Gorlois, the sole surviving member of the Council?" Fugisawa said.

"Except for Billy, who was descended from his son, that being Merlin," Wyrdrune said.

"This much I understand," said Fugisawa. "I think. What I still *don't* understand is the exact nature of the runestones."

"None of us fully understands it, either," Wyrdrune said. "Not even Merlin. It's a spell, after all, that predates even him. The runestones themselves are not the astral spirits of the Council. They're a living enchantment—part of a living enchantment—that is powered by the essence of those spirits. We can draw upon that power, but only when the runestones allow us to. In other words, we couldn't misuse it or call upon it simply anytime we wanted to. There has to be a direct threat from the Dark Ones."

"Or one of their acolytes, which is what I suspect this Kanno might be," said Modred. "If, indeed, he is our killer."

"And the runestones will tell you that?" said Fugisawa.

Modred nodded.

"How will you know?"

"In the presence of the power of the Dark Ones," Modred said, "the runestones emit a glow. The closer we are and the greater the power, the brighter the glow."

"And there's no way they can make a mistake?" asked Fugisawa.

"There's only one thing that will trigger that reaction from them," Wyrdrune said. "If Kanno is the killer, we'll know very soon."

The phone in the back of the limo rang. Modred picked it up. It was the chauffeur on the intercom.

"We're approaching Kanno's shop," said Modred.

He spoke into the phone and told the chauffeur to pull up across the street. Kira took off her glove. The sapphire runestone burned brightly. She glanced at Wyrdrune. He removed his headband. The emerald in his forehead was glowing with a bright green light. Modred did not have to unbutton his shirt to know that the runestone in his chest was giving off a bright red glow.

"It would appear that Don Kobayashi was right," he said.

"So it *is* Kanno," said Fugisawa. "What happens now?"

"That all depends," said Modred.

"On what?"

"On whether or not you intend to arrest us for breaking and entering."

Fugisawa grunted. "It seems to me that I just caught a glimpse of someone moving around in there. As a duly appointed officer of the law, it's my duty to investigate. There might be a robbery in progress."

Modred smiled. "It might be wiser for you to remain here."

"I won't be able to investigate from here," said Fugisawa, getting out of the car.

"Suit yourself," said Modred. "But I warn you, whatever might happen in there, don't try to interfere. It could be worth your life."

"Didn't you say Kobayashi had some men watching this place?" Kira asked Fugisawa.

"That's right. Five men, I think he said."

"I don't see anybody around."

"You won't," said Fugisawa. "Not if it's a hit squad."

"What do you think they'll do when they see us going in?"

"Probably call in for instructions."

"Think they'll try to stop us?"

"We'll find out soon enough, won't we?"

They crossed the street and walked up to the front door of the shop.

"What do you think?" said Kira. "An alarm system or a warding spell?"

"Could be both," said Wyrdrune, kneeling in front of the door.

"If it's an alarm system, there'll probably be a switch inside," said Kira. She reached into the pocket of her leather jacket and pulled out a cased set of lockpicks. "I'll get through this in a snap."

"And if it's a warding spell, it's probably keyed to the front door lock," said Wyrdrune. "If it was forced, or picked—"

The door suddenly opened from inside and they both sprang back with alarm. Modred stood inside the shop, holding the door open, a wry look on his face. He had simply teleported inside.

"Merely an ordinary alarm," he said, "which I've turned off."

"Hell, I could've done that," said Wyrdrune, somewhat sheepishly.

"Yeah, and with your luck, you would've wound up in New Jersey," Kira said. "Come on, warlock." She grabbed him by the collar of his cassock and pulled him inside. Billy and Fugisawa followed.

As they entered the darkened showroom, a high-pitched voice cried out, *"Who's there? Who's there?"*

The beam from Fugisawa's pocket flashlight caught brilliant, shining scales, silvery and green and gold. It was a paragriffin, about the size of an owl, with jeweled scales and cut jade eyes. It shifted its weight from one foot to the other on its perch, cocking its gleaming head this way and that, ruffling its wings and giving off a faint, tinkling sound as the wafer-thin, metallic scales rang like hundred of tiny wind chimes.

"Who's there? Who's there?"

Fugisawa exhaled heavily and lowered his gun.

"Take it easy, Lieutenant," said Modred. "It's only a magene."

There were small cages on shelves lining the walls, containing the fascinating creatures created by Kanno and his apprentices. Some simply sat and stared at them, others, like the paragriffin, reacted nervously to their intrusion. Each was a masterpiece of thaumagenetic engineering.

Some were "bonsai beasts," creatures that occurred in nature, only with their genes magically manipulated with a skill that only a master thaumagenetic engineer possessed. They developed normally, but never grew beyond a miniature size. Full-grown, black-maned lions the size of gerbils paced back and forth in their cages, their roars sounding like a house cat's purr. There were miniature panthers and tiny snow leopards, adult black bears the size of guinea pigs, even an Indian elephant no bigger than a house cat.

There were terrariums containing tiny replicas of jungle lagoons, with hippopotami the size of box turtles partially submerged in the artfully created pools. The shelves along one wall held rows of saltwater aquariums containing different species of sharks and porpoises and even whales, all no bigger than a carp. But most striking were the thaumagenetic hybrids. Furry snats—little catlike creatures with elongated bodies and antennae—clinging to the walls and ceilings of their cages. Raptorgriffins—hawks, falcons, and eagles, their bodies alchemically transformed in painstaking stages through different cycles of their growth; creatures that were part flesh and blood, part living metal. They sat on perches in their cages, their metallic wings glittering with an iridescent sheen, their eyes, like living camera lenses made of precious stones, following them as they moved through the shop.

"I've never seen anything like this," Wyrdrune said with admiration. "The man's a genius."

"He's also a killer," Kira said. "Keep your eyes open."

They went through the shop and into the thaumagenetic laboratory in the back. Fugisawa swept his flashlight beam across the tables holding computers and surgical tools and jewelers implements and chemistry equipment, the shelves holding books and scrolls and various carefully labeled containers.

"I didn't really expect to find anybody here," he said.

"There is *something* here," said Modred, frowning. He glanced at Wyrdrune. "Do you sense it?"

Wyrdrune nodded, looking around. "There's a lot of power here," he said. He pointed. "Where does that door lead?"

Fugisawa walked up to it and started to reach for the doorknob. Billy grabbed his arm.

"Careful," Merlin said. He gestured at the door and mumbled something under his breath. The door slowly swung open.

Fugisawa played his beam through the door, revealing a flight of stairs leading down. "Basement," he said.

"That's where it's coming from," said Wyrdrune.

"There's something down there," Modred agreed.

"What?" asked Fugisawa.

"I don't know yet. But we're about to find out."

"We could use a bit more light," said Wyrdrune.

"Warlock, wait . . ." said Kira.

But he had already spoken a spell under his breath, holding his hands up a foot apart, at about chest level, palms slightly cupped. Green thaumaturgic energy crackled from his fingertips, then shot forth and swirled around in midair in the space between his hands, forming a spinning ball of bright green fire about the size of a cantaloupe. It bathed Wyrdrune's face in an eerie glow, then grew brighter as it spun around, illuminating the area around them.

"There," he said. "That ought to do it."

Suddenly the glowing orb of fire flared brightly and took off, as if of its own accord. It streaked past a startled Fugisawa and narrowly avoided hitting Kira. She cried out and ducked just in the nick of time. It described an arc around the room, then came back at them once again.

"Duck!" said Kira.

Billy held his hand up like a traffic cop as the glowing ball streaked toward him. It stopped suddenly, hovering in midair and pulsating, inches from his palm. Gradually its strobing pulsations stopped and it settled down to give off a warm and steady glow.

"Sorry about that," said Wyrdrune sheepishly. "I guess it sorta got away from me."

"You guess?" snapped Kira. "Jesus, who needs a necromancer with *you* around?"

Fugisawa glanced at him nervously.

"You're being anxious," Merlin said, guiding the glowing ball of fire back toward him. "Don't rush things. I taught you better than that."

"Yes, sir," Wyrdrune said, taking control of the ball. "I'm sorry. I won't let it happen again."

"That's what you said last time," Kira said wryly.

"Let's go," said Modred. "We're wasting time."

Wyrdrune guided the glowing ball down the stairs ahead of them.

"Does he know what he's doing?" Fugisawa asked Modred in a nervous whisper.

"He knows," Modred replied. "He just doesn't always do it very well."

"Thanks for reassuring me," said Fugisawa.

Modred smiled at him. "Are you sure you wouldn't rather stay up here?"

"Not a chance," said Fugisawa. "After you."

Wyrdrune, Billy, and Kira had already preceded them down the stairs. Modred went down after them. Fugisawa took a deep breath, blew it out slowly, and followed.

The stairs led down to an ordinary basement storeroom. The green glow illuminated crates and boxes full of lab supplies and feed for the creatures upstairs, as well as stored office equipment, old ledgers, shelves containing billing envelopes and blank invoices, dusty filing cabinets holding old records...nothing out of the ordinary.

"There's nothing down here," Fugisawa said.

"Nothing we can *see*," said Wyrdrune, frowning. "But there's something down here, all right. I can feel it."

"Whatever it is," said Modred, "it's below us. There must be another room underneath this one."

"And the entrance to it is spell warded," Merlin said. "Which means that it could also be a trap. Everyone stand absolutely still."

Nobody moved.

"Wyrdrune, put out your light."

The glowing globe faded and shrank, collapsing into itself as Wyrdrune canceled the spell. They were plunged into darkness. Fugisawa felt a tightness in his stomach as he heard Merlin start to chant in an ancient, guttural tongue that had not been spoken on earth since the days of the Druids.

"Dhor bir nixh thahr . . . vaxh vohr yll naxh . . . byn vahr vohl tahnyeh . . ."

The air in the basement seemed to grow heavier. The darkness seemed to thicken.

"Dhor bir nixh thahr . . . thahr vahr yll tohr . . . mihr kyhn vohl tahnyeh . . ."

A faint bluish mist formed in the air above Billy's head. It undulated lazily, revolving slowly and sending out foggy tendrils as it took form, growing brighter and brighter, coalescing into a small, billowing storm cloud illuminated from within by the crackling of miniature blue lightning. As it spun around, faster and faster, thundering with thaumaturgic discharges, Fugisawa felt a breeze that gradually grew into a shrieking wind, blowing through his hair and plucking at his clothes. Stray pieces of litter in the basement were picked up and swirled around the room. Boxes overturned. Glass shattered. Things went flying off the shelves. Merlin continued chanting, his voice growing louder and louder, until Fugisawa and the others could barely stand upright in the fierce wind generated by the miniature thaumaturgic storm.

Then Merlin threw his arms up over his head and the swirling cloud exploded in a blinding flash of light, sending out jagged bolts of blue lightning in all directions. Fugisawa and the others ducked as the glowing bolts flew around over their heads like miniature heat-seeking missiles, darting this way and that, until they all came together in one spot, striking one section of the wall and igniting in a wash of burning blue flame that outlined an unseen thaumaturgic portal, a hidden door that had been spell warded against detection.

Suddenly the lights in the basement came on.

"All right, nobody move!" said a voice in Japanese.

There were two men standing on the stairs leading down from the shop, aiming 9-mm machine pistols at them. Three more men came down, passing behind them. They reached the foot of the stairs and covered them while the two men on the stairs above them came down.

Fugisawa held up his hands slowly. "Take it easy," he said. "My name is Fugisawa. You must be Kobayashi's men. I—"

"We know who you are. Everyone just stand very still. First one of you tries any magic, we start shooting. Understood?"

"*Wakarimasu*," said Modred. "You'll have to forgive my friends. They don't speak Japanese. I'll have to translate what you said for them."

The man narrowed his eyes suspiciously, then nodded. Modred repeated what he said, without adding anything of his own.

The Yakuza man smiled and nodded. "Good," he said in heavily accented English. "No tricks. I speak English, you see." He switched to Japanese and told two of the men with him to check them for weapons. They relieved Kira and Billy of their knives, found nothing on Wyrdrune, then took Fugisawa's 9-mm, as well as the backup .32 he wore in his ankle holster, and Modred's 10-mm Colt.

The man who seemed to be in charge snapped his fingers and

took Modred's 10-mm. He admired the big gun briefly, then stuck it in his waistband.

"So, you are the famous Morpheus," he said. "You speak Japanese very well."

"If you know who I am, then you should also know that we're all working for the same man. We came here looking for Kanno, same as you. Are the weapons really necessary?"

"Merely a precaution. What is that behind you?"

"A hidden doorway that was spell warded against detection," Modred said.

"Is it safe to go through?"

"I'm not sure," Modred replied. "We were about to find that out when you interrupted us."

The Yakuza man frowned, then spoke quickly to the men behind him. They hesitated and he angrily repeated his order again. They glanced at him, uneasily, then came over to Fugisawa and beckoned him through the door with their machine pistols. Fugisawa glanced at Modred, then walked up to the glowing doorway and stepped through. He disappeared from sight.

The two Yakuza men hesitated nervously, then at a barked order from their leader followed Fugisawa through the portal. A moment later one of them came back through, his eyes wide, and beckoned the others to follow.

Herded by the gunmen, Wyrdrune, Kira, Billy, and Modred stepped through the portal and found themselves on a crumbling stone stairway. Fugisawa and the two gunmen who had gone through first stood waiting at the bottom of the stairs.

They descended into the large underground chamber, with its ceiling of interlacing steel girders shrouded in spiderwebs and dust. They came down into a pentagonal-shaped plaza, with a large pool in the center filled with a bubbling liquid that gave off a phosphorescent glow. In the center of the pool, upon a pedestal, was an altar that appeared to be made of solid gold. It was covered with dried and crusted blood. There were braziers placed around the plaza, burning some sort of incense that gave off a cloying, sickly sweet odor, and there were torches mounted on the walls.

"Remind you of something?" Kira said softly.

Wyrdrune nodded. "The catacombs, in Paris."

"What *is* this place?" asked the leader of the Yakuza team.

"It was a shopping mall," said Fugisawa, "constructed below street level. They must have built over it during one of the renovations."

One of the men walked over to the glowing pool and stretched his hand out towards the bubbling liquid.

"I wouldn't do that if I were you," Modred cautioned him. "It could be acid."

The man jerked his hand back as if he had been bitten.

"Well, it seems that we have found the killer's hiding place," said the Yakuza leader. "We'll simply wait for him to return." He glanced at Modred and smiled. "It looks as if Don Kobayashi won't be needing your services, after all."

"Don't be a fool," said Fugisawa.

"And you have become superfluous, as well," the man said, gazing at Fugisawa coldly. "This is all very convenient. We won't even have to worry about disposing of the bodies. No one will ever find you down here."

"You're being dangerously overconfident," said Modred calmly. "If you should kill us, I can promise you that you will never get out of here alive. None of you. You are no match for Kanno. Or for his mistress."

The Yakuza man frowned. "His mistress? What are you talking about?"

One of the other men suddenly cried out and pointed. A woman was coming toward them from the far end of the mall. A young Japanese woman dressed in a long, white, diaphanous gown. She seemed to be wearing nothing underneath it. She was barefoot and she moved toward them with a slow, peculiar gait. There was something wrong with her. Something jerky and mechanical about her movements.

"You!" shouted the Yakuza leader. "Stop where you are! Who are you?"

But the woman made no response. She simply kept on coming, oblivious of the guns pointed at her. Her face seemed vacant. Lifeless. Her eyes were dark, glazed, expressionless pools.

"I said, stop where you are! Who are you? Answer me!"

"I don't think she can hear you," Modred said. "She's dead."

"*Dead?*"

"Fugisawa," Modred said quickly, "back away."

Fugisawa stepped back out of the path of the slowly advancing woman, unable to take his eyes off her. His stomach churned with revulsion. She was close enough now for them to see the unearthly, translucent pallor of her skin, the bloodless lips, the lank dark hair covered with dust and cobwebs. Small spiders scampered through the long and matted strands. And behind her, moving out of the shadows, they could see the ghostly shapes of other animated corpses. Leila's victims, naked, their bodies caked with dried blood and dust, gaping holes in their chests where their hearts had been ripped out. They advanced toward them slowly and inexorably, with that same shambling, marionettelike gait.

The Yakuza man closest to her cried out and fired his machine pistol. The 9-mm jacketed hollowpoint slugs tore into her body, penetrating it as easily as if she had been made of paper. She jerked as the bullets struck her, exiting through her back, but she did not fall. Black, coagulated blood oozed sluggishly from her wounds. The man kept firing until he emptied his entire clip and then he threw the gun at her. It struck her in the face, gashing her forehead. She reached out and seized him by the throat. He tried to break away, but her grip was too strong. He pummeled at her with his fists, but his blows had no effect. She continued to strangle him, relentlessly.

The other gangsters had seen enough. They turned and bolted back up the stairs. Their leader paused only long enough to raise his machine pistol, aiming it at Modred, but before he could fire, there was a searing flash of white light and a broadsword came whistling through the air, chopping off the gunman's arm at the elbow. For an instant, he stood still, staring in shock at his severed arm, spouting a fountain of blood, then he screamed. The scream was cut off abruptly as the broadsword whistled through the air once more, severing his head. It bounced down the stairs like a basketball and came rolling to a stop at Fugisawa's feet, an expression of horror and agony fixed on its features.

Fugisawa stared in stunned disbelief at the incredible vision coming toward him. Billy had disappeared and in his place stood a knight in full, gleaming armor, a hulking figure that towered over him with a huge broadsword clutched in one hand and a shield in the other. A blinding white light came from the narrow slit in his steel visor. For a moment Fugisawa thought the armored giant would attack him, but he brushed past him and waded into the throng of animated corpses that were closing in on them, swinging his broadsword like a scythe. He cut them down like wheat, severing their bodies in two with powerful strokes, mowing them down relentlessly. They fell without a sound, pieces of their dismembered bodies twitching on the floor like dying snakes.

Fugisawa watched the carnage slack-jawed. The huge knight didn't make a sound as he sliced his way through the walking dead like a terrible juggernaut. He backed away and then felt a hand grasping his upper arm. He flinched and glanced around. Modred was standing beside him.

"What . . . who . . . ?"

"Gorlois," said Modred.

In moments it was over. There was nothing but dismembered bodies on the floor, jerking spasmodically and then lying still. The huge knight turned and his blade, miraculously unbloodied, scraped back into its scabbard. Then the light coming from behind his visor flared like a supernova and Fugisawa threw his arm up to cover his eyes. When he looked again, blinking from the afterimage, colored pinpricks dancing before his eyes, he saw Billy standing there amid the chopped-up corpses, breathing heavily.

"Gor' blimey," he said softly.

Fugisawa's knees buckled.

"Steady," Modred said, holding him up.

The dizziness passed quickly and Fugisawa gulped in a deep breath of air. "If I hadn't seen it with my own eyes, I would never have believed it," he said a in a shaky voice. He was staring at Billy with astonishment.

"The corpses must have been part of the spell protecting this place," Wyrdrune said. "Leila's victims." He glanced at Fugisawa. "The Ginza murders that you didn't know about.

She kidnapped people, brought them down here, and sacrificed them on that altar to increase her power.''

"I've never seen anything so horrible," said Fugisawa.

Modred bent down over the headless body of the gunman and retrieved his pistol. "You'll see a lot worse, if we don't stop her soon," he said.

Kira looked at Wyrdrune and saw that the stone in his forehead was still glowing. She frowned and glanced at the runestone in her palm. It was still burning brightly. "I don't understand. If she isn't here, then why—"

"The shop!" said Modred. "Quickly!"

They ran back up the stairs and passed through the portal into the basement of the shop. Fugisawa came through right behind them and was brought up short by what he saw. The bodies of the fleeing gunmen, what was left of them, were scattered all around the basement. There was blood and viscera everywhere, as if they had exploded. Fugisawa fought down the gorge rising in his throat.

"Damn it!" Modred swore. "They were *here!*"

They raced up the stairs and into the lab, then went through the shop and into the street. It was deserted. They ran across the street, to where the limo was parked at the curb. Wyrdrune leaned into the driver's window.

"Did you just see anybody coming out—" He broke off and recoiled. "Oh, my God!"

There was nothing left of the chauffeur but a mass of blood and gore.

CHAPTER
Ten

HE WAS OFF THE CASE, JUST AS HE'D EXPECTED. WATANABE had called him into the office and given him his little talk, all about what a good job he had been doing and how everyone knew how hard he had been working, but what with the pressure from the media and commissioner, who was getting a lot of heat from the mayor's office, it would be best if the case were reassigned, a fresh perspective, no reflection upon him, etc., etc. He had tuned out halfway through Watanabe's hypocritical little speech. The case would be assigned to young Sakahara. He was to turn over all his notes, so that Sakahara could have a chance to look them over before the big-shot I.T.C. investigator arrived. And he also agreed to take a few days off, with pay, of course, a well-deserved rest for working so hard. Akiro didn't even feel angry. He just felt tired and helpless.

He went back to his office and told his secretary he was taking some time off, then checked in with Sgt. Soichiro Kitano, administrative coordinator of the task force, a veteran of almost twenty years. Kitano understood and commiserated with him, promising to keep him posted, unofficially, on the progress of the investigation. And he learned from Kitano that while he had been in Watanabe's office, watching his career go down the drain, there had been some new developments. Very disturbing developments.

Apparently, sometime last night, after the bodies of the hooker and the Yakuza man had been discovered in the Ginza alley, the body of a chauffeur was discovered in a limousine parked across the street from Kanno's shop in the Shinjuku district. It appeared as if his body had exploded. Blood and entrails everywhere, all over the inside of the car. A gruesome scene. The door to Kanno's shop had been found open and several more bodies—or, more accurately, remains—were discovered in the basement. They, too, seemed to have exploded. Or been torn apart. No one was even certain how many victims there had been. Two, three, perhaps four.

Kanno's apprentices had seen no sign of him since they had left the shop the previous day and they were afraid that something might have happened to him. For all anyone knew, he might have been one of the victims. It was impossible to identify the bodies, because there was so little left of them.

Sakahara had left to pursue the investigation. He wasted little time.

Kitano had already established that the limo had been rented to a Mr. Michael Cornwall, who had taken two of the most expensive suites at the Imperial Hotel. However, after checking with the hotel, they had discovered that Mr. Cornwall and his party had checked out the previous night, when the limousine arrived to pick them up. The bill had been paid in cash. There had not yet been time to follow up on the address that Mr. Cornwall had given the hotel, but it would probably turn out to be a false one. He had given his occupation as "management consultant."

"But the hotel staff remembered Cornwall and his party very well," Kitano said. "They described him as being tall, well built, good-looking, in his forties, very elegantly dressed, blond hair and beard, tinted glasses, and a British accent. He was traveling with a party of three. A young girl, American, in her late teens or early twenties, dark and very pretty. Gave her name as Kira. No last name. There was a young boy, perhaps fifteen or sixteen years old, also British, but cockney, working class, not like Mr. Cornwall. One of those punks with an outlandish hairstyle, short on the sides and like a horse's mane in the center, a ponytail down to the middle of his back. He gave his name as Billy Slade. And the other member of the party was a young adept who used the magename Wyrdrune. Mid-twenties, long, curly blond hair, headband, warlock's cassock. And he was traveling with an interesting familiar. A talking broom."

"A talking *broom*?" said Akiro.

"Yes, like a kitchen broom, only with arms. But that isn't the most interesting part. Guess who was with them when they left?"

"All right, who?"

"Fugisawa."

Akiro frowned. *"Lt. Fugisawa?"*

"The very same."

"Are you certain?"

"He identified himself to the desk clerk. It seems he came to the hotel to make inquiries about Cornwall and his party and went up to their rooms. He stayed for perhaps an hour or more, then left with them when they checked out.''

"What the hell? Does Sakahara know this?''

"Not yet. I just got off the phone with the hotel. I was about to call him. Why, you want to tell him yourself?''

"No, no, go ahead and call him. I'm off the case. Officially.''

"But you'll pursue it on your own time?''

"Yes, but I'd rather Watanabe didn't know that right now.''

"I won't say a word.''

"What the devil is Fugisawa up to? Have you been able to get in touch with him?''

"Not yet," said Kitano. "But he's going to have a lot of questions to answer. Assuming, of course, that he wasn't one of those bodies in the basement. I don't envy Sakahara. He's walking into one hell of a mess. You're lucky to be out of it.''

"I'll never be out of it," Akiro said grimly. "Not until I solve it. I'm not giving up on this one. See if you can find Fugisawa.''

"If he's still alive," Kitano said. "We've got a bulletin out on Cornwall and his party. Suspicion of murder. There's no question that necromancy was involved. But at least we've finally got an idea who we're looking for.''

"I wonder," said Akiro. "This seems too convenient. The killer's been very careful not to leave us any clues. He, or they, would have to know that we could easily trace them through the rental of the limousine. Why kill the chauffeur? If they were going to kill Kanno, why take a limo to his shop? It doesn't make sense.''

"Maybe we'll know more when we're finished checking up on Cornwall's background.''

"Maybe. How long ago did Sakahara leave?''

"Ten, fifteen minutes ago. He went straight to Kanno's shop.''

Akiro thought a moment. "I have a hunch. Before you call him with this information, check the database and find out when Cornwall and his party arrived in Tokyo.''

"I should have thought of that. Hold on, it shouldn't take long." Kitano sat down at his computer console and called up the data, checking through the list of names of people who had recently arrived in the country. After a few moments he said, "I've got it." He groaned. "Your hunch was right. Cornwall and the others only just came in from America. Reservations at the Imperial were booked from New York, well after the murders had begun. They weren't even in the country when this whole thing started. He's not our killer."

"Fugisawa went to see him for a reason. We have to find out why. And what happened between the time they checked out of the hotel and the limo arrived at Kanno's shop. If those remains have not yet been identified, there's a chance that Cornwall and the others are the victims." He paused, thinking. "These killings don't sound like the others. The common denominator is Kanno. You've been updating the database on our adepts?"

"Of course. We're narrowing it down a lot."

"Check on Kanno for me. Let's not step on Sakahara's toes. Make it look routine, just part of the process of elimination that we've been pursuing. Question Kanno's apprentices. Get a list of his clients and check his appointment book at the shop. Find out everything you can. See if he has any alibis for the times and dates of any of the murders."

Kitano frowned. "You suspect Kanno?"

"I don't suspect anyone right now. I'm merely being methodical. We seem to have two sets of murders, on the surface, apparently unrelated. However, Kanno is the one common denominator between them."

"What about Fugisawa?"

Akiro shook his head. "I've already checked him out. He's got alibis for at least six of the murders."

Kitano stared at him. "You don't leave a thing to chance, do you?" He shook his head. "And Watanabe's removed you from the case. The man's an idiot."

"He's under a great deal of pressure," Akiro said, wondering why he was making excuses for him. "What have you got on the male victim from the alley last night?"

"The Yakuza? He's got a sheet. Fumio Hattori. One of Don Kobayashi's people."

"Don Kobayashi. Where can I get in touch with him?"

"He owns a club in the Ginza, the Paradise. And he's got offices in the Takamura Building."

"I wonder what his connection with this is. I'll be in my office."

He went back to his office and told his secretary that he wasn't in and didn't want to be disturbed unless Kitano called him. Then he asked her to see if she could get Yohaku on the phone right away. He sat down behind his desk, a look of concentration on his face. He hoped that Fugisawa wasn't dead. He knew something. Only what? A moment later his secretary buzzed him.

"I have Master Yohaku on the phone," she said.

Akiro picked up the phone. "Sensei? This is Akiro Katayama, of the Bureau of Thaumaturgy. You remember me?"

"Of course," the mage said. "I am glad you called. I was going to get in touch with you today. I must see you."

"I'd like to see you, too, Sensei. There have been some new developments. Have you spoken with Kanno recently?"

"No, I haven't. But that is what I wanted to speak with you about."

"There is a chance he may be dead."

"*Dead?*"

"We don't yet know for certain. There's been no word from him. Some bodies were discovered in the basement of his shop early this morning. They have not yet been identified. I was just on my way there. If it would not be too great an inconvenience, would it be possible for you to meet me?"

"Certainly. I will leave at once."

"If you arrive before I do, Sensei, there will most likely be police there. I have been . . . there is a new agent in charge of the case. A young man named Sakahara. If he is still there, please tell him that I will arrive shortly and would like to speak with him."

"Of course. You are leaving now?"

"Yes, I should be there in just a little while."

"Good. I will see you there."

Akiro hung up the phone. Then he opened up the lower right-hand desk drawer and took out his gun, a stainless steel .357 Magnum revolver with a three-inch barrel nestled in a black nylon, belt clip holster. He had not worn it in years. He took a deep breath, clipped the holster to his belt inside his jacket, and left the office.

"Damn, they were so *close*," said Wyrdrune with an angry grimace.

They were sitting in Fugisawa's small apartment near the Shibuya Station. None of them had eaten for hours, so they had stopped at Makudonarudo for some take out. The old and well-established fast-food restaurant chain, better know in the West as McDonald's, served exactly the same cuisine as the American original, with a few idiosyncratic Japanese additions, such as iced coffee and orange-flavored milkshakes. It seemed a little strange to be sitting cross-legged at a low table, on the woven tatami mats in Fugisawa's elegantly traditional Japanese apartment, eating hamburgers and french fries, but after what they had experienced in the past few hours, a Big Mac was refreshingly familiar.

"She's building up to something," Modred said. "She's consumed a great deal of life energy and grown very powerful. And she knows we're closing in. She won't be going back to that underground hideout again."

"Unless she figures it's the last place we would look for her," said Kira.

"It's possible," Modred replied, "but I don't think she'll take that chance. She isn't stupid. Killing that chauffeur was a calculated act. She didn't want to leave any witnesses. And that limousine can easily be traced to us. I still think we should have disposed of it."

"I told you, that would have been a mistake," Fugisawa said. "It would have turned up missing and then they would have come looking for you to find out why. This way, you can claim the car was hijacked while you were visiting the Paradise Club. And I could say that I was with you, taking the report, when the murders occurred. That gives you all an alibi."

"Boy, have you *seen* this place?" the broom said, swishing into the room and carrying a tray with coffee cups. "Not a speck of dust! And this is a bachelor, no less, living by himself! The kitchen is clean, no dirty dishes in the sink, everything is put away, the clothes are neatly folded, he doesn't just toss them on the floor like some people I could mention...."

"Not now, Broom," Wyrdrune said. "We're trying to talk. This is important."

"Well, excuse *me*, Mr. Big Shot. Everything's always so important, far be it from me to interfere."

"Broom...."

"I know, I know, you're busy saving the world. I'm just along to fold your underwear. Who cares about me? I don't count for anything. I should just stay in the broom closet, where I belong."

The broom sniffed and swept out of the room. Wyrdrune covered his eyes and sighed. "I'm getting a migraine."

Fugisawa chuckled.

"I think we should go and confront Kobayashi," Kira said. "Make the bastard cooperate. He can put a lot of people on the streets. We stand a much better chance of finding Kanno with him than without him. And wherever Kanno is, Leila can't be far away. They've got to be holed up somewhere."

"In a city the size of Tokyo, that could be anywhere," said Wyrdrune. "But she's got a point. It'll be hard enough trying to find them without having both the police and the Yakuza out looking for us."

"And the I.T.C. as well," said Fugisawa. "I've heard they're sending in a field agent to oversee the Bureau task force."

The phone rang. Fugisawa went to answer it. The conversation was brief.

"That was headquarters," he said. "They've been trying to track me down. They've found the chauffeur and the bodies in the basement. They haven't discovered the entrance to the underground mall yet. If any trace emanations are detected from the warding spell that conceals the entrance, they'll probably be attributed to the spell that killed those gunmen. But they do know about you. They've traced the limo to you and they checked with the hotel. They know that I came by to see you and that we left together. They want me to come in and make a report, answer some questions."

"Things seem to be getting sticky," Wyrdrune said. "I'm sorry we got you into this."

"I was already into it up to my neck," said Fugisawa. "We're going to have to get our stories straight."

"It may be necessary to confide in Katayama," Modred said. "How well do you know him?"

"Not very well, but he's got a solid reputation. He's always gone straight by the book."

"What do you think he'd do if you told him the truth?"

"I honestly don't know," said Fugisawa.

"We may have to find out," Modred said. "We could use some help on the inside. But I gather you don't think much of his abilities."

"Katayama may be in over his head on this case," Fugisawa said, "but he's not a fool. And to cover you with the department, we could use the story of the limo being stolen to provide you with an alibi. I don't think anyone would question it, not with me vouching for you."

Modred pursed his lips thoughtfully and glanced at the others. "What do you think?"

"I think it's worth a try," said Wyrdrune.

"Kira?"

"Having the cops on our asses won't make things any easier," she said.

"We could meet with Katayama," Wyrdrune added. "See how he responds. If he becomes difficult, we could use a spell to cloud his memory and make him forget he ever met us."

"I don't like resorting to that," said Merlin. "It's an easy solution, but spells of forgetfulness often tend to cause psychological problems for the people they're used on. They're difficult to effect with precision. I'd like to avoid that if possible."

"Considering what's at stake, we may not have a choice," said Wyrdrune.

Modred nodded. "If the police start to inquire too deeply into our affairs, it could present a problem. Do you think they'll accept the story of the hijacked limousine?"

"No reason why they shouldn't," Fugisawa said. "Nobody can prove it wasn't stolen. The chauffeur can hardly deny it, can he? I'll say that I came to the hotel to question you as part of a routine investigation and you were on your way out to do some slumming in the Ginza. I needed to see Kobayashi anyway, to question him about his man who was found murdered in the alley, so you graciously offered me a ride. When we got to the Paradise Club, you decided to go in and check it out. And while you were inside and I was with Kobayashi, the limousine was hijacked. I happened to be right there, so I took the report. I just hadn't gotten around to submitting it yet.''

"I don't know," said Modred dubiously. "It all sounds a bit too serendipitous.''

"Take it from a cop," said Fugisawa. "If you're going to lie, make the lie as close to the truth as possible. Besides, I'll be backing up your story and no one has any reason to suspect me of complicity. I don't see any reason why they shouldn't accept it. And I can sidetrack them from checking you out any further.''

"I still think we should have disposed of the car," said Modred.

"No, I told you, that would have been a mistake," Fugisawa replied. "You could still claim it had been hijacked, but this way, having it found with the chauffeur dead in front of Kanno's shop, and the bodies in the basement, it ties in neatly with the killer. It works for us. I can establish that Kanno's been frequenting the fleshpots on the Ginza. And that he's been keeping a separate apartment that he hasn't told anyone about. The key to the whole thing is Kobayashi. The killings have been taking place on his turf and they've been affecting his business. It stands to reason that he'd have his people out, looking for the killer. Well, they found him, but they got too close. That explains the dead Yakuza in the alley and the bodies in Kanno's shop. Kanno hijacked the limo and its driver after the murders in the alley. Kobayashi's men ran him down at his shop and got killed for their trouble.''

"I suppose we could induce Kobayashi to cooperate," said Merlin.

"You probably won't have to," Fugisawa said. "He made a bad mistake, having his people try to take us out. That wasn't like him. It was a dumb, desperate move. He's already in trouble with his bosses for not being able to control what's happening on the Ginza. We'll be offering him a way to save face, a way that's even better than having his men kill Kanno. This way, he'll be able to publicly take credit for helping to identify Kanno as the killer. I think he'll jump at the chance. And so will Katayama.''

"Sounds like it might work," said Kira. "I say we go ahead with it."

"Me, too," said Wyrdrune.

Modred nodded. "All right. Call Kobayashi and present it to him. Set up a meeting. Then make arrangements for us to meet with Katayama. See if you can get him to come here."

"I'll get right on it," Fugisawa said, heading for the phone.

"What worries me most is what Leila's planning," Modred said. "Whatever it is, she must be getting ready to execute it. These Dark Ones are like vampires. They kill surreptitiously, one or two victims at a time, gradually building up their power, but the stronger they become, the hungrier they get. And Leila's not only hungry, she's vengeful. She'll try to cast a spell that would make her powerful enough to overcome the runestones. And that means a great many people would have to die."

"We've gotta try putting ourselves in 'er place," said Billy. "What could she do to kill a large amount of people at one time and absorb their life energy?"

"What did the Dark Ones do when they escaped the pit?" said Kira. "Hell, they caused disasters all over the world."

"Yes, but that was all of them acting in concert, directing their energies through Al'Hassan," said Modred. "By herself, Leila would not be strong enough to accomplish something like that. She would have to concentrate her energies on one localized disaster in order to control the spell."

"Where do large numbers of people gather in one place?" asked Wyrdrune. "Sporting events? Concerts? Shopping centers? Train stations during rush hour? Airports? Hell, in a city as crowded as this, it could be anywhere. There're masses of people everywhere you look. There's no way to second-guess her."

"It would have to be a very powerful spell," said Modred.

"We may simply have to count on the runestones detecting it and hope that we can get there in time to stop her."

"Yeah, only that didn't quite work the last time," Kira said. "We got there all right, but not in time to keep the Dark Ones from escaping. And a lot of people died."

"There isn't anything that we can do about that," Modred replied. "I've told you before, many more people are going to die before we're finished. Hundreds. Perhaps thousands. Fighting the Dark Ones is like trying to irradicate a deadly epidemic. Until a cure is found, there's going to be a lot of death."

"I know," said Kira with a sigh. "But knowing it and accepting it are two very different things."

Fugisawa finished talking on the phone. "I just spoke to Kobayashi," he said. "And he claims he never gave an order for those men to take us out."

"What did you expect him to say?" asked Wyrdrune wryly.

"Curiously enough, I believe him," Fugisawa said. "He seemed extremely upset about it." He glanced at Modred. "And he was particularly anxious that I convince you he had nothing to do with it. He said that if those men tried to kill us, they must have been acting on their own, perhaps hoping to impress him. And he says that anything he can do to convince you of his honorable intentions, anything at all, he'll do without question. And he not only agreed to cooperate with you, but he actually volunteered to be placed under a spell of compulsion, so that you could satisfy yourself that he's telling the truth. He's afraid of you and he doesn't want you coming after him."

"Indeed?" said Modred. "So when and where are we supposed to meet?"

"Sunset. At the Nijubashi Bridge. It's a place I've met with him before. In the meantime, he'll corroborate whatever statement I choose to make. And he's pulled the contract on Kanno. He's put the word out that if anybody spots him, they're to get in touch with us immediately. I gave him the number of my pager. Within the next hour, everybody on the streets will be on the lookout for him."

Modred smiled. "Well done, Lieutenant. Very well done, indeed."

Fugisawa shook his head. "I've been on the streets too long. You know, there's a saying in the department. You work the street long enough, you become the street." He sighed. "All these years, I've been an honest cop. Never looked the other way, never took a bribe, never crossed the line. Now I'm in bed with a godfather of the Yakuza and the number one hit man in the business. I'm about as far over the line as you can get. But the hell of it is, this is one case where two wrongs seem to make a right."

"It's a complicated world," said Modred. "But then who would know that better than a police officer?"

"Yeah. It's not as if it's the first time I've ever cut a deal with a man on the wrong side of the law. But it's the first time I've ever really liked one."

"I appreciate that," said Modred. "And I'm sorry it's giving you a problem."

Fugisawa grimaced. "I keep wanting to ask you how many people you've killed. But I don't really want to know. Considering how long you've lived, the numbers must be frightening."

Kira glanced from Fugisawa to Modred and moistened her lips. What Fugisawa was articulating were the same feelings she could not resolve herself.

"I make no apologies for who I am or what I've done," said Modred quietly. "No excuses. No justifications. I've broken the law, but then I also predate the law, unless you're talking about the laws of God or Buddha or what have you, which I have never considered myself bound by. I have never killed anyone who had not himself killed. However, that's not intended as a justification. It's merely a principle I had set for myself, a line beyond which I chose not to cross. I've turned down many contracts because of that, for what it's worth. But there was never any shortage of contracts I could accept with a clear conscience. And though you might think it's ironic, I *do* have a conscience. I am not a sociopath. I'm merely an exterminator. A predator who feeds on other predators. That doesn't necessarily make me any better. It merely makes me useful. You see, I discovered long ago, long before your great-great-grandfather was born, that right and wrong are never absolutes. They are merely concepts defined by relativity. *All* life exists at the expense of other life, one way or another.''

"So you're a cynic, too," said Fugisawa.

Modred smiled wryly. "I prefer the term 'post-romantic.' It seems somehow more accurate as a description of Camelot's last survivor."

"I wish you weren't such a damned charming son of a bitch," said Fugisawa. "It would be easier if you were a thorough bastard."

"But I am a thorough bastard," Modred said with a smile. "Both figuratively *and* literally."

"If it wasn't for the Dark Ones, you know I'd try to bring you in."

"I know that. And I also know it would be pointless. No jail on earth could ever hold me. You'd have to kill me. But then, that would make you just like me, wouldn't it?"

Fugisawa stared at him for a moment. "I'd better go see Katayama."

CHAPTER
Eleven

THERE WAS A CROWD OF CURIOUS ONLOOKERS ON THE SIDE-walk outside the shop, just beyond the police lines marking off the crime scene. There were news reporters there, as well, and Sakahara was talking to them when Akiro arrived. He couldn't help feeling a touch of envy when he saw how much better young Sakahara was at talking to the media than he could ever hope to be. Not that it really mattered anymore, he thought. He showed his ID to the police officers keeping the crowd back and went through. He stood and watched as Sakahara wrapped up his question-and-answer session with the media.

Kunimitsu Sakahara was thirty-two years old, very serious-looking, and built like a bantam rooster. He was short, even for a Japanese, and to make up for it he had adopted a somberly aggressive, coolly professional manner, with a style of speech that left no doubt that he was a man who knew exactly what he was talking about. He reeked of competence and assertiveness. He paid a great deal of attention to his appearance, dressing well and conservatively. He could have been a young corporate executive. He had that take-charge, brook-no-nonsense way about him. He handled all their questions expertly, with the skill of a politician. He gave his answers without any hesitation, kept them short and to the point, and didn't tell them any more than he wanted them to know.

"Who were the victims, inspector?"

"At this point, we haven't yet established that. Identification is going to be difficult, due to the condition of the remains. As soon as we know for certain, that information will be released, pending notification of next of kin."

"Was Kanno one of the victims?"

"As I just said, we have not yet been able to identify the victims."

"But you don't know that he *wasn't* one of the victims?"

"I think I've already answered that."

"So Kanno is missing, then?"

"We have not yet been able to locate him. At this point, we're not assuming anything. We're investigating all possibilities."

"What about the driver of the limousine? Have you established who hired the car?"

"The driver has been identified, but we are not in a position to release his name until his family has been properly notified. As to the identity of the party who hired the car, that information is being withheld pending a full investigation. And just to save you some time, the limousine company has been requested not to reveal that information until we have completed our inquiries."

"So was it the Ginza Monster, Inspector?"

"We have not yet established the identity of the perpetrator and I would not care to engage in irresponsible speculation."

"But what about the condition of the bodies? Was it the same as in the Ginza murders?"

"No, as a matter of fact, it was not. However, that proves nothing, one way or the other. We are not discounting any possibilities."

"So you're saying it *could* have been the Ginza Monster?"

"It could have been anyone," said Sakahara. "As I said, we are not discounting any possibilities. Can you account for *your* whereabouts last night?"

That produced a laugh.

"Inspector, is it true that Inspector Katayama was dismissed from the Ginza Monster case for incompetence?"

Katayama stiffened. The reporters were all intent on Sakahara and had not yet spotted him.

"That's ridiculous," snapped Sakahara. "That sort of innuendo makes for irresponsible journalism. You owe your audience better than that. Inspector Katayama is a fine officer and it is my privilege to work with him on this case. As a matter of fact, I see him standing over there and if you people will excuse me, I must go and confer with him. You will, of course, be notified of any further developments in the investigation as they occur. Thank you very much. That will be all for now."

He turned on his heel and quickly walked away from them, ignoring further shouted questions.

"I heard that," Akiro said as he came up to him. "That was very nice of you. Thank you."

"No need to thank me," Sakahara said. "They're all a bunch of vultures. I'm glad you're here. I was hoping to catch you at headquarters, but I was called away on this. I just wanted to tell you how sorry I am about what happened."

"No reason to be sorry. It wasn't your fault."

"I know that, but I still feel awkward about it. What they did to you stinks. I admit I wanted this case, but not like this."

"Well, I appreciate that."

"Look, I understand you've been given some time off and if you want to take it, I don't blame you. But I'd really appreciate your help on this. It's really your case, I don't care what Watanabe says. Please don't get the wrong idea. I don't want to take all the credit. If you're willing to do it on your own time,

I'd really like for us to work together. And I don't mean for you to stay in the background. Maybe I can learn a few things.''

Akiro was touched. "You should have been a diplomat, Sakahara."

The younger man stiffened slightly. "I meant that sincerely."

"I'm sorry, I'm sure you did. I didn't mean that the way it sounded. And I'm grateful for the offer. I don't like to leave things unfinished. But I have a feeling Watanabe would object."

"He told you to brief me on the case, didn't he? Well, you're going to be briefing me. He didn't say how long it had to take, did he?"

Akiro smiled. "No, he didn't."

"Fine. It's settled then. Has there been any word from Fugisawa?"

"No, not yet. They were going to try him at home."

"I think he's onto something and I want to know what the hell it is. I just hope he's not one of the bodies down there. Come on in and have a look. It's pretty damn grisly. I hope you've got a strong stomach. Several of the men lost their breakfasts."

"Yohaku is going to meet us here shortly. You should make sure the men will let him through."

"The old man himself? No kidding?"

"He said he had something for me. And I also need to speak with him."

"Okay, I'll make sure he's allowed through."

He went to have a quick word with the men, then they went inside.

"There was no sign of the door being forced," said Sakahara. "And if someone tried to pick the lock, the alarm would have gone off. So whoever got inside must have either had a key or they teleported in. The alarm was turned off, but the apprentices swear they turned it on when they left. Of course, it's possible they're lying. Or just covering up for having forgotten to activate it. No question about necromancy. The trace emanations down there are pretty strong."

They went down into the basement. Akiro caught his breath when he saw the gory scene.

"It shook me up, too," said Sakahara. "Looks like the

bodies just exploded. It had to have been a spell. I can't think of anything else that could have done this. You feel it?''

Akiro nodded. The thaumaturgical trace emanations were very strong, indeed.

''You think maybe Kanno got too close and the killer did him in?''

''Perhaps, but that doesn't explain the other bodies. The apprentices are all accounted for, I presume.''

''Yes. There were only two of them and they're both okay. Scared out of their wits, but okay. I don't think they were faking it. They were practically hysterical when I got here. Kitano said that Cornwall and his associates had alibis for some of the killings?''

''Yes, they weren't even in the country.''

''So there's a chance this could be them.''

''It's possible.''

''And if Fugisawa was with them, he could be here, as well.''

''That, too.''

''Damn. I hope not.''

''So do I. Was anything stolen?''

Sakahara shook his head. ''No, nothing. And there's a fortune in magenes up there. There's something else, too.'' He pointed to where some evidence had been bagged and temporarily placed on one of the crates. ''Whoever these people were, they were armed with machine pistols.''

Akiro bent down and examined the guns in the clear plastic bags. They were caked with blood.

''Don't the Yakuza use these?''

Sakahara nodded. ''Yeah, but they're not the only ones. If they were Yakuza, the question is, what would they want with Kanno? And what happened to Cornwall and the others who came in the limo?''

''Inspector Katayama?''

They turned at the sound of the voice. ''Down here, Sensei,'' called Akiro.

Yohaku came down the stairs. He got halfway down and stopped, his eyes wide.

''Are you all right, Sensei?''

''Yes. Simply startled at the strength of the emanations here.''

"You may not want to see this, Sensei," said Sakahara. "It's pretty gruesome."

"No, I will come down. I must see. There is something..." He stopped at the foot of the stairs and gasped at the horrible sight.

"I'm sorry you had to see this, Sensei," said Akiro. "Allow me to present Inspector Sakahara. He is now in charge of this case."

"Thank you for coming, Sensei," said Sakahara. "It's a privilege to meet you. I'm only sorry it had to be under these circumstances. As you can see, these men—assuming they were all men—were killed by necromancy. That accounts for the trace emanations you've picked up."

For a moment Yohaku said nothing. He merely stared around at the blood-spattered basement storage room, his eyes slightly unfocused.

"No," he said, shaking his head. "No...."

Sakahara frowned. "No? Are you suggesting they weren't killed by sorcery? But surely..."

"No, that is not what I meant," Yohaku said. "We are looking at the results of necromancy, to be sure, but there is something else...."

His gaze slightly unfocused, he moved forward hesitantly, almost like a blind man feeling his way, his hands held out before him. He seemed oblivious of the sticky blood that he was stepping in.

"What is it, Sensei?" asked Akiro, frowning.

"There is something hidden here," Yohaku said. "I sense a strong spell of warding and concealment...." He turned, his eyes staring off into space. "It is somewhere very close...there!" He pointed at what appeared to be a blank brick wall.

Sakahara and Akiro came forward.

"I don't see anything," said Sakahara. "And my perceptions are not as great as yours, Sensei. What is it?"

"A portal," said Yohaku. "A hidden portal."

"Where?"

"Right there, before you."

Sakahara felt the wall. It was solid and unyielding. He looked at the old mage with confusion.

"This only confirms my worst suspicions," said Yohaku. He blinked and his gaze cleared. He turned to Akiro. "I was searching for spells that I could use to help you find this necromancer. And I consulted some of my old scrolls and volumes, some of which date back over a thousand years and deal with the subject. I had not looked at them in years. And yet, when I went to examine some of them, I discovered that someone else had looked through them. Someone who had somehow overcome the warding spells I use to protect my library. There were only two people who had access to my home and might have done this. My housekeeper, whom I trust implicitly and who is not an adept, in any case, and one other, whom I also trusted. And that trust had been betrayed."

"Kanno?" said Akiro.

"Yes. Kanno. Step away, please."

They backed off as Yohaku closed his eyes and started to chant in a guttural language neither of them understood, though both had been schooled as adepts. Clearly, this was an advanced spell far beyond their level. As Yohaku chanted, the atmosphere in the basement seemed to grow thicker and heavier. A roiling mist began to form in the air above the old mage. They felt a cool breeze that rapidly grew stronger as the mist formed into a small cloud that crackled with thaumaturgic discharges. The breeze became a howling wind and they grabbed at the railing of the stairs to steady themselves.

The old mage stood at the center of the thaumaturgic storm, his white robes billowing, his long white hair streaming in the wind. Suddenly he threw his arms up and the roiling cloud above him exploded into tiny, jagged bolts of lightning that darted around the room as if they were alive, whizzing over their heads like angry hornets until they came together all at once, striking the brick wall before them, shattering upon it, and bathing it in an aura of blue flame . . . and a hidden portal was revealed, framed in crackling fire.

Akiro exhaled heavily and exchanged astonished glances with Sakahara.

"Come quickly," said Yohaku. "I fear that we are about to witness a horror that will make what we have seen here pale by comparison."

They followed the old mage through the portal, down a flight of stairs . . . and stopped, struck dumb by what they saw. An underground mall that had been long abandoned and forgotten, a strangely glowing, bubbling pool that cast a sickly light over their surroundings, a blood-spattered altar made of solid gold . . . and a scene of unutterable carnage. Dozens upon dozens of dismembered, decomposing bodies, scattered all around, covered with insects and squirming rats. The stench was indescribable.

"My God," whispered Sakahara.

Yohaku stood staring at the horror with a stricken expression on his face. His shoulders slumped and he suddenly looked very, very old, indeed.

"I had prayed that I would be proved wrong," he said in a broken voice. "We have found the hidden lair of the necromancer."

"It was Kanno," said Sakahara numbly. "Kanno is the Ginza Monster!"

"And it was I who taught him what he knows," said Yohaku. "May God forgive me for what I've done."

"It wasn't you, Sensei," said a voice from behind them.

Akiro and Sakahara spun around.

"Fugisawa!"

"The one who taught Kanno what he knows was here," said Fugisawa. "Her name is Leila. And she's a monster far worse than anything you could imagine."

CHAPTER
Twelve

THEY CONDUCTED A QUICK SEARCH OF THE NECROMANCER'S sanctuary, then went back up into the basement, and after

Yohaku sealed up the portal once again, Fugisawa told them everything. He left out one piece of information that he did not think they needed to know. He did not tell them about Morpheus. What Modred had once been would only cloud the issue, he thought. He downplayed his own relationship with Kobayashi, telling them only that Kobayashi had agreed to cooperate to serve his own interest, and that he had been unofficially assisting Fugisawa in his own investigation, which was what had led them to Kanno.

Initially, he had intended to speak only with Katayama. He had not counted on Sakahara being placed in charge of the investigation or on Yohaku being there, but that had turned out to be fortunate. Knowing how hard it had been for him to accept the existence of the Dark Ones, Fugisawa had expected to have a difficult time convincing Katayama, but Yohaku's presence had made his task a great deal easier.

"No, it must be true," he had said, when the others expressed their skepticism. "There are certain writings, ancient writings, known only to a very few, that make mention of an immortal race known as the Old Ones. They were said to be powerful necromancers who ruled the world when it was young, making humans serve them. But, according to the legend, they warred amongst themselves and their power destroyed them. The few survivors scattered, to hide amongst the humans and to prey on them as vampires and shapechangers, practicing their witchcraft and summoning up demons. . . . I had always believed it was an ancient legend from which many other myths had been derived, but now I see that it was based in fact."

"So you actually believe that we're faced with one of these creatures, Sensei?" asked Akiro.

"Lt. Fugisawa appears to be convinced. And the evidence here is overpowering. The trace emanations in this place indicate enormous power, far greater than my own, and if we are to discount the bearers of the runestones, I am one of the three most powerful adepts on earth."

"Four," said Fugisawa, correcting him. "Ambrosius still lives."

Yohaku stared at him with astonishment. "Merlin is alive? You have *seen* him?"

"And spoken with him," Fugisawa said. "But you would not recognize him now. He is . . . much changed."

He explained about the possession of Billy Slade.

"Amazing. Do you know where he is? Can you take me to him?" asked Yohaku, his old eyes dancing with excitement.

"At this moment he and the others are all at my apartment," Fugisawa said. "I had hoped to take Inspector Katayama there to discuss this with them, but under the circumstances, I think it would be best if we were all to go."

"What should we do about this place?" asked Akiro.

"For now, I think it would be best if it were to remain sealed and warded," Yohaku said. "Lt. Fugisawa is absolutely right. If news of this were to get out, it would cause a worldwide panic. And I think it would be best if this knowledge were to go no further than the four of us."

"What about the I.T.C. agent who's due to arrive this afternoon?" asked Sakahara. "We can hardly keep this from him. The I.T.C. must know, as must the Bureau."

"I felt the same way, initially," said Fugisawa, "but Modred has convinced me otherwise. The Bureau and the I.T.C. are both very large bureaucracies that are vulnerable to leaks. The battle with the Dark Ones must be fought in secret, by a network of trusted individuals."

"You don't mean to include Kobayashi, surely?" said Sakahara.

"Kobayashi can be induced to help us without knowing all the facts. We're meeting with him tonight. In the meantime, it would be best if you did not reveal what you found here to the I.T.C. Or your knowledge that Kanno is the killer. They'd put out an alert for him and all that would succeed in doing is getting people killed. He's become much stronger now, and with Leila behind him, they wouldn't stand a chance. Not even you would be a match for her, Master Yohaku. Only the power of the runestones can defeat her."

"In that case," Yohaku said. "We should go and meet your friends at once and decide upon a course of action. If this Dark One is preparing some catastrophic spell that will kill thousands, then time is of the essence."

* * *

Shiro Kobayashi paced nervously back and forth across the floor of his apartment. It was all going wrong. They had discovered the identity of the Ginza killer and it was only a matter of time before his father's men ran Kanno to ground.

Last night, Morpheus and his confederates had been spotted going into Kanno's shop with Fugisawa. The men watching the shop had called in for instructions and Shiro saw his chance. He issued orders to the men to kill them, but they had failed and been killed themselves. The media was attributing the deaths to the Ginza Monster, but Shiro knew that Morpheus must have been responsible. He and his confederates had checked out of their hotel and disappeared. And then Fugisawa called and suddenly his father had changed his mind about having Kanno killed. He had issued orders to all of his men to be on the watch for him, to report to him directly the moment he was spotted. Under no circumstances were they to hit Kanno. If he was spotted, they were instructed to keep him under surveillance and not to get too close. And now there was this meeting with Fugisawa this evening. It was all becoming clear.

His father had cut another deal with Fugisawa. He would help the authorities find Kanno and take the credit for his capture. In return, they would give him credit for assisting them and discovering the identity of the killer. The favorable publicity he would receive as a result would make him look good and would impress his superiors on the council. Instead of losing face, he would come out of the whole thing with his stature in the organization greatly enhanced. And the arrangement Shiro had made with Nishikawa would all come to nothing. He could simply kiss all that money good-bye.

The one slim hope he'd had that Morpheus would exact retribution for the attempt upon his life was also fading. Fugisawa was apparently in contact with him and when he'd called, Shiro heard his father telling him, almost pleading with him to convince Morpheus that he'd had nothing to do with the attempt to kill him. He claimed that it had all been a mistake, that the men had acted on their own, and that he would do anything he could to make it right. And the meeting tonight was part of that. Morpheus would be there, along with Fugisawa. Shiro was certain that he knew exactly what would happen.

His father would pay Morpheus off. Morpheus would leave Japan. Then, with him out of the way, his father and Fugisawa would work together to bring Kanno in. Shiro swore softly to himself. That damned cop should have been a Yakuza himself. He was a diabolical manipulator. The Yakuza would do his work for him in return for Fugisawa's helping his father to save face with the members of the council. Kanno would be caught, Fugisawa would show up the Bureau and get a big promotion. Damn him!

But there was still one chance. One chance to save his deal with Nishikawa. He glanced at the table. There was a black leather briefcase on it, his father's briefcase, monogrammed with his initials. Shiro had filled it with papers giving details of Yakuza criminal operations his father was in charge of. He had taken a big chance in doing that. If those papers were discovered missing before he could put his plan into effect . . . and what if Nishikawa chose not to go along with it?

Nervously Shiro lit a cigarette and picked up the phone. He dialed Nishikawa's number.

"This is Shiro," he said when his call was answered. "I need to speak with Don Nishikawa at once. It's very important."

He waited anxiously, chewing on his lower lip.

Nishikawa finally came on the line. "You have something for me, Shiro?"

Shiro quickly outlined the situation for him.

"That doesn't look very good for us, Shiro," Nishikawa said. "It would seriously jeopardize our plans. Unless, of course, you have an idea for a solution?"

"I have, Don Nishikawa. I have a plan that would neatly solve the entire situation and allow you to get my father out of the way and take over all his operations, with the council's blessing."

"Indeed? I'm interested to hear it."

"I have my father's briefcase. It's monogrammed with his initials. I've filled it with documents describing in detail certain operations he's running for the organization. Tonight, at sunset, he's having another meeting with Fugisawa at the Nijubashi

Bridge. I will find an excuse to be elsewhere when the meeting occurs. All you have to do is have your soldiers hit the meeting. Kill them all. Then, in return for full payment for my services, I will turn over the briefcase to you. With that and the photographs I've given you, it will look as if my father has been passing information concerning Yakuza operations to the police. I will leave the country and you will be able to take credit for eliminating a traitor to the organization.''

For a moment Nishikawa said nothing. ''You would set up your own father for a hit?''

''It's the only way. I've gone too far to back out now.''

Shiro was starting to sweat. He dragged deeply on his cigarette as he waited anxiously through another silence.

''The meeting is tonight, you say? At sunset, at the Nijubashi Bridge?''

''That's right.''

''And you're quite certain that you have that information that would implicate your father?''

''I have it right here. It's yours as soon as the job is done.''

''Meet me one hour after sunset, at the usual place. Be sure to bring the briefcase.''

There was a click as he hung up.

Shiro leaned back in his chair with relief and exhaled heavily. Nishikawa had bought the plan! It was all going to come together after all! By tonight, he would be free at last. Free of his father, free of the Yakuza, free to go to America and—

There was a knock at the door.

''Who is it?''

''Yuro Taniguchi.''

Taniguchi? What the hell? He'd been one of the men watching Kanno's shop. They were all supposed to be dead! A knot formed in Shiro's stomach. He remembered that the news media had reported that there were perhaps three or four bodies found in Kanno's shop, it was impossible to tell. . . . Obviously, Taniguchi got away somehow. And he could reveal that it was Shiro who had given them the orders to go in and take out Morpheus and Fugisawa and the others. And if that was revealed now . . .

"Just a minute!"

He ran to his desk and got his automatic, with the silencer attached. He tucked it underneath his jacket, into his waistband, at the small of his back. Then he went to the door and opened it.

"Yuro! I was afraid you were dead! Come in, tell me what happened!"

Taniguchi had a blank expression on his face. He walked stiffly about two steps into the room and then collapsed on the floor. Shiro stared at him with astonishment, then heard a slight sound and looked up to see Kanno standing in the doorway.

"*You!*"

He clawed for his gun, but before he could reach it, he felt his arm grabbed from behind and twisted up and back with violent force. He cried out with pain and suddenly felt himself being lifted off his feet and hurled across the room. He struck the wall and fell down to the floor. Stunned, he looked up and was astonished to see that the person who had picked him up and thrown him clear across the room was a beautiful young woman with coppery skin and flaming red hair. She looked down at him and smiled. Kanno came in and softly closed the door.

"You knew about me," Kanno said. "You had your men watching the shop. You knew about the apartment, as well. I wonder what else you know. You're working for them, aren't you?"

Shiro stared at them, wide-eyed. "I don't know what you're talking about," he said.

"I think you do. And you're going to tell us everything."

Shiro pulled out his gun, but before he could fire, the woman made a languid motion with her hand. The gun was wrenched out of his grasp and flew across the room. Her eyes began to glow and suddenly Shiro was lifted off the floor and pressed up against the wall with incredible force. He gasped for breath, and then he felt something like icy tendrils wrapping themselves around his brain.

He told them everything before he died.

Sunset at the Nijubashi Bridge.

The guards at the gates did not stop Don Kobayashi as he

entered the grounds of the Imperial Palace with his men. Takeo walked beside him as they headed down the manicured paths toward the bridge, several men walking before them, several behind, all of them armed and alert.

"You've heard nothing from Shiro?" said Kobayashi.

"Nothing," said Takeo. "There was no answer at his apartment. No one seems to know where he is."

"He should have been here," said Kobayashi truculently. "He was told."

Takeo made no reply.

"You don't think much of him, do you, Takeo?"

"He's your son."

"I asked for your opinion."

Takeo hesitated. "I am not comfortable with him."

"Nor am I," said Kobayashi. "Does that surprise you? He's a smart boy, but he's been a disappointment to me. I had hoped that he would take my place someday and run the business, but I know that isn't where his heart is. He wants to go to America, did you know that?"

"No. He never mentioned it."

"I had hoped that with the increased responsibilities I'd given him, he would come around," said Kobayashi. "But lately, I've been forced to realize that he lacks the proper qualities to follow in my footsteps. I think that I will let him go."

"To America?"

"Why not, if that is what will make him happy? Tomorrow, I will tell him my decision. Let him go to New York and be a clerk on Wall Street. You will take his place, Takeo. I have always been able to reply on you."

"I am honored, Don Kobayashi. Thank you."

"This entire business has left a bad taste in my mouth. I will be glad when it is over."

They reached the bridge and the men took up their positions.

"I have always liked this place," said Kobayashi. "I have always felt at peace here."

He walked out on the bridge.

* * *

They left for the meeting with Kobayashi shortly after dinner. It had been an unusual afternoon. In telling them what he had said to Sakahara, Katayama, and Yohaku, Fugisawa had subtly managed to indicate to them that he had told the three newcomers nothing about Morpheus and Modred had nodded his approval, then they filled in the Bureau agents and the mage on what they did not know. They told them the story of the Dark Ones and the runestones and about the encounters that they'd had with the necromancers in the Middle East, in London, Los Angeles, and Paris. It had a sobering effect on them, especially after what they had already seen.

Sakahara had left early, to return to headquarters to meet the agent from the I.T.C. and brief him on the details of the case. He had agreed with the necessity of not telling the I.T.C. any more than what was known officially. He had also agreed to act as their secret liaison with the Bureau, their man on the inside. Fugisawa had seen that the others were favorably impressed with him.

Yohaku was contrite. He felt responsible for Kanno, for having so seriously misjudged him, but Merlin sought to reassure him, telling him about how he himself had misjudged Al'Hassan, whose greed, ambition, and lust for power had resulted in the freeing of the Dark Ones. It was fascinating, watching Billy and Yohaku talk. Or Merlin and Yohaku. The old man deferring to the boy, the boy sounding like an older man and talking to him like a teacher to a favored pupil.

Katayama had said little. At one point Wyrdrune asked him why he was being so quiet, what was on his mind.

Akiro sighed. "This was my last case," he said. "A short while ago I had thought that if I could only solve it and bring the murderer to justice, then I would not so much mind taking my forced retirement. I would have been able to leave the Bureau with some sense of accomplishment. The job would have been finished. But now I see that the job has only just begun. And I will be retired from the Bureau, knowing what I now know about the threat the Dark Ones pose, knowing that I will be unable to do anything to help."

"That isn't true," said Wyrdrune. "You will have helped us to stop Leila and Kanno. And we *will* stop them. We must.

And just knowing that we'll be able to call on you if we ever need your help will make what we have to do a little easier.''

"It's kind of you to say that.''

"He's not just being kind, Akiro,'' Kira said. "We don't know how many necromancers are still out there. We can't be everywhere at once. We need people we can count on, people we can trust. People to keep watch. We know about Leila. There are a lot more like her that we don't yet know about.''

Modred had glanced out the window. "The sun is going down,'' he said. "We'd best be on our way.''

Don Ito Nishikawa raised his head and glanced out the window as the pretty young masseuse worked on his back, skillfully probing pressure points with her fingertips. The sun was going down.

"You are so tense,'' the masseuse said. "Too much worry. Try to relax.''

He could not relax. He hoped that he had not made a big mistake. He did not like depending upon Shiro Kobayashi. But he had committed himself. He felt sure that young Kobayashi would deliver what he'd promised. And then he would be paid. Only not quite in the manner he expected. Don Nishikawa had no intentions of letting Shiro live. He was taking no chances. To that end, he had hired Tanaka to accompany his own assassins and perform the hit. He could not afford any mistakes. Kobayashi and Fugisawa both had to die in order for the plan to succeed.

It would be very soon now. Soon he would know.

The sun was sinking lower in the sky. Kanno sat in Shiro Kobayashi's apartment, watching the sunset and waiting tensely. He would have to time it perfectly. He knew that the moment he got close to them, the runestones would detect his presence. He had to make his move at almost the same time the Yakuza assassins made theirs. He glanced at Shiro's blood-stained body, lying on the carpet. Leila had believed that he was working with the avatars, her enemies, the bearers of the runestones, but instead, ironically, what he had done had given her the perfect opportunity to make her final move.

They had come very close. Far too close. Leila had been

furious when she realized that the avatars had discovered her sanctuary. Once before, they had defeated her and she was determined to pay them back for that. There had been three of them. Leila had not been alone. He had not known until only a short while ago that the avatars had killed two of the Dark Ones who had been with Leila in Paris. She had never told him about that before. He had believed the Dark Ones were invincible, but he realized now that Leila feared the runestones, the enchanted gems that contained the life essence of her ancient enemies. These mortals who had bonded with the runestones possessed the same powers as the immortal Dark Ones. Leila feared them and her fear had played right into Kanno's hands.

She meant for him to kill them, or at least distract them long enough for her to complete her spell. Kanno knew that Leila did not care if he lived or died. She only meant for him to serve his purpose, and if he survived, she would reward him. Kanno intended to survive. Not because he wanted a reward from her, not because he sought to please her, but because he wanted to destroy her. He would kill the avatars, absorb their life force and become as strong as they were. As strong as Leila. Even stronger. The one chance he had was the element of surprise, which Shiro Kobayashi had unwittingly given him.

The power struggle between the leaders of the Yakuza played right into his hands. The moment Don Nishikawa's assassins struck, Kanno would make his move. And, at the same time, Leila would make hers. At this very moment, she would be preparing her spell. She had teleported to a location approximately sixty miles west of Tokyo, to the cloud-shrouded summit of Mt. Fuji.

With an elevation of 12,388 feet, Fuji was a majestic, almost perfectly proportioned volcanic cone, capped with snow. Its name meant "to burst forth." The last five thousand feet to the summit was an immense cone of cinders, completely bare of any vegetation. It had been formed some twenty thousand years ago in a week-long eruption of fire and lava. Revered as sacred since ancient times, "Fuji-san" was quiet now. There were several well-worn trails leading to the top, divided into ten different stages. Approximately four hundred thousand people climbed Mt. Fuji every year. It was a very popular thing to do in Japan. There were souvenir shops, restaurant, and shrines located at each stage, as well as at the summit. There were also mountain huts, which for a fee provided accommodations with futons, toilet facilities, and optional meals of dried fish and rice and pickled vegetables. Climbing Fuji-san was a Japanese adventure, a pilgrimage, and during the peak season, at all hours of the day and night, long lines of hikers stretched along the rocky trails. Night hikers liked to climb with flashlights and then watch the sunrise from the peak. A grand and awesome sight, Japan's most notable geographical feature, Fuji-san had slept for a long time.

Now Leila would awaken it.

Tanaka had selected his position carefully earlier in the day. He had picked out an old cherry tree on the opposite side of the moat surrounding the palace grounds, one that offered a suitable perch with an unobstructed field of fire. Dressed in a black ninja outfit, loose enough to conceal the street clothes underneath, and wearing a black hood that covered his entire head and face, leaving a slit for the eyes, he had climbed the tree and assumed his position with the semiautomatic .223 caliber sniper's rifle that he had removed from its special case. The case, which looked like an ordinary briefcase, was hidden beneath a nearby shrub. All he would have to do was make his two shots, drop down from the tree, retrieve the case, break down the rifle, strip off the ninja suit, and leave. He could accomplish the entire procedure, from the moment that he pulled the trigger, in slightly over a minute and a half. Plenty of time to make his getaway, especially considering the fact that his first shot would signal the attack by Nishikawa's men, who were concealed in the shrubs around the bridge and along the paths.

He rested the rifle on the forked branch in front of him, drew back the bolt and chambered a round from the magazine, then sighted through the starlight scope. The crosshairs centered on Kobayashi's forehead. He was standing on the bridge next to his lieutenant, Takeo. Tanaka kept his finger off the trigger. His other target hadn't yet arrived. He had carefully studied the photographs of Kobayashi and Fugisawa, to make sure there would be no mistakes. He swept the bridge with his scope.

Several people were approaching. He frowned. More than he'd
expected. That could present a problem, if one of them were to
get in the way. He would have to wait until they got into a
favorable position. He picked out Fugisawa. Now all he had to
do was wait.

Leila stood at the summit of Mt. Fuji, watching the sun set.
Below her was a vast expanse of clouds. It looked as if she
were standing on a rocky island in the middle of a white,
billowing sea. The sun was staining the sky red. She was not
alone. There was a crowd of people at the summit, watching
the sun go down, taking photographs, enjoying snacks, con-
gratulating each other on having made it to the top. In moments, she thought, they would be very sorry they had made
the climb. She smiled, raised her arms, and began to chant.
People turned to stare at her. At first, some of them chuckled,
some pointed, others took a photograph. And then a wind
started to come up.

Leila raised her voice as she chanted. The climbers shouted
excitedly and pointed as thaumaturgic energy sparked and
crackled from her fingertips, discharging into the air in jagged
bolts of magic lightning. The clouds around the mountain
began to roil as the wind grew in intensity. Her entire body was
outlined with an aura of pulsating thaumaturgic force as she
channeled the life energies of all her victims through the spell.
The wind now blew with gale force, tearing at the people's
clothing and knocking over several of the concession stands.
The hikers screamed and started running panic-stricken for the
trails as the sky grew black and red, lit up with jagged fire.
And from deep beneath the earth, there came a distant rumbling.

"You have some explaining to do, Fugisawa," said
Kobayashi, frowning as he glanced from Fugisawa to the
others. His gaze lingered uncertainly on Modred before it
returned to Fugisawa once again. "You seem to be burning the
candle at both ends." His gaze fell on Yohaku and he bowed
respectfully. "I am honored, Master Yohaku," he said, "but I
am curious as to the reason for your presence at this meeting.
And I should like to know why Inspector Katayama is here, as

well. I had thought that our arrangement was confidential, Fugisawa. I do not care for surprises. What are you up to?''

"Please, calm yourself, Don Kobayashi," Fugisawa said, stepping up to him. "There is no reason to feel apprehensive. I—"

A shot suddenly cracked out and a hole appeared in Kobayashi's temple. Even as he fell, another shot came right on the heels of the first, striking Fugisawa in the head.

"Down!" shouted Modred as gunfire erupted all around them. Men dressed in black ninja suits were springing up out of the bushes, firing automatic weapons.

They dropped down flat as bullets whizzed around them. Kobayashi's men started to return the fire, but they had been caught standing out in the open and Nishikawa's assassins quickly cut them down.

"You bastard!" swore Takeo, pulling his gun, but before he could fire, Wyrdrune made a quick gesture with his hand and the pistol was torn out of Takeo's grasp.

"Don't be an idiot!" said Wyrdrune. "They're shooting at *us*, too! Kira?"

"I'm all right!"

"Where's Master Yohaku?" asked Katayama.

The old mage had disappeared.

"He's teleported," Modred said. He crawled over to Fugisawa's side and quickly examined him. He shook his head. "He's dead."

"So is Don Kobayashi," said Takeo. "It was a setup! But if not you, then who . . . ?"

"I intend to find out," said Modred grimly, glancing in the direction that the shots had come from. "Kira, stay here with Katayama. I'm going after that sniper. Wyrdrune, Merlin, can you take care of those men?"

"Count on it," Wyrdrune said through clenched teeth. "Go!"
Modred vanished.

Takeo picked up his gun. Akiro already had his in his hand.

"Stay here!" said Wyrdrune. "Merlin!"

"I'm with you," Merlin said. An instant later they had teleported.

Akiro started to get up, but Kira pulled him back down. "Stay put, damn it!"

"I must go help them..."

"Believe me," she replied, "they don't need your help. Now keep your goddam head down!"

The last of Kobayashi's men fell and Nishikawa's men moved in toward the bridge. A group of the black-clad assassins suddenly found their path blocked by an old man in white robes. They opened fire with their automatic weapons, but Yohaku simply extended his arms and the bullets all stopped before they reached him, suspended in mid air, each of them surrounded by a glowing aura. All at once, they turned around their axis, facing back the other way, and sped back toward the gunmen like lethal fireflies. In panic, the assassins tried to flee, but each burst unerringly struck the man who'd fired it and one by one they crumpled to the ground as the magically redirected rounds shredded their bodies.

Wyrdrune and Billy appeared simultaneously behind two other groups of men who were running toward the bridge. Blue bolts of thaumaturgic fire lanced from Billy's eyes and struck several of the assassins in the back, killing them instantly. Wyrdrune spoke a kinetic control spell and the others suddenly felt their guns seem to come alive in their hands. It happened so quickly that before any of the selected killers could react, their own weapons turned them toward each other and opened up on full auto, of their own accord, with the result that they mowed one another down.

"Wyrdrune! Behind you!" Merlin cried.

Instinctively Wyrdrune leapt to one side and rolled as another machine pistol clattered behind him. He heard the bullets whistle past him. There were two black-garbed, hooded men behind him. He gestured toward them and the guns flew out of their hands. Faced with an adept, the men knew they were committed. One of them quickly reached into a pouch at his belt and rapidly hurled three throwing stars at Wyrdrune, one after the other. Wyrdrune used his kinetic control to turn them in midflight. They described a graceful arc in midair and spun back like miniature boomerangs toward the man who'd thrown them. His scream was cut short as the lethal stars embedded themselves deeply in his chest and forehead. The second man, disarmed of his automatic weapon, knew that it was pointless to run. He reached behind him and unsheathed a gleaming sword from the scabbard on his back.

"All right, you want to play samurai?" said Wyrdrune. He gestured toward the body of the man who threw the stars and the sword in the scabbard on his back unsheathed itself and floated free.

The second man's eyes grew wide as the sword came flashing toward him, as if wielded by an invisible attacker. Steel rang on steel as he parried desperately, backing away from the magically animated blade that lunged at him repeatedly, driving him back relentlessly. The swords clanged against each other as the man fought wildly against an opponent he could not wound or kill. He was a skilled swordsman, but it was a fight he could not win. He cried out as the flashing blade bit into his upper arm, then swept around and sliced into his torso, moving faster and faster, with a speed impossible to defend against, finally delivering the coup de grace as it drove itself into his chest and penetrated to the hilt, emerging from his back.

But the remainder of Nishikawa's men were quickly closing in from both sides of the bridge.

"I can't just cower here!" said Akiro furiously. Before Kira could stop him, he got up and started scuttling across the bridge in a crouch.

"Katayama! Get back here!" Kira cried.

"Let him go," said Takeo. "What's one coup, more or less?"

"Give me that," she said, twisting his gun out of his grasp.

Startled, he was caught unprepared. She wrenched the pistol away from him and clipped him on the side of the head with the barrel. He grunted and collapsed. Keeping low, she quickly moved off after Katayama.

The remaining gunmen had realized that they were overmatched. They turned and fled. Merlin sent bolts of thaumaturgic energy lancing after them. Each one found its mark and the assassins fell. All save one, who kept on running.

Wyrdrune raised his arms, but Merlin stopped him.

"No! We need one of them alive," he said. He teleported, reappearing on the path just ahead of the fleeing man.

The assassin stopped, wide-eyed, and quickly brought up his weapon. It went flying from his grasp. He grabbed for his sword, but it sprang out of its scabbard as if by its own volition and went spinning end over end into the bushes. He fumbled for the pouch on his belt, but his trousers suddenly fell down around his ankles. Panic-stricken, he struggled out of them and took off running in the opposite direction.

"A man should not go running about without his trousers," Merlin said. He gestured at the discarded pants. The black trousers sprang up, as if filled by invisible legs, and gave chase.

The assassin glanced over his shoulder and screamed as he saw his own pants chasing him down the path. He sprinted for all he was worth, but the pants gained on him quickly. They flew through the air and wrapped themselves around his ankles, tackling him. He fell sprawling, his legs trussed up by his own trousers. He thrashed on the ground, struggling to free himself, then looked up and saw the young boy who had bested him walking toward him purposefully. His eyes were glowing with blue fire. If he had been wearing his pants, the assassin would have wet them, but before his body could react to the terror that had seized him, he felt an icy cloud enveloping his mind and he ceased his fruitless struggles.

Tanaka had dropped down out of the tree as soon as he saw Fugisawa fall. He was unconcerned about the remainder of the battle. He had done his job and he had performed it flawlessly. The rest of it was Nishikawa's worry. He moved with quick and calm precision. He ran over to the bush where he had hidden his case, pulled it out, set the rifle down on top of it, and quickly stripped off his ninja suit. He rolled it up and stuck it underneath the bush, then reached for his sniper rifle to break it apart. And suddenly a voice spoke out behind him.

"Going somewhere?"

He spun around, bringing up the rifle, and Modred, moving with uncanny speed, smoothly drew his Colt 10-mm and shot him. The powerful slug smashed into the sniper's shoulder, tearing through flesh and pulverizing bone, exiting out the other side. Tanaka was hurled backward by the impact and the rifle fell from his grasp. He tried to scramble for it, but Modred kicked it out of his reach.

"Who hired you?" Modred asked in Japanese.

Tanaka simply glared at him.

Modred shot him in the left kneecap. Tanaka howled with pain.

"You can die fast or you can die slow," said Modred. "Take your pick. I can use a spell of compulsion on you to get what I need anyway, but why waste the energy?"

He calmly shot him in the other knee.

Tanaka screamed.

Suddenly the runestone in Modred's chest flared, sending a wave of heat through him. He gasped, his eyes grew wide, he spun around... and a powerful bolt of thaumaturgic force struck him squarely in the chest, blasting its way completely through his torso. The ruby runestone was driven through his body and out the other side. It fell, flickering, to the grass. His life rapidly ebbing from him, Modred looked up and saw a hazy figure advancing toward him. His vision swam. He summoned up his last ounce of strength and tried to raise the Colt, but it twisted in his hand like a snake and wrenched itself out of his grasp. As the figure came closer, Modred could no longer see it clearly. He gasped for breath with a hideous, rasping sound and suddenly there was a roaring in his ears and he felt as if he were falling, spinning down and down, being sucked away into a void...

Kira doubled over with pain, dropped her gun, and screamed. The sapphire in her palm was blazing. Instantly she knew. *"Modred! No!"*

At the same time, the emerald runestone sent a searing wave of pain lancing through Wyrdrune's forehead. He cried out and brought his hands up to his head, collapsing to his knees. He gasped as the pain washed over him and the awful realization struck him. He did not know how he knew, but it meant that Modred was gone.

Kanno stood over Modred's body, staring at it with puzzlement. No life force had been released. There was no sign of any runestone. Nothing. He swore furiously and walked over to where Tanaka lay in agony, clutching at his ruined knees. He drained him of his life force and left an empty, bloody husk lying on the ground, then disappeared.

Ignoring the pain, Kira snatched up her gun. "Oh, God," she said, "Wyrdrune..." She took off, running hard.

Wyrdrune was on his hands and knees on the path, his vision blurred with pain. He shook his head, trying to clear it, and suddenly saw a glowing ruby appear on the ground beneath him. He stared at the runestone on the ground before him as it strobed, then blazed with a blinding light. A thin red beam lanced out from it and struck him in the chest. He cried out, clutching his chest with pain...and in that moment, Kanno materialized behind him. He raised his arms...

...and Akiro, running down the path, came to an abrupt halt, raised his .357 in both hands, crouched, and fired three times. The bullets struck Kanno in the chest and hurled him backward, off his feet.

Akiro hurried to Wyrdrune's side and bent over him. "Are you all right?"

Wyrdrune, still on his hands and knees, nodded weakly. Then Akiro heard a rustling sound. He glanced up just in time to see Kanno's body, wriggling through the grass like a snake, disappear into the bushes.

"Stay here," Akiro said.

He got up and followed Kanno through the bushes. Moving cautiously, he pushed his way through the hedge. It was quickly growing dark and he could not see well. He swore and listened. There was a rustling sound over to his left. He turned, bringing up his gun, and something reared up before him with a deafening roar. Something out of a nightmare. Something that was long and sinewy, reptilian, with iridescent scales and a long neck that ended in a large, triangular head with gleaming eyes and rows of razor-sharp, dripping fangs. Startled, Akiro jerked back with a cry and stumbled, tripped over a root and fell. His gun discharged into the air. And he saw something rising up into the darkening sky, something like a serpent with leathery wings. It went streaking off into the distance, moving with incredible speed, rising higher and higher, faster and faster...and then it simply vanished.

Merlin came up, leading his prisoner, who had the glazed, unfocused gaze of someone under a spell of compulsion. Kira and Yohaku came rushing up at the same time.

"I know who was responsible for this," Merlin told them. "A rival gangster by the name of Nishikawa..." his voice trailed off as he spotted Wyrdrune kneeling on the ground. *"Wyrdrune! What happened? Are you all right?"*

Wyrdrune nodded.

"Modred's dead!" said Kira, tears streaming down her face. "I felt it. My God, I *felt* him die! He's gone!"

"No," said Wyrdrune, looking up at her. "No, he's not."

"But I know—"

"The dragon!" Akiro said, coming out of the bushes with a wild expression on his face. "I saw it! I saw the dragon! It was Kanno! I found his body in the bushes. He's dead. But I saw the dragon! It flew off—"

"Quiet!" said Wyrdrune.

The runestone in his forehead was glowing brightly. His gaze met Kira's. The sapphire in her palm was giving off a blinding light. There was a far-off rumbling in the distance.

"Leila!" Wyrdrune said.

"She knew about this!" said Merlin, perceiving the situation instantly. "She used it as a diversion!"

"But... where is she?" asked Akiro. "How will you find her?"

Wyrdrune looked off into the distance. "There," he said.

They followed his gaze.

"Mt. Fuji?" asked Akiro.

"We've got to stop her," Wyrdrune said.

"But *how*?" Kira asked with anguish. "Modred's dead! We can't form the Living Triangle!"

"Oh, yes, we can," said Wyrdrune. He opened his cassock and tore open his shirt. The ruby runestone blazed in the center of his chest.

Kira stared at him. "But—but how..."

"There's no time," said Wyrdrune. "Your hand!"

She held up her hand, palm out. A bright green beam of thaumaturgic force lanced out from the emerald in Wyrdrune's forehead and struck the sapphire in her palm. A blue beam leapt from her hand to the ruby embedded in his chest. The Living Triangle was formed, the aura of its light grew brighter and brighter, blocking them from view. Akiro and Yohaku shielded their eyes as the glowing triangle began to revolve, spinning around and around, faster and faster, rapidly rising up into the sky. There was a crack of thunder and it disappeared.

She was all alone at the summit now. As the mountain began to tremble, people ran screaming down the trails, bowling over and trampling those who were coming up behind them. Only those who had been at the summit and had seen her start to cast her potent spell knew what was really happening. The panic spread up and down the trails like wildfire and it was instantly infectious. The crowd surged down the trails, in the grip of mass hysteria as the panic flowed down the slopes of Mt. Fuji like the burning lava that would soon start streaming down its surface.

The wind around the summit was blowing with hurricane force and dark thunderclouds roiled above the mountain. Bolts of thaumaturgic force and jagged lightning split the sky. The ground beneath it trembled. The molten magma deep beneath the earth was surging upward. Soon, it would break through the crust. The earth would split and fissures would form, belching forth steam. In a matter of moments, the pressure would become too great and the ground would heave and buckle. The ancient volcano would come alive again, erupting with tremendous force, sending forth salvos of rock and ash. Lava would flow down the trails, it would cook the fleeing hikers and the ash would rise up high into the sky, where the magic thunderclouds would charge it with a lethal energy far deadlier than any natural radiation. It would cover the area for miles, falling on the city, poisoning everything it touched. And Leila would be above it all, absorbing all the life energy that was released as death rained down on Tokyo. Her flame-red hair billowed in the wind like a corona; her eyes were wild with anticipation; her lips were stretched back from the gums in an obscene rictus of concentration as she channeled forth the energy to fuel her spell.

She stretched her arms out to the side and threw back her head, her long hair streaming in the howling wind. She opened her mouth and a piercing, inhuman shriek escaped her lips, louder than the whistle of a locomotive. She began to change. Her face started to elongate. Her robes tore as her arms sprouted into giant leathery wings. She rose up into the air, floating on the howling wind currents, taking the form of a pterodactyl, circling above the groaning mountain. And suddenly something came streaking up at her through the clouds.

Before she could realize what it was, it clipped her and she felt a searing pain as powerful jaws snapped and tore flesh from her body. She shrieked and fell, spiraling back down to the mountaintop. The spell broke as she lost her concentration and writhed in agony upon the ground, where she resumed her natural form. A large chunk of meat had been torn from her side and her blood fountained out upon the ground. The dragon came swooping down upon her, roaring in defiance.

"*Kanno!*"

She grimaced as she tried to block out the pain and channeled all her energy into the spell to throw at the attacking dragon. She did not know why Kanno had suddenly turned on her, unless it was because he had been planning to betray her all along, to wait until the time was right, till she had cast the spell that would release the massive flow of life energy that would renew her and imbue her with tremendous power. Yes, of course! She cursed herself for not anticipating it. Just as he had betrayed the mage who taught him, Kanno had intended to betray her all along, to strike when she was vulnerable and seize for himself the power that she would release. The fool! He deserved to suffer endless agony and torment for his duplicity and arrogance, but she could not spare the time to mete out the punishment that he deserved. And time was of the essence. She was badly hurt and she would have to kill him quickly before the bearers of the runestones could respond to the emanations of the potent spell she had unleashed.

She gathered all her strength and focused it into a tight beam of thaumaturgic force that lanced out at the dragon swooping down on her. The blast struck the creature and it shrieked with pain, dropping like a stone below the clouds with a bellowing roar of agony.

Gasping with pain, Leila tried to summon up the strength to

heal herself. Wounded as she was, the bolt of force she'd thrown at Kanno had cost her. Grimacing with the effort, she focused her energies on the gaping wound in her side. The blood stopped flowing and the torn tissues started to magically regenerate themselves with astonishing speed. Sweat poured from her as she drew energy from deep within herself to heal the wound. Moments later the skin had closed and only a raw redness remained where the dragon's jaws had torn the flesh away. She gasped as she slowly raised herself to her hands and knees, still drawing on her power to renew her strength.

With an angry roar, the dragon shot up from beneath the cloud banks, its tail thrashing the sky as it rose above her, folded back its wings, and came hurtling down at her in a screaming dive. She tried to summon up another bolt of energy, but the dragon was too quick. It struck her with tremendous force and bore her up into the sky high above the mountain, its wings beating as it coiled around her, crushing her. The jaws came snapping down at her, but before they could close, a huge talon gripped the dragon just below the head, the claws sinking deep into its skin.

Leila's mouth opened, the jaws unhinging and gaping wide, revealing rows of serrated teeth, and her body hardened into dark green scales like armor plating. Dark, vertical pupils gazed out from golden eyes with nictitating membranes and a long forked tongue flickered out to strike at the dragon's eyes. Locked in mortal combat, the two huge reptiles soared high above Mt. Fuji, jaws snapping at each other, talons raking, and then the leathery wings stopped beating at the sky and both creatures fell, landing with a jarring impact on the summit of the volcano.

For a moment neither of them moved, and then one of them began to twitch and shudder as Leila slowly regained her human form. She disentangled herself from the dead beast beneath her and crawled away, coughing up blood. Her entire body throbbed with pain. Several ribs felt broken. Red foam flecked her lips as she drew great, shuddering breaths. Her energy was almost spent. She would have to use all that remained to heal herself and make good her escape. The fury that she felt was boundless. So close! So close! As she drew on her last remaining energy to heal the damage to her ruined body, she knew there would not be enough remaining to effect the spell that would reawaken the volcano. Already, the rumblings beneath her were decreasing in intensity. But there were still the hikers, fleeing panic-stricken down the trails winding up the slopes, many of them fallen, lying injured, trampled by those who had run over them in their mad plunge down the trails. As she felt her strength returning to her, she thought that it would be a simple matter to reach out to them, drain them of their life force and gain the necessary energy to fuel the spell, take those who are closest first, then use the power she would gain from them to reach out farther, to the throngs stampeding down the trails. . . .

And then she saw something glowing in the sky above her.

"No!" she cried out, blanching with fear. *"No!"*

A shaft of light came down, enveloping her, and she screamed in agony as it bathed her in its magic aura. Her skin blistered and burst, her blood boiled, her hair erupted into flame. Her eyes were cooked out of their sockets and her flesh melted from her bones. In seconds, there was nothing left of her but a steaming, viscous pool upon the ground.

The earth gradually ceased to tremble. The conjured clouds began to dissipate. The wind slowly died down as the glowing object in the sky descended to the summit of the mountain. There was a blinding flash of light. Wyrdrune and Kira stood facing each other on the mountaintop, looking drained and tired. The light slowly faded from their runestones.

Kira stared at Wyrdrune, bewildered. "What happened? How—how could we have done it without Modred?"

Wyrdrune smiled. "We didn't," he said. He touched his chest. "Modred's here."

"But . . . *how*? I don't understand. . . ."

"Kanno took him by surprise," said Wyrdrune. "But the runestone absorbed his life force before Kanno could. And now it's part of me."

"You mean . . . like Billy and Merlin?"

Wyrdrune shook his head. "I—I don't know. I'm not really sure."

"Then he really isn't dead?"

"In a way, I guess he is," said Wyrdrune. "And in another way, he isn't. His life energy lives on. I can *feel* it within me." He glanced down at what remained of Leila and breathed a heavy sigh. "It's over now. We've won."

"Until the next time," Kira said.

He met her gaze. "Yes. Until the next time."

She came into his arms and they stood together on the summit, holding on to each other tightly.

EPILOGUE

"THE NEWS MEDIA REPORTED IT AS AN EARTHQUAKE," KIRA said as she finished up the story. "A lot of people were hurt trying to get down off the mountain, but fortunately, nobody was killed. A few witnesses reported seeing Leila whipping up the spell, but nobody took that very seriously. It could have been much worse."

"What happened to the guy who ambushed you?" asked Makepeace. "Did the police arrest him?"

"They never got the chance," said Wyrdrune. "Don Nishikawa killed himself. Committed ritual seppuku. Although it's possible he may have had a little help. Shiro Kobayashi's body was discovered in his apartment. Leila must have killed him. Or maybe it was Kanno. Anyway, it doesn't matter now. Fugisawa got a department funeral, with full honors. It was too bad about him. He was a good man. Sakahara and Katayama got the credit for solving the Ginza murders, with Yohaku's help. And instead of being retired, Katayama's been promoted. The I.T.C. agent who came down to take charge of the case was so impressed with him that he arranged a transfer for him. So we now have one more connection in the I.T.C. I've got a lot to be thankful to him for. He saved my life."

"Too bad about Modred," Makepeace said.

"Yes," said Wyrdrune. "Merlin cremated his body and took it back to England. I have a feeling Modred would have wanted that. Merlin wouldn't say where he was going to bury the ashes, but I think I can guess."

"With Morgana?"

Wyrdrune nodded.

"But you said that Modred isn't really dead? He's part of you now, like Merlin is with Billy?"

"In a way," said Wyrdrune. "But I don't think it's quite the same. Billy is possessed by Merlin's astral spirit. There are two separate personalities there. Modred's runestone absorbed his spirit, or his life force, and passed it on to me. I don't know how that's different, but it is. I don't feel as if I have another personality inside me. It's strange, but it feels as if we're both the same. Don't ask me to explain it. I'm not sure I can."

"Well, you both must be very tired," Makepeace said. "I think I should leave you to get some much needed rest."

"What about Archimedes?" Wyrdrune asked.

"I think that can wait until you've had some sleep," said Makepeace. "Although I think you're in for a considerable surprise. Pirate has worked miracles. You won't recognize the little fella. He's all grown-up now."

"I kind of liked him as he was," said Kira.

"You might like him even better now," said Makepeace. "He's really an amazing little machine. Pirate can take some of the credit, but Archimedes did the rest all by himself."

"So you actually managed to crack the data bank security at General Hyperdynamics?" Wyrdrune said.

"Archimedes did even better than that," said Makepeace with a grin.

"What do you mean?"

"You're not going to need that hyperdimensional matrix unit," Makepeace said. "You've already got one."

"I don't understand."

"You know about AI personality matrices?"

"The programs that assign identity to a computer?" Wyrdrune said. "Make it behave like a male or a female, give it emotional responses, that sort of thing?"

"Exactly. Well, it turns out that the hyperdimensional matrix unit at General Hyperdynamics is female. And she fell in love with Archimedes."

"You're kidding."

"Nope," said Makepeace with a chuckle. "The little fella's got himself a girlfriend. And she'll give him anything he wants. You won't have any trouble accessing any database you want, anywhere in the world. If Archimedes can't handle it himself, Mona will be glad to get it for him."

"*Mona?*" Kira said.

"The G.H. computer," Makepeace replied. "Smart lady. Very sexy, too."

"I don't think I'm ready for this," said Kira.

"You look like you're ready for some sleep. I'll stop by with Pirate in the morning and we can introduce you to the lovebirds."

He got up and left.

"Lovebirds?" Kira said.

Wyrdrune shrugged. "I guess computers need love, too."

"Well, I don't know about you, but what I need is some rest."

They went into the bedroom. She washed up first, then stripped down and got in bed. It felt good to be back in her own bed again. And it felt strange knowing that she would wake up in the morning and not see Modred.

"Kira?" Wyrdrune said.

She heard him over the sound of running water in the bathroom.

"Yeah?"

"You really miss him, don't you?"

For a long moment she did not reply. "Yeah. I guess I do."

"I know how you felt about him. I mean, I understand."

"Do you? Well, at least that makes one of us."

"I think he understood, too. Or at least, he does now."

The sound of water stopped.

"Let's not talk about it now," she said. "Just come to bed."

There was no reply.

"Warlock?"

"I'm right here."

The sound of his voice galvanized her. It was different. It was . . . She turned toward the bathroom.

Modred was standing in the doorway.

She gasped and sat up in bed, staring at him wide-eyed.

"I'm sorry," he said. "I didn't mean to frighten you."

"Oh, my God . . ."

"It's still me, Kira. Or rather, it's us. Both of us. We're both here."

"How . . . ?"

"I honestly don't know. But it seems that I can do this. Shapechange from one form to the other. The way Gorlois does with Billy. It should make things rather interesting."

"Jesus Christ," she whispered. "I don't know if I can handle this."

"I'm sorry. I didn't mean to upset you. I'll change back."

"No," she said softly, meeting his gaze. "Don't."

She held her breath as he came to bed.

WELCOME TO A FANTASTIC WORLD OF DANGER AND INTRIGUE!

Simon Hawke takes you where you've never dreamed...into a fantasy universe of wizards, wonder and terrifying excitement.

☐ **THE WIZARD OF RUE MORGUE**
0-445-20740-3/$4.50 ($5.95 in Canada)

☐ **THE WIZARD OF SUNSET STRIP**
0-445-20702-7/$3.95 ($4.95 in Canada)

☐ **THE WIZARD OF WHITECHAPEL**
0-445-20304-8/$4.50 ($5.50 in Canada)

Questar
SCIENCE FICTION

Questar is a registered trademark of Warner Books, Inc.

**Warner Books P.O. Box 690
New York, NY 10019**

Please send me the books I have checked. I enclose a check or money order (not cash), plus 95¢ per order and 95¢ per copy to cover postage and handling,* or bill my ☐ American Express ☐ VISA ☐ MasterCard. (Allow 4-6 weeks for delivery.)

___ Please send me your free mail order catalog. (If ordering only the catalog, include a large self-addressed, stamped envelope.)

Card # _____

Signature _____ Exp. Date _____

Name _____

Address _____

City _____ State _____ Zip _____
*New York and California residents add applicable sales tax.   503